A TALE OF THE MOJAVE

a novel
by

Arley Owens, Jr.

SHORTY MAE PRODUCTIONS

This is a work of fiction.
Any resemblance to any person, living or dead—any organization, enterprise, place, or event—is coincidental. The characters and settings are either imaginary or used fictitiously.

Bible quotations from the
Authorized King James Version

Cover Art: CL Owens
Editor: Pitman Sanders

First Printing Oct 2012
Printed in the U.S.A.

Soft Cover Edition
ISBN: 978-0-9848195-2-2

SHORTY MAE PRODUCTIONS
P.O. BOX 81102
MIDLAND, TEXAS 79708

To Cristi,
the queen of my heart

Special Thanks and Much Love to:
MILDRED HOWARD,
my junior high English teacher,
the first to spot the writer in me.
DYLAN J MORGAN,
whose nose for improvement,
eye for error, and excellent suggestions
greatly helped me whip the
manuscript into shape.
SUE SMITH,
my indefatigable proof reader.
AL CARTY and HAMISH MCBRIDE
for plowing through the first draft with me.
And SANDI MARTIN,
my baby sister, who couldn't get past
the first three chapters at first because
"They were too scary!" which provided
the exact shot in the arm this ol' boy
needed to push on.

Let the wicked forsake his way, and the unrighteous man his thoughts: and let him return unto the Lord, and he will have mercy upon him; and to our God, for he will abundantly pardon.

- Isaiah 55:7

For precept must be upon precept . . . line upon line; here a little, and there a little.

- Isaiah 28:10

Somewhere in the Mojave desert . . . .

ONE

Each time the Jeep slammed to earth after being hurled airborne, his head smacked the roof with teeth-jarring ferocity. He'd shout or grunt, or merely grimace, but Poppy Quinn never slowed down. The worn engine could only manage eighty-five, but he kept it there—bolting down a path too hazardous to navigate at half that speed. Never one to seek automotive thrills even as a young man, he'd become all the more cautious behind the wheel in middle-age. He wasn't being a daredevil by choice—circumstance had forced him to drive like one. Grimly focusing ahead, Poppy prayed the rocky canal would lead to some form of civilization.

* * * *

Bob Talasota's whitewalls were getting radically mauled by the friggin' rocks. He hoped they could keep handling the pounding without blowing out. If only he hadn't decided to check out Vegas on his way home the Skylark wouldn't be suffering such abuse. No way would anybody believe the reason he'd taken this rough trail, but to hell with that—he'd love to get raked over the coals about it by his home-boys back in Brooklyn. That would mean he'd lived to tell the tale. What he wouldn't give to be back there right now instead of being tossed around in his ride at ninety miles an hour.

Closing in fast on a Jeep, he had no room to pass and couldn't slow down. "You'd better step on it, pal, or I'm liable to ram your ass big time!"

* * * *

A brutal jolt drove her rib cage against the steering wheel of her prized sixty-five Mustang. Denise Jones cried out again, but more from the fear engulfing her than pain. Already driving far too fast on a course never meant to be navigated by an automobile, she'd have accelerated even more if the car ahead hadn't prevented it. She was close enough to note the man driving had black hair, broad shoulders, and also traveled solo. Occasionally the stony conduit curved and she could see a Jeep in front of him.

A helmeted leather-clad man on a motorcycle was gaining on her. An RV jostled along behind him, growing more distant, though she knew the driver had to be pushing it to the limit.

Her cell phone had no signal so she wouldn't be able to call for help if she crashed: a distinct possibility given the fact that no one on this dried up riverbed was willing to slow down.

* * * *

Though still sandwiched between two cliffs, Poppy shouted out a hallelujah when the ground turned from rock to hard dirt. A Buick shadowed him, almost touching his bumper, and he wished the driver would slow down because he couldn't go any faster.

He'd never seen anything like what compelled him to keep his right foot cemented to the floorboard. A while ago he'd been leisurely driving down highway one-twenty-seven in a region of desert somewhere between the Mojave Preserve and Death Valley. An odd sensation had trickled up his spine and a second later a small town appeared out of nowhere. Going seventy at the time, he'd slowed down at the outskirts, but soon gunned the engine in panic while passing through. A short distance on the other side of the macabre community, the road ended at the base of a sandy mountain with a craggy passageway venturing off to the right, and he'd taken it without hesitation.

Turning back had been unthinkable.

A biker with a dark shield concealing his face managed to maneuver around the Buick. Squinting with anxiousness as the motorcycle swerved left of him, Poppy tried to make more room, veering precariously near the stone cliff to his right. He held his breath—there couldn't be more than three feet between the Jeep and left precipice. A moment later he exhaled with harried relief when the suicide machine made it through the narrow space and shot on ahead.

You saw it too, didn't you.

The passage had become relatively smooth, but still very constricted. One wrong move and the Jeep would bang against one rocky barricade or the other, and start ping-ponging between the two, wadding itself into a metal tootsie pop with him winding up as the chewy treat in the center.

"Oh merciful Lord, get me through this . . . ."

* * * *

Damned fool biker, what a stunt! "What? You think you're Evel Knieval or somebody? You wanna kill yourself, use somebody else's coupe to do it."

Bob had instinctively hung the bird when the asshole passed, screaming for him to back off before they both wound up dead. He'd been trying to find a way past that Jeep for the last twenty minutes, but the corridor never got wide enough for two cars to maneuver side by side. Not so for a hog, but the dude had been crazy trying to squeeze through such a slim gap.

He took a quick look in the rearview mirror at the hot brunette riding his ass, her thick brown hair bouncing atop her shoulders. If she'd been ahead of the Jeep they'd be red, white, and blue like the flag, he thought idly. Her Mustang had Illinois tags. The guy steering the white bucket of bolts in front of him hailed from Texas according to his.

The clamor of the vehicles grated on his tattered nerves. When he'd hit that weird town the radio went static. Scared shitless, hands frozen to the wheel, white noise had blared for miles before he'd been able to will his pale-knuckled fingers to relax their death grip long enough to turn it off. Since the CD player had gone on the blink too, he had nothing to listen to but whining engines and spinning wheels. But snappin' to the groove of the music so smooth, wasn't what he wanted at the moment. Glancing at the empty passenger seat, he let out a harsh sigh. It would be so *decent* to hear a friendly voice.

So very decent indeed . . . .

* * * *

Thank God the biker hadn't caused a three car pile up and gotten himself smashed up as well. Denise couldn't believe the driver ahead had given him the finger when he passed. Once he made it around the Jeep she'd lost sight of him, as she had the RV behind her.

Her thoughts swirled with desperation as she tried to conjure a theorem to scientifically explain how she'd wound up at that town, and what she'd seen while driving through it. The pavement had started breaking up and then—rising from underground like a ballistic missile leaving a hidden silo before acquiring speed—a thing more frightening than a nuclear blast cast its six yellow eyes upon her. The screams erupting from her throat as she swerved around it, had continued until well after she'd been forced down this makeshift road.

Had an unknown prehistoric species managed to avoid whatever catastrophe extinguished the other dinosaurs of the era, or was that reptilian humanoid actually the devil—Satan himself, rising from hell on an invisible elevator? Though refusing to believe such a notion, she couldn't deny the paranormal way she'd encountered the odd settlement, or the unbearable evil emanating from that entity.

Logic dictated this couldn't really be happening, that any moment now she'd wake up in her comfortable bed at Franklin Park. She dwelt on that possibility for a moment, allowing a comforting fantasy to play out. Any second now she'd wake up—go through her typical morning routine, drive to the Chicago branch of Northwestern University, and greet her students, gathered to hear a lecture on paleontology. A mental image of their eager faces dissipated with yet another bend in the path, and cruel actuality reasserted itself. Though she'd truly been plunged into a nightmare, this was no dream.

If the riverbed hadn't turned to sand, making for a much smoother ride, her other problem would have been impossible to deal with. She'd almost wet her pants from fear upon seeing the creature, but now biological necessity had emerged and that's exactly what would happen if she didn't find a place to pull over soon. Stopping the car and relieving herself on this dusty trail wasn't an option. The RV had to be heading her way if the beast hadn't gotten to it, and with her luck she'd get caught with her pants down. She'd begun to ache as her bladder grew more insistent by the second. Shifting in her seat, trying to relieve some of the pressure, she even took her foot off the accelerator for a moment.

Nothing helped.

The discomfort became unbearable. Tears welling, she gritted her teeth, straining as hard as she could—fighting the demanding urge to relax her cramping abdomen and obtain sweet relief. To her horror, a section of corrugated earth appeared and the Mustang vibrated over it, forcing an abrupt end to the agony. Liquid warmth flooded her inner thighs, saturating her jeans. She'd pissed herself . . . it felt marvelous, almost erotic . . . she was very ashamed.

* * * *

The high cliffs on both sides of the passage grew smaller in the distance, but the route seemed to be heading towards a mountain. Poppy hoped it didn't end there. The biker had gotten so far ahead he'd disappeared from sight, but the Buick remained on his tail, riding ahead of a Mustang.

He had no idea where he was. The road he'd been on before the town appeared was supposed to take him to a place called Handelton where he'd planned to spend the night. According to the map he shouldn't have encountered anything but desert until then. Something had altered his course, and he feared the supernatural event had been engineered by a malevolent spirit from hell.

A passage in Revelation sprang to his mind: *And they had a king over them, who is the angel of the bottomless pit, whose name in the Hebrew tongue is Abaddon, but in the Greek tongue hath his name Apollyon.*

The dreadful prophecy referred to the swarm of locusts with scorpion tails that would be released from the bottomless pit at the end of time. Could it be that day had come and he'd actually laid eyes on Abaddon? If so, would the nightmare soon begin, or had he stumbled onto their exit before the time they were destined to be unleashed? Of all the plagues recorded in the last book of the Bible, he found that one the most fearsome. According to scripture the pain would be so unbearable men would seek death, yet it would flee from them.

It was nearing six o'clock and he hadn't eaten since early that morning. He'd planned to have a hearty meal at Handelton but now had no way of knowing how long it would be before his mounting hunger could be satisfied.

A short while later he feared it never would.

TWO

As he neared the mountain Poppy could see the biker inexplicably trying to race over it. Though the boulders on both sides of the canal were too close together for his Jeep to get through, either direction could be negotiated by a motorcycle. Going straight ahead was utterly impossible. A typical desert dune composed the bottom of the edifice, but a rocky cliff, almost perpendicular, rose at least fifty feet to the peak. Only a madman would think he could drive a motorcycle up it. Poppy feared the poor soul's mind must have snapped at the sight of the creature.

The riverbed grew wide, funneling out on both sides before ending at the impassible ridge. As Poppy slowed to a stop at its base, the Buick swerved to his left, halting in a cloud of dust. He got out of the Jeep and stretched. It felt good to be motionless, but his gut churned with anguish at the sight of another dead end.

And this one didn't offer a detour.

A young man got out of the Buick and leaned back, pressing his hands against the base of his spine, obviously trying to loosen muscles tensed from being in the same position too long. "Man . . . that was one hard-ass drive for nothing. What the hell was that thing back there? You saw it too, right?"

Poppy could barely hear him over the growling motorcycle. "Yes, I saw it."

The man walked towards him with an extended hand, mustering a grin that couldn't disguise fear. "I'm Bob Talasota."

"Poppy Quinn, pleased to meet you. Wish it was under better circumstances."

"Me too, Pops. You don't mind if I call you Pops, right? I mean—Poppy-Pops—got a ring to it."

He didn't care for the nickname, especially the way it sounded through a Yankee accent, but didn't say so. Obviously scared, Bob was apparently trying to compensate by acting cocky. If that helped him deal with the situation, so be it. Whether the same instinct would have emerged under normal conditions, Poppy didn't know, but he felt an immediate, almost paternal affection for Bob Talasota.

The Mustang pulled up before they finished shaking hands.

* * * *

Denise shut off the engine and slammed her hand on the dash. *What the hell am I supposed to do now? I'm not about to go back through that town!*

Staring blankly through the windshield, she watched the biker trying to climb the impassable peak that blocked any chance of driving away from this nightmare. His insane efforts seemed to punctuate the hopelessness of the situation and she started crying. A moment later she saw two men walking towards her, and frantically wiped her eyes dry.

Recognizing the hair and shoulders of the younger one, she knew the other belonged to the Jeep. Not about to get out of the car where they could see she'd peed in her pants like a little baby, she rolled down the window and leaned her head out.

"Dead end, huh?"

"I'm afraid so," said the elder gentleman with a Texas drawl, thick as cream. Tall and lean with wavy silver hair, she was surprised he didn't wear a cowboy hat to complete his western attire.

The t-shirt stretching across the other guy's muscular chest fit so tightly it appeared to be an epidermal layer rather than white fabric. His jeans weren't much looser, and he walked with a rhythmic bop as if keeping time to a beat. Though quite handsome, he seemed grossly overconfident.

"Yo, I'm Bob Talasota. This here's my new friend Poppy Quinn. And you are?"

His tone confirmed the conceit she'd suspected, but she forced a polite smile. "Denise Jones."

"Thanks for finally backing off my tail a little. I was afraid you were going to rear-end me. Might as well get out and stretch your legs, 'cause I don't think you want to go back the way you came unless you're like Mister Motorcycle over there. I think he must have lost the correct change back down the road a ways." He pointed towards the biker with his thumb held like a hitchhiker, never taking his eyes off her.

"Um . . . I think I'll stay here for now."

"Look, lady, we don't bite, at least I don't. Do you, Pops?"

Poppy Quinn gave her a smile that both reassured her safety and apologized for Bob's forwardness. His intent couldn't have been conveyed more perfectly if he'd spoken the words. He exuded a charismatic erudition that belied his redneck apparel, and she found the contradiction very appealing. In spite of the horrid situation, she couldn't help feeling intrigued.

* * * *

Something troubled Denise Jones besides winding up at this dead end, and Poppy sensed it had something to do with getting out of her car. Fearing the Yankee would persist in trying to persuade her to do so, he said, "You know, Bob, the thing for us to do is scout out this area and find a way out of here. Miss, if you'll excuse us."

"You're right, Pops," Bob answered, still eyeing the pretty brunette. "We can't go back, and we sure as hell can't stay here."

* * * *

Thank you, Mister Quinn! Denise shouted in her mind as he and the presumptuous Bob wandered off. She quickly climbed into the back seat, pulled off her wet jeans and panties, replaced them with a fresh pair of both from her suitcase, and got out of the car.

Heading the direction they'd taken, she cut her eyes to the left, glancing with pity at the man revving up his motorcycle for yet another vain attempt to accomplish the impossible. The engine quit roaring and she screamed.

The hill had absorbed the biker.

"Why is all this shit happening . . .?!" knees buckling, she hit the ground wailing. Bent forward like an Islamic woman doing penance—shoulders heaving, bowels cramping with terror, the sheer absurdity of the situation raping her mind—she pounded the desert sand as if the answer could be beaten from it.

Denise soon found herself being pulled to her feet by the two men she'd just met, each demanding to know what was wrong. Still sobbing, she pointed towards the spot where the cursed mountain had sucked the unfortunate lunatic and his motorcycle inside itself.

Bob frowned. "What, the biker made it over? Freak me out. How the hell did he do it?"

"No, no, no, he didn't make it! The damned thing swallowed him somehow . . ." she buried her face in her hands. "What is happening?!"

* * * *

That is *the question, isn't it, Miss Jones.* Poppy stared at the ominous intersection of dune and cliff she'd pointed to. *And they had a king over them—*

He shook off the passage before it could catch hold again.

Bob stood slack-jawed and speechless, gaping at the hill.

Poppy knew he had to take charge of the situation—they couldn't afford to panic. He pulled Denise to him and gently nudged her head to his shoulder. "Please calm down. We'll get out of this."

Her sobs were deep and violent, but he only encouraged her to continue. "That's right, let it go . . . just let it all go, we'll get out of this . . . ."

When her emotions finally leveled off and tears quit soaking his shirt, she looked up at him with bleary eyes. "I'm sorry . . . you're right. There has to be a way to escape from this nightmare."

He released her and put a hand on Bob's shoulder. "What do you think happened?"

"Jeez . . ." Bob slowly turned his way, face pale with fear. "I don't know."

Poppy gave the beefy deltoid a reassuring squeeze and lowered his hand. "Let's analyze what we do know then. First off, I'd like both of you to give me your perspectives on what you saw in that town."

"Why, Pops? We all saw it. What good is rehashing it going to do?"

"Humor an old man, would you?"

Denise sniffed and ran a finger beneath her nose. "I'll tell you what I saw—a hideous monster I'd have never believed existed if I hadn't seen it with my own eyes."

"I know, but I want a more detailed account. I was driving along with nothing but highway and desert ahead, then suddenly I was entering a town. The shock from that intensified a thousand-fold when I saw a section of pavement heave upwards like it was made of rubber, and start ripping apart as a dreadful thing I can only describe as a dragon-like man-beast rose through it. I floored the accelerator before seeing its legs, but judging by the upper torso, it must have been at least twenty feet tall if not more."

She nodded. "Dragon-like man-beast describes it perfectly, that's the same thing I saw. The street split and that thing rose up."

"Me too," said Bob.

"I see." He looked skyward, unable to hide the anxiety their statements induced.

"What, Pops?"

He let out a wary sigh and leveled his eyes. "That town was like a two dimensional movie set, and I suspect everything it had to offer was on that lone street."

Denise squinted with confusion. "What I saw was in three dimensions."

"I don't mean two dimensional in the literal sense. The buildings didn't appear to have any depth to them, like they were stage props or something."

"I didn't pay much attention to them because of that friggin' monster," said Bob, "but now that you mention it, that pretty well sums it up for me too."

Apprehension glistening in her big brown eyes, Denise glumly uttered, "I agree, now that I know what you mean."

"Now to the troubling part."

Bob snickered, humorlessly. "Come on, Pops, you just covered the troubling part."

"No he didn't, Bob. I know what Poppy's talking about now."

"Well fill me in, toots."

As if reacting to an intolerable insult, Denise bared her teeth and got right in his face. "Nobody calls me that, and don't you *ever* do it again!"

"Whoa . . .!" Bob's hands flew up in a defensive posture. "I meant no disrespect, it just popped out. Don't take it personal."

Jaw tight, shoulders squared, she kept glowering at him, eyes blazing with indignance.

"Aw man, don't be like that—I promise I won't do it again. Come on, I'm sorry, okay? Pull in your claws already."

Poppy started to intervene on Bob's behalf, but she seemed to be considering his apology, so he held back.

Denise drew a shallow breath and sighed, features once again displaying anxiety over their situation rather then anger. "Forget it, you couldn't have known. Sorry I bit your head off."

"So I'm forgiven?"

"Yeah, Bob, you're forgiven, just don't do it again, I can't stand that word—it hits me like being called a whore. Anyway, correct me if I'm wrong, Poppy, but what you're troubled about is the fact we didn't see each other when we encountered the creature."

"Exactly," he solemnly verified. "Nor did I see the biker. I was the only driver on that road when it happened, and didn't notice anyone behind me until after I took the detour that brought us here."

Bob shrugged. "Well I don't see what all the fuss is about. You didn't see me when you went through because I was behind you, and you got out too fast for me to see you. I vacated too quick to see Denise, and she didn't see us because we'd already gotten the hell out of Dodge. So what gives?"

"Don't you see?" said Denise. "We all saw the same thing—that beast breaking through the pavement. Chunks of asphalt fell as it rose from the ground, so there's no way it could have been a Disney-like apparatus that continually rises and resets for the next person on the joy ride to see it go through its motions. That means we should have seen each other, but we didn't."

"Oh jeez . . ." the Yankee's face dropped, signaling his enlightenment.

"That's the troubling part," Poppy wearily confirmed. "I don't know how or why, but we've somehow gotten entangled in a supernatural phenomenon that obviously extends beyond that mysterious town, in light of what just happened on the hill there. Needless to say, we need to find a way out of here, and panicking won't accomplish that. We've got to stay calm. Let's find a spot to sit down, and come up with a plan of action."

Spotting a cluster of small boulders at the base of the mountain where the right wall of the riverbed intersected it, he led them there. Denise poked around on one before cautiously sitting down.

Bob chuckled. "Making sure you won't fall through?"

"You got it."

"Believe I'll do likewise," the Yankee stated seriously.

Poppy followed their lead before seating himself. They only had a couple of hours till nightfall, and needed to act before darkness set in. "Okay, we can't drive over or alongside the hill in either direction, so we're going to have to walk around it. We can either try now, or stay here for the night and head out in the morning. Do either of you have any supplies on you? Water, food, anything of that sort?"

Bob shook his head. "I ate the last of my road snack before hitting the town."

"I don't have anything except some breath mints and aspirin," said Denise.

Poppy grinned. "Okay, so we don't have food or water, but at least we're covered for bad breath and headaches."

That pumped a laugh out of Bob and a short giggle from Denise, which relieved him. A sense of humor assured neither had allowed fear to numb their wit . . . at least not yet.

"So what'll it be, Pops? We staying or going?"

He squinted at the sky. The sun had dropped behind their nemesis, and its shadow inched further eastward by the minute. "We don't have much daylight left so we shouldn't venture too far from the vehicles, since we'll have to sleep in them if we can't get to the other side. Our best bet is to split up, check both directions, then meet back here. Pick your poison, Bob. You go one way, I'll go the other."

Denise sprang to her feet. "If you think I'm staying here alone, you're crazy! I'm going with one of you."

"Of course, I'm sorry. Why don't you go with Bob?"

She put her hands on her hips and frowned. "Why don't we just all stay together?"

"We can't tell which side of the ridge will go shallow first," he explained, "and we don't have any supplies. Splitting up gives us the best chance to see if we can make it to the other side before nightfall. We'll meet back here in an hour if neither side is possible to get around within a thirty minute walk—we don't dare risk more time than that. Hopefully we'll find the edge of it, and there'll be a town or house or something we can reach before sundown. If not, we'll have to try again first light when we'll have a whole day's supply of sunlight to work with. Does your watch keep good time, Bob?"

"Takes a lickin' and keeps on tickin'."

He rose from the boulder and glanced at his own. "Okay, let's synchronize, marking thirty minutes from now. Be careful. Head back here if you don't find anything within that time frame, and if the mound becomes negotiable, don't try going over it. Remember what happened to the biker."

"You don't have to tell me, Pops. Ain't no way I'm going up that friggin' haunted hill."

"Good. Since Denise is going with you, don't bother coming back if you're able to go around it and see something promising that you can reach before it gets dark. I'll do likewise. If you have to come back, wait five minutes or so and if I'm not back by then, head my direction. It'll mean I found something and vice versa."

Denise leered at him. "And if it means you're dead or we're dead, what then? Why don't we just all stay together and pick one direction or the other?"

Poppy mustered a reassuring smile which didn't seem to placate her at all. "If you wind up heading my direction, just come back if you don't see a way around the hill within a thirty minute span from here. That'll mean something happened to me."

"Or vice versa," she retorted, acerbically.

* * * *

After walking north for fifteen minutes Poppy noticed a section of the gradient where gathering sand had formed a slope against the cliff that could be negotiated. There wasn't enough time to explore much further, and the hill stretched easily beyond an hour's walk, so he either had to return to the vehicles or ignore his own advice and try to cross over.

He stared at it for several moments before deciding. Already beginning to feel weak from hunger, he'd grown quite thirsty too. Hoping Bob and Denise wouldn't be as foolhardy if they found a place to climb over, he dug an arrow in the sand with his boot heel to show them what he'd done if they wound up coming this way, and started upwards.

This wasn't the smart thing to do, but he couldn't bear the thought of bunking in his Jeep for the night on an empty stomach. If he spotted the remotest possibility of sustenance—even a prickly pear—this risky action would be worth it.

Providing he didn't wind up feeding the hill.

* * * *

Bob's cadence and relaxed expression indicated he'd also gotten over the jitters they'd both been feeling since the biker vanished, but she'd become fearful they'd never get around the sandy man-eater. Denise grabbed his arm and stopped walking. "Hold up, it's useless. That damn hill goes all the way to the horizon."

He checked his watch and turned to her. "Why don't we just cross over here? It's not that steep anymore."

"How much time have we got before we have to start back?"

"We've been hiking for twenty-five minutes."

She peered at the ramp of dirt that had been increasingly swallowing the cliff along the way, making it crossable despite some rocky protrusions. "Not much time left. It looks so normal and harmless, doesn't it. Of course it looked that way to the biker too, and that turned out to be his last mistake. I don't think we should try it."

Bob heaved a sigh. "I've been giving it some serious thought. Maybe he just hit some sort of quicksand. Remember he was all over it before that one spot got him. I'll go first. If I make it to the top without getting eaten, come on up too, and be careful to follow the same path."

"I don't know . . ." she crossed her arms beneath her breasts.

Bob hooked his thumbs in his pockets, and winked at her. "Tell you what—if I lose my cookies, the Skylark's yours."

"Like I'd touch anything made by General Motors. You saw my car, it's a classic. I had it restored to mint condition, down to the original cherry red. Ford rules."

"Rules . . .?!" he hacked a sarcastic cough. "Ford sucks, is more like it."

"No, Bob, GM sucks," she retaliated, then shoved him. His pectorals were rock hard.

He lightly banged her shoulders with his palms. "Says who?"

"Says me, you Bronx ox." Welcoming another opportunity to touch his chest, she pushed him again.

"I resent that. I'm from Brooklyn, so that makes me a Brooklyn ox." He jammed harder and she lost her balance, landing on her backside.

"Oh no!" Slapping a hand over his mouth in a failed attempt to keep from laughing, he extended the other.

She couldn't help giggling like a silly schoolgirl. All the fear and tension that had been mounting since she'd entered that eerie town dissipated for a moment. As he helped her up, they locked eyes. Sensing the wrong kind of confidence building in his, she lowered hers to his chest.

His powerfully built thorax expanded with a deep breath. "So what do you think? Mind if I give it a try?"

"Promise you'll jump and roll, or somersault backwards if anything weird starts to happen. It might mean some bumps and bruises—maybe even a broken bone—but that would be better than becoming that damn thing's lunch."

"Right you are, my lady . . . ."

Cautiously taking one slow step at a time at first, Bob apparently became convinced he wouldn't fall through, and trotted the rest of the way, reaching the top without incident. Whatever he saw on the other side greatly alarmed him. He hurried back down yelling, "Run back to the cars! Oh friggin' mother of pearl, run!"

He needn't have bothered telling her twice. One look at the terror on his face had set her feet in motion.

* * * *

Unless the creature had gotten its evil claws on them, Bob and Denise would most certainly be coming back. Head hanging low, Poppy sat on the same boulder he'd used for a chair earlier. Never had he felt such utter helplessness. It took all the mental resolve he possessed to keep despair from launching him past the brink of sanity. They were trapped in a paradox: it didn't matter if they went over the hill or back down the riverbed, because both choices were one and the same. He hadn't seen the creature, but the hole from whence it sprang still remained on the only street of that baffling town.

Everything looked exactly as it had before. While eyeballing it from atop the ridge, he'd been able to confirm the suspicion he'd shared with Bob and Denise. The few buildings situated on both sides of a short strip of asphalt had nothing behind them but desert sand. The whole scene appeared as lifeless as a stage-set without any actors. From his vantage point he'd also spotted the mountain where the two lane highway dead-ended beyond the ominous hamlet.

And they had a king over them, who is the angel of the bottomless pit, whose name in the Hebrew tongue is Abaddon, but in the Greek tongue hath his name Apollyon . . . .

Bob and Denise came running up. He forced the scripture from his mind, and tried to conceal his anxiety. They needed him to be strong.

They were both ranting: Denise begging for an explanation, frequently interrupting Bob's breathless account of what he'd seen on the other side. Like him, Bob hadn't spotted the creature, only the breach in the road. Denise kept sobbing, and Bob was almost hyperventilating. Poppy urged them to calm down, explaining that he already knew they'd somehow circled back to the mystifying community with no name, and a devil as its only inhabitant. He reminded that panicking would only make matters worse.

Bob—bent over with hands on knees, trying to catch his breath—finally quit jabbering. Denise started wiping her eyes.

Poppy asked if they believed in God.

"Yeah," said Bob, still heaving, "I'm Catholic."

Denise's face, which had been flaccid with defeat, stiffened into a frown. "Why? Do you think we're in hell?"

Before Poppy could answer, a noise made him turn to see a large recreational vehicle coming around the last bend in the riverbed.

"The RV made it!" Denise shouted with elation as if they were being rescued. "I'd forgotten all about it."

The vehicle halted behind her Mustang, and the three of them walked towards it. Seeing no one behind the wheel, Poppy opened the door so the driver could hear from the back where he or she had obviously gone. "Hello? My name's Poppy Quinn."

A moment later he shrugged his shoulders to express his ignorance as to why no one responded.

"Must be shy," said Bob, taking his turn at the door. "Yo, RV driver, you're among friends here!"

No one answered.

"What's the deal here, you deaf or what?"

Still no answer.

"Hey, I'm coming aboard, just want to make sure you're okay, don't be scared."

Poppy felt a sense of dread like he had when the town appeared, and an awful intuition came over him. When Bob went in back of the motorized camping trailer, he held out his arms to Denise. "Come here."

She complied and he hugged her tightly. "I don't think Bob's going to find the driver but please don't panic, we've got to keep our heads."

Silently she raised her beautiful dark eyes. Piercing, unblinking, and soaked with desperation, they remained riveted to his until Bob stepped out of the vehicle.

"This is going from weird to weirder. Man there ain't nobody aboard this bus."

Poppy pulled away from Denise and went inside. It had the

look and smell of being brand new. Behind the dash sat two captain chairs in front of the kitchen area, complimented by a couch nestled beneath a bunk jutting from the wall. A full-size exit door stood before the entrance to a narrow hallway with a bathroom on one side, two folding doors on the other. It terminated at a bedroom. He opened the folding doors and saw they enclosed a shallow closet with men's and women's clothing hanging above a shoe rack. The bedroom and bathroom, like the rest of the vehicle, were uninhabited.

The sense of foreboding he'd experienced had proven to be a valid premonition. Despair once again tried to engulf him, but when he looked in the cabinets and refrigerator, primal instinct took over. He tried the faucet at the sink and water sprang forth. Not bothering to search for a glass, he cupped his hands beneath the clear stream, lowered his head, and plunged his parched lips into the cold wetness. It tasted stupendously wonderful. After quenching a raging thirst, he turned off the tap, wiped a sleeve across his mouth, and shouted, "Come on in, guys! We have food and water!"

THREE

Since he intended to consume it all, Poppy didn't need a plate. He carried his bounty to the table, jerked the lid off one of two cans of corned beef hash, tore open a bag of potato chips, sat down, and grabbed his fork. Wolfing the grub unashamedly as a hog, he washed it down with diet cola, then reached for the other container of blended meat and potatoes. Bob guzzled three glasses of milk while emptying a large package of powdered doughnuts. Only Denise displayed any table manners as she began to dine on a Salisbury steak frozen dinner she'd patiently let cool a bit after taking it from the microwave. She'd rolled her eyes at the beginning of their eating frenzy, but never vocalized her obvious disgust at having to witness such gluttony.

Stuffed to the gills, Poppy got up and swiveled the driver's chair around so it faced the interior. Easing into it, he grinned at Bob who was leaning back, hands behind his head, eyes closed, looking totally sated. Denise picked at a portion of apple crumb cake occupying the smallest compartment of her readymade meal.

Taking note of an air conditioner mounted on the ceiling, Poppy stood up and put a hand over one of the vents. He dropped back in the chair frowning—another troublesome fact had presented itself. "Something's puzzling me."

Bob's lips curled into a lazy smile. "About who drove this bus? Man, right now I don't care if the devil himself sent it here. We got food and we got shelter."

"No, I don't mean that."

"What then?"

"Do either of you recall breaking a sweat or even feeling uncomfortably warm?"

The Yankee's eyes flew open as he dropped his arms and bolted upright. "No, the friggin' temperature's been perfect ever since I got out of my car."

Face pale, mouth ajar, Denise glanced fearfully around. "Just like it is now, inside this RV."

"Maybe the air conditioner's on," said Bob in a wishful tone.

Poppy shook his head and pointed. "That's the air conditioner up there, and it's not running. That's what got me to wondering."

Bob looked up at the unit. "Even if it *was* running, that wouldn't explain why we didn't feel hot like we should have when we were outside. We're in the friggin' desert in the summertime, but it feels like a perfect seventy degrees."

Denise glanced at the windshield and said, "It's almost dark. Maybe that's why we're comfortable. The desert can get pretty chilly at night. I bet we'll feel the temperature drop."

Bob sneered at her. "Who's kidding who here? We should have been sweating rivers when we ran back here, and you know it."

"Not necessarily. Just because it's the desert doesn't mean it can't be seventy degrees once in awhile. I'll admit it scared me at first, but now that I think about it, I don't think it's all that abnormal."

Poppy leaned forward and palmed his knees. "Even at seventy degrees we should have sweated at least a little bit during the scouting expedition, especially you two, as Bob pointed out. We're dealing with a phenomenon that defies the laws of physics. I've got a feeling we're going to find several peculiar things about this recreational vehicle besides the fact it drove itself here."

"Like what?" asked Denise.

"What's your shoe size?"

"My shoe size?" she chortled out incredulously.

"Yeah."

"Why? What's that got to do with anything?"

"Humor an old man, will you?"

"What are you getting at?"

He pointed at the hall. "Behind those folding doors you'll find some women's shoes. I've got a hunch they'll fit you perfectly."

She turned to look, as if verifying the closet's existence. "You want me to try on some shoes?"

"Please."

Bob went to the closet and returned with a pair of black pumps. "These look like your size?"

Frowning with irritation, she removed her sneakers and snatched the heels from him. Fear replaced the frown when she tried them on. "Oh my god, they fit."

Poppy blew out a mournful sigh. "I was afraid they would. Bob, I saw a pair of cowboy boots and men's shoes in there. I'm betting the boots are going to fit me and the shoes are going to fit you. Want to check it out?"

The Yankee eyed the folding doors but made no motion towards them. "You're scaring me, Pops."

"What size are you?"

"Eleven and a half."

"I wear a ten, and I don't wear anything but boots, so if my theory's right the shoes will be too big for me and the boots too small for you."

Bob again went down the hall, came back with a pair of cowboy boots with riding heels, and stood like a pale-faced sentinel, waiting for him to try them on.

Poppy exchanged his ostrich quill for lizard skins. "They're a perfect fit just as I feared." He swapped again, put the other pair back in the closet, and retook the driver's chair.

Bob stood wide-eyed and rigid.

Denise jerked the pumps off and barefooted her way to the closet. Returning with a pair of loafers, she shoved them against his chest. "Put them on!" she shouted angrily, face dripping with fear.

Reluctantly, the Italian took them from her, sat down on the couch, and untied his black high-top tennis shoes. Pulling them off with two nervous jerks, he cautiously slid his feet into the camper's footwear. "Oh jeez . . . what the hell's going on here?"

Watching him hastily remove the troublesome shoes and put his own back on, Poppy said, "Earlier when I asked if either of you had any food or water, you told me something interesting, Bob. Do you recall what you said?"

He looked up while tying his laces. "Jeez, Pops, don't turn this into a parlor game, just come right out with it."

"You said you'd eaten the last of your snacks before entering the town. Remember?"

"Yeah, so?"

"What was the snack?"

"Powdered doughnuts. What's the big deal?"

"What did you eat just now?"

"Oh I get it. You think the doughnuts were put here just for me, right?"

"I'm afraid so."

"Newsflash! I ain't the only person on the planet that likes powdered doughnuts, and they aren't the only type of doughnuts I eat."

"Did you have anything to drink with them when you were on the road?"

"Yeah, a carton of milk, one of those pint jobs. And I know I had milk just now, but that don't mean nothing. I drink milk all the time, with most anything."

"I had Salisbury steak at a restaurant for lunch earlier today," Denise warily reported with an awe-struck frown while reacquiring her sneakers. "And the order came with a complimentary piece of apple crumb cake. How did you know all this, Poppy?"

He pointed to the ceiling. "When I discovered the air conditioner wasn't on, it got me to thinking about how perfect the temperature was when it shouldn't have been, and while I was trying to reason that out I remembered the last thing I had eaten was corned beef hash with potato chips and a diet cola. Recalling Bob's statement, I knew if he'd eaten powdered doughnuts I was on to something. Your Salisbury steak confirms it."

Her dark eyes flared with bewilderment. "And I hardly ever eat Salisbury steak, and never twice the same day. Wonder what possessed me to choose it here?"

"I don't think you had much of a choice. I'm betting the only type of food and drink we'll find in this camper is whatever the three of us last consumed before we drove through that town."

They checked the cabinets, refrigerator, and drawers. His intuition proved correct.

Bob appeared to be looking for something on the walls, then seated himself in the passenger's chair and started perusing the dashboard. "We've got another mystery. Good thing the lights were already on because I don't see any switches anywhere, and it's getting dark outside."

"Now that you mention it, I don't either . . ." Poppy scoured the dash but found no switches, knobs, or buttons. The absence of one in particular chilled him to the bone. "This vehicle doesn't have an ignition switch, at least none that I can see. I can't find a brand name either."

"Maybe there's one on the outside," said Denise.

"It's too dark to tell now without a flashlight."

She searched the kitchen cabinet and found one stashed beneath the sink. Turning it on, she exited through the full-size door.

Poppy watched the beam dancing laterally like a broken spotlight unable to be lowered stage-ward. It disappeared when she left his viewpoint to check out the rest of the vehicle.

A few moments later she stepped back inside. "I couldn't find anything . . . ."

* * * *

Poppy sat staring at the hill which he could hardly make out through the dusk, thinking about the creature. At any time the serpentine beast might venture over it, or come up from behind them since physical direction seemed to have no bearing here. He knew if that horrid fact hadn't already occurred to Bob and Denise, it eventually would. No one had said anything for quite a while and that wasn't good. Silence would only fuel the mounting fear.

They needed something to discuss besides their plight, anything that might lift morale. Poppy glanced at Bob, pensively leering through the windshield like he'd been doing. He turned to examine Denise. She sat on the couch wearing a somber analytical expression. It didn't take a mind reader to ascertain what they were both brooding over.

At length he thought of a way to get them talking. "An unbelievable event has thrown the three of us together, and do you realize we don't know anything about each other?"

"Who wants to go first on show and tell?" Denise said dryly.

Poppy smiled at her, hoping she'd be cooperative in helping him lighten the mood. "Lady's first."

She inhaled a deep breath and acquiescently turned up her palms. "In case you two have forgotten, my name is Denise Jones. I live in the Chicago suburb of Franklin Park and teach paleontology at Northwestern. I'm presently on vacation, and was on my way to Las Vegas to visit an old friend who recently moved there from—"

"Whoa, talk about the long way around!" Bob spun the chair one-eighty degrees to face her. "Vegas is way north of here. How come you wound up south of it coming from Chicago?"

Something bothered Poppy when she mentioned Las Vegas but Bob's interruption made it flitter away. Before he could put his finger on it again, Denise heaved an impatient sigh and started explaining.

"I didn't, silly. I went to Arkansas first to see my brother, sister-in-law, and nephew, then to Dallas where my dad moved after my parents divorced several years ago. From there I drove to Los Angeles to pay my mother an obligatory visit, and after getting that crap over with, was heading for Vegas for a few days of debauchery before going home. Obviously I never got there. Now it's your turn."

Bob grinned and shook his head. "Not likely. Besides what you do and where you live, about the only thing personal I learned about you just now is that you must really like to drive, with that crazy flight plan of yours. Are you married, single, divorced, widowed, homo, or what?"

She shot him a reprimanding scowl. "Now you're being nosy, Bob."

"No I'm not, just curious. Spill the beans on yourself. Tell us about your childhood, where you grew up, what turns you on. Lay your vitals on us, stuff like that."

Poppy had to laugh. If he was Bob's age he'd be just as curious about her marital status. He studied her face, trying to discern whether or not she wanted to reveal any more about herself. When she didn't give a prompt reply he attempted to bail her out with his biography, but she spoke up before he could start.

"Single, Bob—never married, definitely heterosexual. My

vital statistics are none of your business, but I will tell you I'm five eight. I grew up in Oakland, California, but we moved to Los Angeles my junior year so I graduated high school there, went to college at Berkley, and after earning my doctorate, moved to Chicago where I've remained ever since."

Suddenly she stood up—thrust out a hip, put one hand on it, the other to the side of her head, and mimicking Bob's accent said, "But what youse really wants to know are my measurements and cup size. Yo, guess what? I ain't gonna tell youse, so theah. My turn-ons are none of ya beeswax, but I will tell youse what turns me off—getting lost in the desert, driving down bumpy roads behind pushy shit-for-brains Italian dick-heads who don't know theah head from theah ass, and—"

Hysterical giggles rendered her speechless. Her routine had made Bob laugh so hard he was bent over, slapping his knees, and Poppy's guffaws had apparently been contagious as well.

When the hilarity finally subsided, Denise adjusted her chair and sat where she could see the two of them. Crossing one leg over the other, she grabbed her raised knee with both hands, and leaned forward with a cynical smile. "Okay, Bob, tell us your drab, pitiful, little saga."

"My drab little saga . . ." he shook his head with a grin. "You put it so poetically. Okay, I was christened Roberto Virgilio Talasota at birth, but even though my name may sound like it, I'm not Italian."

"That's bullshit," blurted Denise. "If you're not Italian, then I'm Chinese."

"Oh yeah? Well this all I've got to say to that: *Jack and Jill went up the hill to fetch a pail of water, but didn't know the hill was haunted until in it both had fallen."* Bob stood up, took a bow, and sat back down.

"Come on, no fair, I don't speak Italian. What did you say?"

When the Yankee folded his arms across his chest and smugly grinned instead of answering her, Poppy spoke up. "I understand what he said, but you wouldn't believe me if I told you."

Bob looked pleasantly surprised. *"No fooling, Pops, you speak the lingo?"*

"Yes, but I haven't spoken it in years so you'll forgive me if I'm a bit rusty."

"Very impressive, my man."

"Enough already, you two. Let me in on it—in English if you please. Or you could tell me in German or Russian since I speak both."

"He was reciting his own version of a nursery rhyme."

"Aw come on, Pops, don't give me away."

Denise snickered. "Nursery rhyme, huh. Now why doesn't that surprise me? Okay, you Bronx ox, have it your way. Who would want to know anything about you anyway?"

"That's Brooklyn, babe, Brooklyn. Remember?"

"Brooklyn, Bronx—same difference—who cares?"

Donning an Elvis-like sneer, Bob smoothed the sides of his hair. "You care, and-you-*know-it.* No-*doubt-about*-it."

"Oh that's cute," she said sarcastically.

Poppy wished there was some place he could disappear to so the two of them could be alone, but didn't relish the idea of leaving the safety of the RV. Though he knew they weren't really safe, and wouldn't be until they got out of this . . . whatever this was. But the RV at least had the illusion of safety, so he stayed put and listened to them banter back and forth—Bob insisting she was dying to know all about him, Denise maintaining she couldn't care less. Their sparring had turned very flirtatious, and he felt like a fifth wheel.

After awhile he ignored their jibbing and jiving, and retraced the strange day. He'd left Barstow on Interstate Fifteen, taken the exit for one-twenty-seven about two hours later, and stopped at a convenience store with gas pumps and two covered picnic tables. When he went inside to pay after gassing up, he'd spotted a small deli located in the center of the store. He'd plan to check it out until he passed a shelf of canned foods on the way, and opted for corned beef hash and chips instead. Taking only a plastic spoon from the deli, he'd seated himself at one of the picnic tables and spread out his map, looking for a place to spend the night before reaching Death Valley.

Leaving the store with the intent of bedding down at Handelton, he'd planned to cross Death Valley the next morning, then take highway one-seventy-eight into Nevada.

But he never got to Handelton.

Clearly visualizing the exit sign in his mind, he was positive he'd taken the right road. Although he'd never been on that highway before, countless others had, and they'd made it through to whatever destinations they'd been in search of. Why hadn't he, Bob, Denise, and the biker? And why had the four of them, and no others, been forced to take the detour at the base of that mountain?

He stopped musing when Bob finally quit teasing Denise and began to talk half-seriously about himself.

"Like I said, I'm from Brooklyn, New York. My folks came over from the old country, and I'm the first American-born Talasota in my family. I'm second cousins with Al Pacino, believe it or not, and am distantly related to Robert De Niro as well."

Denise slapped her thigh. "Oh you are not, you liar!"

"Okay, maybe we're third cousins, me and Al, or maybe fourths, I forget. Anyway we're cousins somewhere down the line. I always wanted to be a lawyer but couldn't get through college—too much reading this and memorizing that—so I wound up in construction and worked my way through three apprenticeships as a carpenter, plumber, and electrician. Plan to have my own construction company someday.

"I'm on vacation too. Never been out west, so I took a trip to San Bernardino to see my cousin Al—Barzera not Pacino. We were real close as kids but hadn't seen each other in years, and I didn't know we'd drifted apart till I went to see him. Took me five days to get from Brooklyn to Al's house, and I wanted to get the hell out of there so bad, the few hours I stayed seemed longer than the drive out. I decided to check out Vegas on my way back home, and was on my way there when I . . . wound up here with you guys instead. Your turn, Pops."

It finally dawned on Poppy what had bothered him when Denise mentioned going to Las Vegas earlier. "Bob, you say you were going to Vegas?"

"That's right."

"Then why didn't you take the interstate?"

"Excuse me?"

"Why were you on highway one-twenty-seven if you were heading for Las Vegas from San Bernardino?"

Bob scowled at him. "What highway one-twenty-seven? Man I was cruising down Interstate Fifteen when all of a sudden I was on a two-lane outside that weird burg."

"So was I," said Denise. "And that's exactly what happened to me. I went from the interstate to the town in a flash."

Poppy reeled with terrifying bafflement. "I was on one-twenty-seven . . . I had assumed the two of you were also."

And they had a king over them, who is the angel of the bottomless pit, whose name in the Hebrew tongue is Abaddon, but in the Greek tongue hath his name Apollyon.

He shook off the tormenting scripture and tried to compose himself. Glancing at Bob, then Denise, he figured their frightened countenances were bound to mirror his own.

"What's going on here, Pops?" Bob looked at him like a child seeking reassurance from a parent.

"I wish I knew . . . but all I can do is speculate. Remember when I asked the two of you if you believed in God?"

They nodded.

"Well I do, and I know He created all things—everything that is, all that ever will be. I can't say why we've been snatched away from the normal world, but God knows why. Whether He did it directly, or allowed some other agency to do it, He's seen to it we wound up here. What I've stated so far is fact. All I can do from this point is hypothesize. It may not be sound, and it's rather odd, but I have a theory."

"I'm all ears, Pops."

"Before I continue, would you explain paleontology to us, Denise?" Poppy didn't need a definition, Denise's first mention of it spawned the idea, but he wanted to make sure Bob understood the part pertinent to his supposition. He'd sensed the macho Italian had lied about being in construction, apparently thinking it would impress Denise, and his real vocation would make or break the hypothesis.

"Simply put, a paleontologist analyzes fossil remains of plants and animals."

"Would you mind elaborating a little?" said Poppy.

"Well, the distribution of fossils in the particular layer of strata where they're found, helps in geographical mapping needed to determine the location of oil and mineral deposits—"

"Thank you . . ." he signaled her to stop. "You covered the part I wanted to hear."

"Okay, Pops, now we know what she does. So what's your theory? Lay it on us already."

He cleared his throat. "You want to tell us what you really do for a living?"

"I told you, construction."

"Why would he lie about what he does? That's rude of you to accuse him like that, Poppy."

Donning a disbelieving grin, he focused on Bob without responding to her.

"Come on, Pops, I told you the truth."

"No you didn't. Please don't be ashamed to admit you were pulling our legs, just tell us."

"Why do you think he's lying, Poppy?"

"Because he is."

She hissed a sigh. "Bob, if you're lying, stop it. I want to hear Poppy's theory, and it's becoming pretty damn evident he's not going to share it until you come clean, so if you're lying, come clean."

Poppy waited patiently for him to *come clean*, never taking his eyes off him. Bob pouted like a guilty little boy, caught red-handed but nonetheless stubbornly refusing to admit his guilt. The expression convinced him even more that the Yankee hadn't told the truth.

Denise, meanwhile, became increasingly impatient. "Oh never mind whether he's lying or not, Poppy. Tell us your theory."

"Not until he tells us what he really does for a living."

Minutes went by. Bob shifted uneasily in the passenger's seat but never blinked, obviously determined not to lose the staring match that had developed between them. Silence hung heavy, awkwardness gave way to tension, which continued to mount. From the corner of his eye Poppy saw Denise fold her arms beneath her breasts as she began restlessly tapping her foot.

"Dammit, Bob, just tell him you lied whether you did or not so we can hear his theory."

Donning a lopsided sneer, Bob slapped the arms of the chair and finally broke eye contact. "Oh all right, for crying out loud! I did lie, you caught me. Satisfied? You win, I lose, let's leave it at that."

"No, Bob, I need to know. Your vocation is the hinge-pin of

my theory. Now what do you really do for a living?"

When he didn't answer, Denise said, "What is it you think he does?"

"I'll tell the theory, right or wrong, but only after he answers me. Bob, I have what you might call a sixth sense about certain things, the spiritual gift of discernment, that's why I knew you fibbed. Now I'm sensing you're embarrassed to tell us what you do. Is it illegal?"

That seemed to get to him. Bob heaved a bitter sigh and lowered his head. "I work for the sewer."

"Nothing whatsoever to be ashamed of." Poppy tried to hide his disappointment.

Denise rolled her eyes and threw up her hands. "Good grief, Bob, what's the difference? I can't believe it bothered you to say that."

Crimson faced, he straightened his neck and leered at her. "That's easy for you to say, you don't work for the sewer. And I wasn't totally lying anyway. I did work all three apprenticeships for awhile, and do plan to start my own construction company someday. My uncle got me on at the sewer when I was having a tough time finding a job. I worked my way up to foreman and some pretty decent pay, but it's still the sewer."

"And a very necessary profession and nothing whatsoever to apologize for," said Poppy. "Were you ever in the military?"

"No."

"My theory isn't valid, I'm afraid. I thought our occupations were interlocked in such a way that by combining our respective areas of expertise, we'd be able to solve the mystery and make it back to the real world. I guess it was just wishful thinking on my part."

Denise wrinkled her brow. "How could paleontology have helped us out? I'm very confused."

"I thought we might have been able to learn more about

what to do if you were given a chance to study the hole the creature created when it rose up. Whether or not the rock and soil is native to the Mojave Desert or—"

"Jeez, Pops! Of course it's native to the Mojave, what kind of thinking is that? And here I thought you were super brains. Jeez."

"I don't think it is, Bob. Not that it really matters now."

"Say what?"

"Bob, he's making sense. Wherever we are, nothing is behaving the way it should. The temperature alone ought to tell you we might no longer be in the Mojave Desert. And Poppy's right—if I can have a look at the strata beneath the hole, it might give us a clue to our whereabouts."

Bob stretched his arms, clinching then relaxing his fists above his head. "I can't believe the two of you. You both lack about nine cents having the correct change even thinking of checking out that friggin' hole. What, you think Mister Monster's just gonna sit back and watch you work? Sheesh."

Poppy merely smiled at the insult. "Anyway, my theory's out the window, so we're back to square one."

"No, wait a minute," said Denise excitedly. "Maybe your theory isn't so wrong. Bob works for the sewer, that thing may have risen from a sewer for all we know."

"Be that as it may, I don't see how that would be of any help to us. It was a reach to begin with, and I feel pretty foolish now. When you said you taught paleontology I thought it might explain why Bob and I saw the hole, but not the creature from the top of the hill—as if The Almighty wanted me to take careful note of it, knowing I'd soon learn about your profession. The theory depended on Bob being familiar with astronomical navigation so he could figure out which direction we needed to go, once he got a look at the stars. Assuming, of course, that you'd have been able to determine roughly where we are. Like I said, it was a reach."

"So that's why you asked if he was in the service. You were hoping he'd learned that skill in the Navy."

Poppy nodded. "Or perhaps worked in navigation in the Air Force or Army Air Corps."

Bob narrowed his eyes. "What I'd like to know is exactly how your profession could help us, Pops. Just what is it you do, anyway?"

"I'm a theologian. The creature falls under my area of expertise, I'm afraid."

"You telling me that thing is the devil? Is that what you're saying?"

"Not Satan, Bob, but a devil nonetheless."

Denise glared at him contemptuously. "I'm not sure whether God exists or not, but I certainly don't believe that thing is a devil, Poppy. It's native to this earth, how ever aberrant or out of its own time it may be."

"I agree that it's native to the earth, Denise. Perhaps more so than any other creature. But it *is* a demon, and I believe I may know precisely which one. Some demonic spirits are free to roam the earth, but others were bound and will be loosed at the end of time. I believe the one we saw is a particularly frightening one, whose sole purpose is massive judgment when he's released."

"You're scaring me again, Pops."

Sighing with frustration, Denise gripped her waist with both hands—cinching it so tight her long fingers lacked only a few inches from touching each other. "I'm as scared as you, Bob, but that thing is no demon or any derivation thereof."

"I'm afraid the evidence denies that assertion," said Poppy. "Everything we've experienced has been supernatural."

"It appears to be, I can't argue with that, but in the end there has to be a rational explanation for all this. Think of how supernatural the caveman who started the first campfire must have looked to the others. He was probably worshiped as a god. That creature may look like a devil, but it's just an undiscovered species."

"Oh, Denise . . ." Poppy knew she really didn't believe her argument any more than he did. He couldn't blame her for trying to be pragmatic, but her reasoning was based on fear rather than fact. She couldn't face the obvious because it frightened her to admit their situation didn't lend itself to empirical analysis. "You're straining at a gnat and swallowing a camel. Spiritual law supersedes physical law. Everything that happens in the world we call normal is a direct result of what is going on in the spirit realm. The manifestations we've experienced will always defy rationality. Only God, who created them, can override physical laws or permit any spiritual being, good or bad, to do so. Several were violated in bringing the three of us together here. You can't argue with that."

She tensed her jaw. "Of course I can. Science is making new discoveries every day. What appeared impossible yesterday is commonplace today and fits neatly into the realm of physics. We're bound to be going through a natural phenomena that so rarely occurs it appears to be supernatural. We may have accidentally stumbled across a doorway connecting two dimensions. That creature may be a million years old, and we've somehow gone back to its time, or it may have entered ours, the possibilities are endless."

"Are they?" Poppy gave her a smile he hoped didn't appear condescending. "Then how do you explain this RV, the food, the shoes, the biker?"

"For all we know the driver of the RV is still here," Denise countered, "but exists in a dimensional state we can't see, and the biker accidentally found an entrance leading to that dimension and—"

"Oh give it up for crying out loud!" Bob shouted with an asymmetrical sneer of exasperation. "Do you hear what you're saying? Pops is right—this is supernatural and no scientist is going to be able to explain it. We're stuck in a friggin' nightmare, and trying to rationalize it ain't gonna help us get out of it."

Denise glowered at him, her piercing dark eyes threatening the Yankee as though they could turn him to stone if he uttered another word. She kept it up for several seconds, then her lips quivered and she burst into tears. "I know . . . this *is* a nightmare! Why are we here?!"

* * * *

Night had fully descended on the desert, and it had weight like the darkness God visited on Pharaoh when he refused to let His people go. Poppy stared through the windshield, marveling at the abysmal void shrouding this place of hopeless desolation. There were no stars, and there should have been because the sky had been cloudless at sunset. He wondered if they'd ever see daylight again. The lights burned brightly in the RV, but at the moment it felt like the only illumination in the entire universe.

A deathly quiet had hung in the air since Denise quit crying a good while ago. Like the darkness, the silence seemed to have mass and negative energy. He wanted to offer words of consolation, affirm they still had hope, proclaim victory would somehow be attained. But mere rhetoric couldn't negate the amazing strength of the blackness and dread that bore down on them.

Poppy let out a deep yawn and rose from the captain's chair. Denise had fallen asleep on the couch. Bob's head lay on his muscular arms, crossed atop the table. It looked uncomfortable, and he wanted to wake him and tell him to lie down on the bed. But didn't. The peaceful look on the Yankee's face forbade disturbance, like the sweet face of an innocent child in blissful slumber.

Back behind the wheel, again facing the ebony cosmos that pressed against the windshield, he tried to plan a course of action for them to take when morning came. Assuming it would come, for there was no such certainty in this place. Little Orphan Annie might bet her bottom dollar the sun would come up tomorrow, but he wouldn't, not here.

FOUR

Poppy opened his eyes to find he'd fallen asleep in the driver's chair. Though almost blinded by the brightness reflecting off Denise's Mustang, his heart leapt with joy. The light was beautiful, magnificent, extraordinarily glorious and faith renewing.

Praise the Lord, the sun *had* risen!

Stiff from sleeping in a sitting position, he gingerly rose to his feet, wondering where Bob and Denise were. Slowly he made his way to the bathroom, thankful to find it unoccupied. After relieving himself he went outside to get his toothbrush from the Jeep, and saw them sitting on a boulder.

"Yo, Pops! How's the chair for sleeping?"

Poppy rubbed his lower back, noting Bob had changed clothes—trading his t-shirt for a blue button-up, jeans for khakis, high-tops for wingtips. "Better than the table, I'm sure. What are you doing out here?"

"We didn't want to wake you," Denise answered with a considerate smile. She was holding a can of cherry cola, the same thing she'd drank with her Salisbury steak. Like Bob, she'd donned another shirt—a pink pullover with sleeves ending at the elbows—but her jeans and sneakers looked to be the same ones she'd worn yesterday.

A creepy feeling gnawed at his gut when he noticed the position of the sun. Poppy glanced at his watch and saw he'd slept past noon. Rarely did he sleep more than six hours, and never more than eight, yet he'd been out cold for at least twelve. He opened the back hatch, fumbled through a cheap suitcase for his dental gear, closed both, and made for the camper.

He cleaned his teeth and grabbed a diet cola, wishing he'd drank coffee at the convenience store so a supply would be in the RV. Rejoining his new friends, Poppy again took note of Bob's garments. They looked like they'd come straight off a clothier's rack. "Those duds you're wearing, are they yours or did you get them from the camper?"

"Mine," said Denise. "I'm not about to wear anything from that haunted RV."

Bob stood and modeled for him, doing a graceful pirouette. "Figured they'd fit since the shoes did. You like?"

"Oh you look scrumptious in blue and khaki, Bob." Though grinning, he felt uneasy the Yankee hadn't stuck with his own wardrobe. "I can't believe I slept so long. How long have you guys been up?"

"About an hour," said Bob. "Denise cracked her eyelids not long after I did. Almost caught me in the john."

The aberration in his nocturnal pattern kept nagging at him. He normally couldn't sleep at all with the lights on, yet not only had he slumbered for hours with sunlight streaming through the windshield, he'd done so slumped behind a steering wheel. Something else concerned him as well: they were sweat free on a bright summer day in the desert.

"You guys notice the temperature feels perfect again?"

"We were just talking about that," said Denise.

"And there's another puzzlement. I slept way too long."

Bob snickered. "Oh man, Pops, that's the ultimate. With everything else that's gone down here, you're worried about oversleeping? We ever get out of here I'm going to write a book about it, and put the fact you overslept at the top of the macabre list."

Denise laughed at Bob's sarcasm, but both of them stopped grinning after Poppy explained his normal sleeping habits.

"You know what, Pops? I don't remember going to sleep."

"Nor do I," said Poppy. "Of course I don't think anyone actually recalls the moment they start to snooze, but I usually remember trying to."

"That's what I meant. I was planning on using the couch or the bunk, figuring Denise should get the bed."

"I was thinking the same thing last night. Denise?"

"Well, I hadn't planned on falling asleep on the couch, if that's what you mean. I hadn't given a thought as to where I would sleep. I think you may be making a mountain out of a molehill on this one, guys."

"Could be," Poppy agreed with his lips, but not his heart. He looked at the sky. "Do either of you remember seeing any clouds yesterday?"

"No, don't think so," said Bob.

Denise shook her head. "As I recall, it was just like today. Completely clear."

"So what do we do, Pops? How the hell do we get out of here?"

"Well we don't go over the hill, that's for sure, because we'd be on foot. If we're going through the town, we need to drive. The cars will offer at least a modicum of protection against the beast."

"Are you kidding me?!" barked Denise, brows raised high. "That thing could bite through a foot of steel. There's no way I'm going near that town."

Poppy didn't want to say aloud what should have been obvious, but had to point it out. "Denise, what keeps the creature from coming over the hill?"

Evidently that possibility hadn't dawned on either of them because they both gawked at him with fear-drenched eyes.

A noise made him turn around. The RV's engine had started. Bob sprang to his feet and ran towards it.

"What should we do?!" screamed Denise.

Poppy ignored her as panic seized him. "Bob, don't get in

the RV . . .!"

* * * *

Denise had been hysterical, and his efforts to console her miserably futile since he felt the same way inside. Eyes swollen from crying, shoulders stooped with exhaustion, she sat on a slab of smooth rock, looking as helpless as he felt.

It'd dawned on him what was going on the instant the engine started, but Bob had ignored his warning. The passenger door opened of its own accord a moment before the Yankee had gotten to it. He'd jumped in, tried to get behind the wheel, but had fallen below the dash. Then, the motorized camper with no brand name, no ignition switch, and no driver, peeled out, heading back down the riverbed. It hadn't bothered turning around, just sped away in reverse, leaving a cloud of dust in its wake. Poppy didn't know if Bob was alive or dead, but had no doubt he'd been transported back to the demon's habitat.

Tears filled his eyes as he gazed at the blue Skylark and said a silent prayer for its owner.

Denise began to sob again.

FIVE

Denise had finally quit crying, but her features were still blanketed with grief and despair. Slumping forward, elbows on knees, she stared morosely at the ground, appearing to have lost any hope of escaping this wicked paradox. Poppy had quit trying to encourage her because he could no longer hide his own feelings of hopelessness. God had allowed all this to happen. But why? Silently, he begged The Almighty for an answer.

Involuntarily wiping his brow, a thrill shot through him. He felt moisture. He'd been so distraught, and worried about Bob, he hadn't noticed the temperature rise. The heat felt wonderfully unbearable.

"Denise!"

"What . . .?!" she jerked her head up with alarm, thinking he'd screamed to alert her of impending danger, unaware she'd started perspiring.

"Look at me, I'm sweating! It's hot and I'm sweating, and so are you."

She ran a finger over her forehead, gawked at the sweat on it for a couple of seconds, then jumped to her feet, flinging her hands in the air. "Oh my god, I'm hot! I'm hot! No more fucking seventy degrees, I'm hot! I'm sorry for my potty mouth, I usually don't talk like that, but fucking hell it's hot, hot, hot! Hallelujah it's *fucking* hot . . .!"

He detested cussing, especially the F word, but couldn't help but laugh while joining her in a frenzied dance of jumping up and down, bellowing joyful cheers because they were sweating profusely in the searing desert heat.

When their rollicking jubilation finally wound down, he said, "Come on."

"Where?"

"Back to the normal world, I think it's safe now. I don't know how long things are going to stay that way so we have to move fast, The Twilight Zone could return any second. See that?" He pointed at a bank of billowy white clouds overhead. "They're another sign things are normal. Let's go—I'll lead."

"I'm not going back through that town, Poppy!"

"There's no other way, come on . . . ."

Ignoring her repeated protests, he ran to his Jeep, knowing she'd finally give in and follow him, since she wouldn't want to be left alone. The baked air in the oven-like interior almost suffocated him as he started the engine and switched on the air conditioner. Storming back down the sandy path, he alternated palms to keep the steering wheel from searing his hands. A few minutes later he wrapped his fingers around it as the interior cooled down. This time a different fear made him keep the pedal to the floor: that normalcy would abandon them. They had to get to the other side of the creature's lair before it did.

Poppy glanced at the rearview mirror and smiled as a Mustang appeared on the horizon. Before the sand had turned to rock, Denise was only a couple of car lengths behind him. Periodically he lowered the window and stuck his arm outside for reassurance. Each time he felt heat, his spirit leapt within him and he thanked the Lord.

He'd figured out the food had made him sleep too long, so the clothes and shoes should be avoided. But that cognition had occurred simultaneously with the cranking of the RV engine and Bob being irresistibly drawn to the camper. Whatever dark power was at work must have known he'd warn Bob to take off the clothes so it started the engine, counting on Denise and him instinctively following its victim inside.

Though only speculating, he felt it had to be true because the food and clothing had obviously been put there specifically for the three of them.

If Poppy hadn't wised up, he strongly suspected the evil spirit would have kept the RV at rest and patiently waited, soon bringing the three of them under its control because they'd have no recourse but to continue eating the food. Bob had been petrified when the loafers fit, but the milk and powdered doughnuts had transformed his thinking overnight to such a degree that he'd decided to dress entirely from the mysteriously provided wardrobe, which apparently hastened the entity's ability to dominate human will. The instant Poppy put two and two together the unseen demon had to act, and wound up settling for one instead of three. Then, a short while afterwards things became normal.

But for how long?

If they could only get there in time, the town should be gone because it had no place in the real world. Though they'd seen the ungodly thing after somehow being yanked away from the natural realm, the demonic beast couldn't enter carnal reality until the time came for the legions of stinging locusts to swarm out of the bottomless pit, and inflict pain on their helpless victims for five horrifying months. It didn't matter if the insects and time frame were literal or figurative. Whatever its true meaning, that prophecy forecasted a plague of unimaginable agony, and he hoped its fulfillment lay in the very, very distant future.

Even if the beast wasn't Abaddon as he felt in his spirit, the three of them had been chosen to see it for a specific purpose, and Poppy now thought he knew why. It had nothing to do with their occupations, although the Lord saw to it a theologian witnessed the event. Denise most likely wouldn't believe him, but he'd tell her anyway when they were safely far on the other side of that mysterious stretch of desert, where he prayed the town would no longer be.

* * * *

Denise felt euphoric with hope of returning to the real world, but her heart was breaking over Bob. She couldn't recall ever experiencing such opposing emotions. That stupid Bronx ox, why did he do it? Why hadn't he listened to Poppy? Fighting back tears, she imagined him correcting her: "That's Brooklyn, babe. Brooklyn ox . . . ."

Once again the rocky path jiggled her Mustang, and she gripped the wheel tightly, keeping it centered in the canal. Not about to stay at the foot of that cursed hill by herself, she had no alternative but to follow Poppy, trusting him with her life. She couldn't allow herself to even consider the possibility of him being wrong because that meant they were most likely about to become lizard lunch.

The mountain loomed ahead, blocking her view of the bizarre town awaiting them on the other side. It had all been so unbelievably horrible, but maybe it would soon be over at last. As she watched Poppy stick his arm through the window like he'd done several times before, a sobering thought gripped her mind like a fist: it truly *was* about to be over, one way or the other.

"Oh, Poppy, you'd better be right . . .!"

* * * *

Stunned, confused, and dreadfully afraid upon seeing the town still there, Poppy resisted the urge to retreat after navigating around the mountain, knowing it was now or never. Praying for divine protection, and that Denise would continue tailing him, he clenched his teeth and drove through it. "Praise the Lord!" he shouted while zipping past the few blank buildings, seeing neither the demon nor a hole in the pavement. Through the rearview mirror he watched them dematerialize like a desert mirage evaporating. The pavement was disappearing too, giving way to sand and rock beyond Denise's Mustang, transforming behind it as if she were towing twenty feet of pavement.

The Lord must have made it linger long enough for us to get through! he thought elatedly.

Too afraid things would change again to slow down, he sped down the highway at top end. Denise started honking her horn and waving with joy. He honked and waved back, then focused on the road ahead . . . .

SIX

Shuddering with relief, Poppy pulled into the sparsely occupied parking lot of the convenience store he'd breakfasted at yesterday. Two small boys were jumping off one of the picnic tables, merrily playing a game only they knew the rules to. He smiled at them for a moment, then looked towards Interstate Fifteen, less than a quarter mile away. Endless traffic zoomed across an overpass arching over the two-lane he'd just driven down. Everything looked exquisitely ordinary and normal.

The smell of corndogs and fries greeted his nostrils as he stepped out of the Jeep. Denise, who'd parked beside it, ran to him for a celebratory hug.

"We made it, Poppy! You were right all along, and we made it! Thank you!"

The grin he wore while accepting her embrace, vanished when he saw the RV coming down the service road, slowing as it approached the tarmac. Denise, facing the opposite way, couldn't see it. He put his hands on her shoulders and gently eased her back. "Denise, don't panic, but the RV's here."

Fright contorted her pretty face into a fleshy smear of incredulous despair. "Oh my god, no!"

He dug into his hip pocket. "Calm down and listen to me. We'll get through this, I promise, but we need to gas up. All that high speed driving made for lousy road mileage and I'm nearly on empty. Take this and give me your car keys—" he handed over his wallet. "I'll fill up the vehicles while you get us some food. Get a lot and get a variety, I don't know how long it's going to be until we're free of that cursed camper.

Don't buy any corned beef hash."

He'd tried to inject some humor at the last to lessen her distress, but it didn't work. Fear and disbelief radiated from a face turned cadaverously white as she relinquished her keys with a quivering hand.

Cautiously eyeing the RV, wondering why it hadn't spirited all three of them away during the night while they were sleeping, he eased the Jeep to a gas pump. The youngsters were too busy playing their made up sport to notice the vehicle had no driver. It parked near a corner of the building and left the engine idling.

Terror and confusion had replaced the momentary joy of believing they'd escaped. They had to get on the interstate and keep driving until they reached a spiritual boundary the RV couldn't cross. It shouldn't be here in the normal world, should have remained trapped in the now invisible town, it should—

The thought was so terrifying he scarcely dared think it, but it had to be true. They weren't in the real world yet. Up until that moment he thought he'd crossed the boundaries of the normal realm after leaving this place yesterday. Now he realized that transition had occurred before he got here. *That's why the RV was stocked with corned beef hash and chips!*

He had to get Denise out of there as soon as he filled up the Jeep. With no time to spare, they'd have to leave her Mustang. Poppy topped off the tank and placed the nozzle back on the pump, wishing he didn't have to get gasoline from this location since anything might be a toehold. Trying to appear nonchalant, he walked inside.

A fat lady behind the counter, who appeared to be either Native American or Mexican, smiled at him as he walked in the door. He nodded a greeting but didn't say a word, feeling the less interaction with anyone in this place the better.

Denise stood at the deli where a teenage boy was filling her order.

They dared not partake of the food from here. “Um, Denise, we won’t be needing anything after all.”

Eyeing him with fearful surprise, she stepped over to give him his wallet. “Are you sure?”

He nodded, then turned to the lady behind the counter, hating he’d forgotten the amount on the pump—now he’d have to speak to her. “How much for the gas?”

“For you, Mister Quinn? It’s on the house.”

Poppy’s bowels lurched with alarm, vacuuming all the moisture from his throat and mouth.

The teenager approached. “Here’s your Salisbury steak, Miss Jones.” He tried to hand her a large plastic bag that presumably contained the item, despite the fact the deli offered no such delicacy, only finger foods.

Gawking at the teenager with terrified astonishment, Denise started backing away from him. “Poppy, what’s going on here?”

One of the little boys came barging in. “Hi, Poppy and Denise! Mama, can I have a powdered doughnut?”

An eerie grin crept across the fat lady’s face. “Now you don’t want to spoil your supper, son. Guess what we’re having, Mister Quinn. Roast Talasota with Bob sauce.”

It was insane—totally insane—but though it made no rational sense at all, he knew what they had to do. He grabbed Denise’s hand and ran out the door, leaving the fat lady laughing at him, the small boy and teenager giggling through knowing grins.

Denise rushed to her Mustang but Poppy screamed, “No, come with me, forget about your car!”

She didn’t argue, and within seconds he had the engine pushed to its limit.

“Why are you going this way?! We’re heading back towards the town!”

"We can't get out any other way."

"Poppy, all you have to do is get on the interstate. I'm not going back there, take me back and let me get my car."

"Don't you get it? It won't be real."

"Yes it will, if we drive far enough it will."

He cut his eyes to her. "Where did you have lunch yesterday?"

"Poppy!"

"Humor me!!"

"At a restaurant. I told you that yesterday."

"Well that restaurant was within the boundary of this unreal world or that kid at the deli wouldn't have mentioned Salisbury steak, and the RV wouldn't have been stocked with it. Whatever it is we've stumbled into stretches far beyond the area of the demon's town. Like you, I thought the real world ended right outside there, but the truth is we left normal reality miles before that."

Her complexion turned a sickly pallor as she glared at him, eyes swimming with desperation. "How do you know?"

He refocused on the road. "That convenience store, the one we just left?"

"Yeah?"

"That's where I had the corned beef hash yesterday."

"Well that doesn't mean we can't escape by taking the interstate."

"I'm afraid it does."

"So just what do you propose we do? How is going back to the town going to help? It disappeared, remember?"

"The biker found the exit just like you speculated when you mentioned the possibility of a doorway connecting two dimensions. He didn't die in that hill, he escaped from this hell, and we have to go back there and find the invisible doorway just like he did. He must have been going down the riverbed for the second time when we saw him, having gone back like we did just now, planning to get on the interstate, only to discover there was no way out. How he knew to keep trying the hill, I don't know. But he made it, and so will we."

Her dark orbs blazed with incredulity for several moments before a glint of trust surfaced in them. "I hope to God you're right . . . ."

The pavement ended where the town once stood, but that didn't matter because the mountain, and more importantly the path commencing at its base, remained. After crossing a few miles of desert sand they reached it and banged over the rocks in silence, Denise staring straight ahead, looking as exhausted and spent as he felt. Over the hard-packed sand they went, neither of them uttering a syllable until they reached the hill.

Poppy screeched to a halt beside Bob's Buick and killed the engine. "Try to remember where he disappeared."

She pointed to an area atop the gentle slope of sand where the rocky cliff began.

"Okay, let's go . . . ."

They bounded up the hill towards it.

Feeling like an Indian Brave doing a war dance, he circled the area while stomping the ground, with Denise doing likewise. He kept at it until his right foot sank into the sand as if it were thin air.

"I found it!" He stood deathly still, one foot on solid ground, the other hovering over pay dirt. He held out his hand and she took it.

"I'll go first . . . ."

Poppy spiraled downward in total darkness, falling perhaps a thousand miles an hour or faster, he had no way of knowing. Denise did the same, he assumed, but the tremendous centrifugal force held him paralyzed, so he couldn't cry out to verify it. Before long the corkscrew motion began to decrease in speed. When his body finally quit spinning altogether, he found himself gaping at the most beautiful place he'd ever seen in his life.

He stood on the bank of a crystal-clear river inhabited by swarms of colorful fish. Emerald pastures with meadows of exotic plants and flowers, most of them a species he'd never seen before, lay on the other side of it. The watercourse ran beyond his field of vision leftwards, and wound past a dense forest about a half mile to his right. Turning to his rear, he saw a motorcycle lying on its side in the lush grass. A short distance beyond it, a wall of purple quartz rose endlessly up into a deep blue sky, and stretched horizontally as far as he could see. Denise suddenly materialized between him and the bike, looking dumbfounded. He couldn't help grinning as she surveyed her new surroundings.

She turned to him with an expression of childlike wonderment. "Is this heaven?"

"Looks beautiful enough to be, doesn't it. I have no idea where we are." His voice sounded funny to him, different somehow. Though he felt no pain in either, he wondered if spinning so fast had done something to his eardrums.

After glancing around in every direction, jaw sagging with awe, Denise eyed the motorcycle. "I wonder where he is."

"No telling." His voice still didn't sound right, but since Denise's hadn't altered, he figured it had to be a temporary condition rather than permanent hearing damage.

"Well, what do we do now?"

Poppy checked his watch. "I guess we follow the river. That way we can always backtrack without getting lost. Pick a direction and we'll start walking."

She looked to her left, away from the forest. "Okay, this way."

SEVEN

Finding the door unlocked meant he didn't have to break a window, something he'd have done without hesitation rather than heist any of the other wheels there. He didn't know how to disable the steering wheel lock on modern automobiles, but thankfully this vintage ride didn't have one. It took only seconds to hotwire it.

The interstate looked so tempting and normal, every instinct he possessed demanded he take it, but he knew that was the super-slab to hell. Bob gunned Denise's Mustang down the only other road available.

An overpowering urge had driven him aboard that friggin' bus when its engine started cranking, and he'd blacked out the moment he got in it. He'd woken up on the floor and scrambled out of the RV, finding himself at a convenience store, which seemed familiar. Then he'd spotted Denise's Mustang. Assuming she and Pops followed the haunted camper there, he'd gone into the store expecting to find them, but had found another nightmare instead.

"Hello, Bob, don't you look tasty," a fat lady behind the pay counter had said while sliding a whit stone over the edge of an ax as two little boys rushed in from outside.

They'd eagerly asked, "Mama, is that our supper?"

"Yes, that's our Roast Talasota," she'd answered with a wicked laugh.

As her ominous snickering continued, a huge black dude with no irises, only whites for eyes, had rose from behind the counter—holding a long knife in one hand, a meat fork in the other.

Bolting outside in a blind panic, knowing he'd never make it back to reality on foot, he'd locked himself inside Denise's Mustang. While fiddling with the wires, he'd been scared to death those creeps were going to come after him, smash the windows, drag him from the car, and butcher him for barbecue. Thank God no one had even stepped outside.

From the edge of the parking lot he'd seen a sign directing the way to Interstate Fifteen, and realized why the store had sparked a feeling of recognition. He'd exited for a pit stop there and had gotten back on the freeway daydreaming about how much fun Vegas would be. No way was he getting back on the interstate from that location again.

He'd bought the milk and powdered doughnuts there.

* * * *

She'd been analyzing Poppy as they walked along, admiring his lean profile, silver hair, and that incredible brain beneath those wavy locks. It was at work now—she could tell by his pensive expression—thinking ahead, anticipating what might lie in store, deliberating the proper action to take in each contingency. Up until now he'd been right about everything except his occupational theory, so she had every reason to believe he'd figure a way out of this too.

The absence of a ring didn't automatically make him a bachelor since some married men preferred keeping that finger bare, but she had the feeling he was. He obviously didn't care much for self exposure, but his intellect, sweetness, and sensitivity came through just the same. Those qualities she found immensely attractive, but he had a mysterious spiritual side that evoked emotions she couldn't quite nail down.

Recalling him conversing with Bob in Italian, she wondered if he spoke any other foreign languages.

"Vy gavarite pa rUsski?"

"Nyet," he answered, grinning.

She giggled. "Funny how you understood the question and answered in the very language you claim not to speak."

"It sounded like it might be soviet-speak so I took a wild guess," Poppy said in flawless Russian. *"Just teasing of course. It's one of my favorite languages."*

"Can you speak German?"

"Deutsche? Nein. Goethe's Die Laune des Verliebten est lang, ya vol?"

She laughed again. "So you speak Italian, Russian, and German. Speak any others?"

"A few," he replied with a wink.

"How many?"

"About a dozen I guess."

"Fluently?"

"I suppose."

"You know, Bob and I never did get the skinny on you during show and tell."

"Not much to tell. I'm a theologian as I said, and live on a small farm in Texas."

"Alone?"

"Mm hmm."

"So you're single then."

He nodded.

She kept studying him as they continued along the river. "Where did you go to college?"

"I didn't."

"I thought you said you were a theologian?"

"I am."

"Seminary?"

"No."

"How could you learn theology without going to college or seminary?"

"You've heard of self taught? Well I'm God taught."

She laughed. "Quit teasing. Seriously, where did you go to college?"

"Seriously, I didn't. I didn't even finish high school."

"Seriously?"

"Seriously."

"A natural born genius, huh?"

He turned her way and frowned. "Who said anything about genius?"

"My, what modesty."

She'd never gone for older men but this one amazed her. He dressed like a cowboy, yet spoke like a scholar. It was hard to believe he'd never worn a cap and gown. Poppy's walk began to turn her on, so she forced herself to look straight ahead. This wasn't the time for romance, and he wouldn't be interested in her anyway. Men like him required a rare sort of woman: a feminine brain trust with the sensitivity of Audrey Hepburn and spirituality of Mother Theresa. Being neither a genius nor saint, she'd never be able to fill his needs, just as Bob couldn't hers.

Poor Bob. He was the kind of man she always avoided. The quintessential lady killer—full of himself, figuring *broads* were put on earth as his special playthings *no-doubt-about-it*. She could never fall in love with him like she feared might be happening with Poppy, even if he had somehow survived.

That spooky lady at the store sounded deadly serious when she'd spoken like a cannibal. The thought of Bob being eaten made her nauseous, driving away all romantic musings over Poppy. Realizing she'd soon start crying if she didn't quit thinking about such a gruesome possibility, she reminded herself the Bronx ox was far too strong for that woman and the deli attendant to overpower. That eased her mind for a moment until it dawned on her any of those sinister people could have taken him down with a gun, even one of the little boys. But the real problem was the evil force controlling the RV. His muscles were powerless against it.

Thinking about the way he'd fallen after getting inside that cursed vehicle, she rubbed her eyes, trying not to cry as brutal factuality drove away what little hope she'd managed to retain since the RV carried him away. Bob was bound to be dead.

* * * *

The Mustang reeked of Denise's womanly scent. Bob found the smell intimidating. He'd fallen in love, and wished like hell he hadn't. It felt weird experiencing defeat over a female for the first time in his life. All the chicks dug him, and he'd sampled more than his fair share, but Denise wasn't some shallow bimbo whose greatest attributes were a luscious set of jugs and a pretty face. Not that she lacked those endowments, she had them in spades, but she was too brainy and deep for the likes of him. Hell, she'd earned a Ph.D. for crying out loud, while he'd barely made it through high school. Oh sure, he could pull out all the stops—turn on the ol' Talasota Magicota and make her swoon, but he'd never be able to keep her. She'd eventually grow immune to his charms and dump him like a glass of stale beer, leaving him crying in his.

Knowing he'd never feel this way about anyone else, and not the type to settle for second best, it looked like his Casanova days would never end. Destiny had condemned him to remain a noncommittal hound for as long as the weasel could get stiff enough to shake a mulberry bush. But he couldn't worry about that right now. He'd get drunk and lick his wounds when he finally made it back to Brooklyn. Keeping his ass alive long enough to do that was all that mattered at the moment.

Not liking what he appeared to be seeing up ahead, he hoped his eyes were playing tricks on him.

“Fuck!” he yelled upon discovering they weren’t. The road ended in the middle of nowhere, leaving him no choice but to head back towards the convenience store. Swearing with frustration, he braked to a stop, and got out to take a leak.

Gazing in the distance while draining the weasel, he spotted the mountain where the riverbed began and freaked. This disappearing road had to be the very one he’d been on when that town appeared . . . but now it was gone, thank God. *Maybe it'll be safe to take the interstate now,* he thought, wishfully. *Nah, no way—no friggin' way! But just what am I gonna do now?*

He looked down while zipping his pants and noticed tire tracks in the sand. Something very odd occurred to him. Instead of turning around, he drove across the desert.

EIGHT

Bob heaved a sigh of relief. The fuel gauge had been on empty for the last twenty miles, but the Mustang hadn't stalled. He jerked the gearshift to park, pulled the wires apart to kill the engine, and got out. Quickly, he stripped off the clothes and shoes he'd taken from the RV, leaving them on the ground. He didn't want anything from that ghost-driven bus near him or his car.

On the way to the Skylark, wearing only his boxers, he glanced at the tires on the Jeep and made a victory fist while hollering, "Yes!" Grabbing his jeans from the back seat of the Lark where he'd tossed them after putting on the khakis in the RV, he jerked them on, but couldn't find his t-shirt. He nixed the idea of getting another one from his suitcase in the trunk, for fear of the monster showing up before he even got his tennis shoes tied. Once he'd done that, Bob ran up the hill bare-chested, following depressions in the loose sand, that might or might not have been left by human feet.

Trampling all over an area that had been disturbed, he twisted his ankle in a patch of exceptionally loose sand and fell, face down. Instinctively thrusting out his arms to break his fall, only one did. The other disappeared in the hill, all the way to his shoulder.

He knew one of two fates had befallen Denise and Pops: they'd somehow known to make like the biker and find this spot on the hill as he suspected, or both of them had bought it at the convenience store. If they'd driven there in Denise's car, they were most likely dead, but he'd confirmed the single set of tire tracks leading to the mountain belonged to the Jeep.

That meant somebody drove it back here. If they were still alive, they'd fled the store in Pops' ride, leaving the Mustang behind for reasons unknown. Either that or Pops managed to escape after those bastards got their hands on Denise. He knew this for the simple fact that if Denise alone survived, there was no way in hell she'd have chosen Pops' wheels over her beloved classic.

It didn't take Sherlock Holmes to figure out what they'd wound up doing, since there was no friggin' way they went over the hill. Someone, or some thing, had been all around the spot that swallowed his arm, but the sand was too loose to retain definite impressions. He couldn't even tell which tracks were his. Hoping the others were made by the feet of Denise and Pops, he eyed the mysterious dirt as he slowly stood up.

Taking one last look around, he stepped through.

"Whoa . . .!"

Vertigo seized him as he whirled around like a friggin' tornado while plunging down faster than a bullet, hoping like hell he hadn't made a fatal mistake. About the time he'd concluded he had, and would soon be seeing his maker, the pace began to slow down. Soon thereafter, he finally quit spinning and falling.

Unclenching his eyelids, Bob gaped at the surroundings. Absolutely awestruck, he turned slowly around, taking in a view the likes of which he'd never seen. Breathtaking beauty lay before him in every direction except one—a purple wall seemed to reach above the sky, and zoomed from horizon to horizon. He stepped to the edge of a river, and felt like he was looking at a living kaleidoscope, there were so many multicolored fish lazily swimming around.

Spotting the biker's hog, Bob wondered why the dude had abandoned it. A thrill shot through him as he realized the dips in the sand where he'd fallen through couldn't have been made by those tires. Denise and Pops, or at least one of them, had to have been on that section of turf. Then something else hit him, and confusion overrode his excitement. The biker had been racing all over that crazy hill, yet he couldn't recall seeing any continuous ruts made by a motorcycle, and there should have been plenty of them. He didn't ponder that mystery for long—it would take a bigger brain than his to figure out how such a thing could happen.

"Think," he said aloud, fingertips tapping his temples. "If they made it, they must have started out here because me and the biker did."

He lifted the motorcycle from the ground and mounted it. It was a beautiful customized job: black, with chrome everywhere—four cylinders, electric starter, the whole nine yards. It was built similar to a Harley, but he couldn't spot the make. The biker had left the key in the ignition. Bob twisted it and the hog fired right up. Revving the engine, he relished the angry sound of controlled explosion, and the raw power vibrating between his legs.

"Okay, if they made it, which way did they go? Not up the crystals, that's for sure." He eyed the wall of purplish stone, then looked towards a dense forest. "Doubt they'd swim across the river, so they either went towards the woods or the other way. Pops is a braniac, he'd do the smart thing. I'm not the sharpest knife in the set, so he'd probably do the opposite of what I would do. So what would I do . . .?"

After considering it a brief time, he kicked the bike into first gear and took off. When he got to the trees, he discovered they were so close together, navigating through them on the motorcycle would be more cumbersome than practical, so he killed the engine. Forcing the kickstand out with the toe of his tennis shoe, he eased the rig leftwards until its weight rested on it.

He cupped his hands around his mouth. "Yo, Pops, Denise, can you hear me?!" Bob hollered the question several more times, but no one responded, so he stepped into the forest.

Numerous scents teased his nose—all of them rich and pleasingly fragrant, but the only one he recognized, somewhat resembled pine. It made him think of Christmas trees and last year's family yuletide feast. It would be the last one he'd share with Grandma Pacino who'd passed away two months ago. His eyes turned misty, so he quit reminiscing.

Small shrubs and colorful undergrowth made it impossible to leave discernable footprints. He snapped an occasional branch and left it dangling in order to find his way back to the bike. Ambling around one tree, arbitrarily choosing another, he zigzagged deeper into the woods. After a fair amount of time passed without finding any broken twigs, disturbed shrubs, or anything else indicating somebody had passed through, he decided to climb one of the trees, hoping he might be able to spot them from up above. Selecting a tall one with a narrow trunk, he shimmied up to the branches, and climbed like a monkey until he neared the top. Unfortunately, he couldn't see past the other green peaks nearby.

* * * *

They'd been hiking for an hour. The wall of quartz and winding river apparently had no end, and the landscape hardly deviated from one mile to the next.

Poppy stopped walking, motioning for Denise to do the same. "Let's go back and try the forest. We're not getting anywhere this way, and we'd probably only find more of the same on the other side of the river."

"I'm afraid you're right, and my legs are getting tired. What we need is a boat." Placing hands on hips, she heaved a sigh. "We weren't thinking. We should have taken the motorcycle."

He cast her a disapproving frown and started walking. "We'd have been stealing another man's property. Besides, I don't know how to drive one. Do you?"

Her jaw dropped. "You're kidding me! You mean there's actually something you don't know?"

"There's an endless list of things I don't know. Can you drive one?"

"I had a boyfriend back in high school who tried to teach me, but I couldn't get the hang of working the clutch with my hand and shifting gears with my foot, it just seemed so backwards to me. I loved sitting behind him while he drove though. So how come you never learned to ride one?"

"Too dangerous. No matter how careful you try to be, if you get hit, you're defenseless. The world's best motorcyclists can't prevent someone from running a stop sign and ramming into them. In a car, at least you've got some metal between you and whatever vehicle that rams you . . . ."

Poppy had checked his watch when they left their point of entry, and they should've been close enough to see the motorcycle by now. The distance to the forest appeared to be about the same as his recollection of it when they'd arrived, so the biker must have returned for it. Skid marks about thirty feet ahead confirmed it. He'd peeled out in the direction of the woods.

"Well, Denise, we won't have to worry about being tempted to teach ourselves how to ride the motorcycle and steal it. It's gone."

She glanced at the tracks and frowned. "Why would he leave the bike and then come back for it?"

"I don't know."

"It looks like he was headed for the trees."

"Sure does." He checked his watch. "Let's hope he found the gateway out of this place like he did the other . . . ."

When they got to the forest he spotted the motorcycle leaning on its kickstand. That didn't make any sense. If the biker had walked here and went back for his motorcycle, he wouldn't have done so just to leave it behind once again. And he couldn't have gone the other direction or they'd have seen him. It seemed very unlikely he'd swim across the stream without checking out this side first. Nothing in the lavish countryside warranted getting his leather duds soaked.

Poppy concluded the biker was either insane after all, or someone else rode his motorcycle here. The latter seemed more probable to him, and a wild hope sprang up. "Denise, I think Bob may still be alive."

She stared at him with cautious disbelief, as if she'd been told something too wonderful to be true. "You really think so? Why?"

He vocalized his logic, but ended with a disappointing possibility. "If Bob didn't drive it here, we have another friend besides the biker. But since this whole surrealistic experience thus far has involved only the four of us, my money's on Bob, although I'm at a loss to explain how he got here."

"Who cares, as long as he's alive!" She ran to the nearest tree and yelled, "Bob, we're here by the motorcycle! Can you hear me?!"

"Yeah!" said a heavily accented voice that could belong to only one person. "Don't go in the forest, I'm on my way to you guys . . . ."

* * * *

The instant that Bronx ox came into view she ran up to hug him. Her momentum knocked him off balance and they fell. She landed on top of him with her right cheek grazing his left, her breasts compressed by his firm, exposed chest.

"Oh, Bob, you're alive—you're alive!"

He coughed, took a shallow breath, and laughingly said, "Well I was until a second ago."

Denise knew he must have been very uncomfortable with

his bare back pressed against grass, leaves, and pine needles, but she didn't want to get off of him. It startled her to think that if Poppy wasn't there, she'd plant her mouth on those full Italian lips. Feeling him getting aroused, it took all her willpower to keep from pressing her hips downward. Knowing she wouldn't be able to resist the urge a second longer, she forced herself to stand up, and gazed longingly at the bulge in his jeans as he rose from the ground.

Poppy hugged him, depriving her of the view. "You gave us quite a fright, my friend. It's so good to see you in one piece."

"Good to see you too, Pops."

When they parted, she couldn't pry her eyes off his delicious naked chest. "How did you get here, and just where is your shirt, young man?"

"Wow, it was a trip, let me tell ya . . . ."

As Bob explained what happened since he saw them last, Denise couldn't make the desire go away. Though still afraid she was falling in love with Poppy, she wanted that handsome Italian *badly.* His pectorals sent her into orbit the moment she saw them, and feeling them flatten her breasts had ignited a passion that remained unsatisfied only because they hadn't been alone. She was no floozy—no easy woman by anyone's definition—but she wanted to tear off her clothes and demand he put out the inferno raging in her loins. Oh but that Adonis looked good without a shirt on! Staring unblinkingly at Bob's upper body, she realized Poppy would soon take note of her lust, so she tried to look away.

But at that precise moment an epiphany occurred:

They weren't in heaven, they were in Eden. Bob was Adam, she was Eve, and the unattainable Poppy was God. She shouldn't be wearing clothes, Eve didn't wear clothes in Eden. Denise gasped with excitement—that's why Bob had no shirt, further verifying her vision. He must take off the rest of his clothes as well, and so must she. They were in Eden and were supposed to be naked—they had no business covering their bodies in paradise, they should be naked.

She whirled round and round, analyzing the enchanting garden, looking for substantiation that this was indeed what she felt it had to be . . . Eden . . . Eden . . . *Eden.*

But the trees were wrong, they bore no fruit. There had to be fruit trees, and of course the Tree of Life and Tree of Knowledge. She stopped turning and stared at the beautiful waterway as the truth dawned on her. They were only in the periphery of Eden. The actual garden lay elsewhere, perhaps down the river. The river—of course! It was the River of Life and it flowed right straight to Eden.

Intoxicated by the enlightenment, having never felt so beautiful, so desirable, so . . . uninhibited, she began to disrobe.

* * * *

Like Bob, he stood speechless as a mute idiot, gaping at the place where Denise had taken off her clothes. The emotions swirling around his thoughts were impossible to demarcate. Somehow she knew to do this. A mere paleontologist understood what the brilliant theologian did not. But how? She questioned God's existence, she'd said as much, and yet she—the doubter, and not he, the staunch believer who'd most assuredly give his life rather than deny Christ—had comprehended it. More importantly, she believed it, and hence, she escaped.

It wouldn't do him any good to follow suit. All he'd get for shedding his clothes would be a good razzing from Bob. He couldn't make himself believe it in the sense she had, for that took childlike faith. Some perception about this place had formed in her mind and she'd believed in it enough to take off her clothes in front of two men she didn't even know existed until yesterday. That action required the faith of a child, the kind of faith God takes hold of and nurtures, eventually revealing Himself through.

He'd never be able to go backwards and pretend he didn't know, therefore he couldn't attain such innocent belief. His own escape would elude him until he completely understood the reason for this place. Unlike Denise, he was far too advanced to perceive this gorgeous pastoral setting as anything more than mere illusion. Though certainly real enough to imprison him, it was an exotic stage prop, much like the town with the creature, who pointed towards the day that men have dreaded since Adam—the end of time.

Poppy hadn't gotten round to telling her what dawned on him when they'd raced back through the town and wound up at the convenience store. This paradox they'd been pulled into had a specific purpose. Though it appeared malevolent in the beginning when they'd been abducted from conventional reality, not a hair of their heads had been harmed. He felt it had something to do with preparing for the end times, and this conditioning centered on Denise, with he and Bob playing lesser roles. Until he'd turned up alive, Poppy thought Bob's part of this had been fulfilled. He figured his own role was to verify Denise's testimony when they got back to the real world. People weren't likely to believe a preacher alone, but an agnostic paleontologist with nothing to gain would have credibility, especially since nobody could have accounted for Bob's disappearance. Now she once again had two witnesses. Of course it was only a theory, he had no proof, so she most likely wouldn't have believed him anyway.

What he did know, and clung to at the moment, was the scripture proclaiming God wasn't the author of confusion. Since he hadn't knowingly rebelled against The Almighty, he felt confident he'd come to understand what this place represented, and subsequently be freed from it. But he feared it wouldn't be any time soon.

Another Bible passage came to mind—God speaking to the hiding Adam: "Who told thee that thou wast naked?"

"Um . . . Pops, where did she go?"

Poppy finally took his eyes off the pink pullover, blue jeans, bra, and panties lying on top of a pair of sneakers, and looked at the bewildered Yankee. "She escaped, Bob. She's back in the real world."

"Whoa! You mean to tell me all we gotta do is strip and we're out of here? What are we waiting for, Pops, let's get naked . . .!"

NINE

The sound of music blaring forced her eyes open. She cut them to the radio alarm clock, slammed a hand on the snooze button, and closed them again. A vague memory troubled her as she tried to go back to sleep. It would neither go away, nor crystallize into coherency. Attributing the disjointed reflection to her brain hovering between dreamland and the brink of consciousness, she adjusted her pillow and pressed back into it. Then something dawned on her and Denise launched up on her elbows, wide awake.

She was back in Franklin Park.

How could I drive all the way from Las Vegas to Chicago and not remember it?

The radio shrieked again and she turned it off, squinting at it, still trying to remember. Currents of anxiety raced through her at the realization she couldn't recall anything about her stay at Vegas.

Jerking the covers off, she swerved her feet to the floor, assuming a sitting position on the edge of the bed, breasts swaying in the process. She glanced down at them. A peculiar feeling swept over her at being nude . . . she didn't know why since she usually slept that way.

For several minutes she sat there, scanning her bedroom, trying to reason everything out. The antique chair she always draped her clothes on when retiring stood empty, and she couldn't locate her shoes. Reeling with confusion, she went to the living room to see if she'd undressed there last night.

She hadn't.

After a search of the entire house turned up nothing,

perplexity began to edge towards angry frustration and fear. She went back to the bedroom, snatched panties and t-shirt from her chest of drawers, threw them on the bed, and went to the closet for jeans and shoes . . . .

The strange impression she'd felt over waking up naked intensified as she soaped and rinsed her bare skin in the shower, still trying to remember the last part of her vacation. Her nerves were tied in knots of apprehension by the time she toweled herself dry. She still couldn't summon a single memory of being in Las Vegas or driving home.

Foregoing a bra since she had no plans to go anywhere, she pulled the t-shirt over her head. Something stirred. A mental image surfaced, but refused to come into focus—stubbornly remaining a distorted abstract in the back of her mind. It seemed to have some connection with the way her nipples had stiffened when the white fabric slid over them. Straining to recall, she stood bottomless, hands fisted, lids screwed shut, teeth clinched.

But the dots wouldn't connect. "Shit! Why can't I remember?"

She put on the rest of her clothes and went to the kitchen. Anxiety had weakened her appetite, but she made herself pull a box of shredded wheat from the cabinet, and dumped a few spoon-size briquettes in a bowl. Still trying to force something, anything to come back to her, she took a half gallon carton from the refrigerator. Much the same as waking up nude and the t-shirt had, the milk vexed her. Frowning, she drenched her cereal, returned the bothersome container, and sat down.

Scooping up a chunk of dairy-soaked wheat, she froze before it crossed her lips. *Why did I set my alarm when I'm on vacation?* The spoon slipped from her hand and bounced off the bowl, spinning like a propeller to the floor, catapulting its load in the process.

"Fuck!"

Rarely using the expletive, she wished she hadn't now because hearing it invoked the same troubling, impossible to discern impression everything else had that morning. Had she apologized for saying it recently? It seemed like she had, but to whom?

It dawned on her she'd forgotten to brush her teeth, normally the first thing she did after rising, so she abandoned the idea of breakfast and went to the bathroom, but couldn't find her toothbrush.

Must have left it in the car with my bags.

Digging through a narrow closet beside the lavatory, she pulled the last one from a three-pack . . . .

She spent the entire morning stretched out on the couch, brooding over her memory lapse. The last twenty-four hours of her life remained a total blank. Resisting an urge to call her friend Peggy in Las Vegas, she rose and ambled to the kitchen at the insistence of an empty stomach. The milk was sour, she discovered after taking a sip, which she quickly spat in the sink while emptying the glass into it.

Nothing looked appealing. At length she decided to get a Reuben and slaw from a nearby deli. She pulled off the t-shirt on her way to the bedroom, and it tugged at her memory again while sliding across her breasts, once more turning both nipples hard as stone. Angrily, she wadded up the disturbing garment and threw it on the dresser, glared at it while fastening her bra, then went to the closet and put on a blouse.

She'd apparently also left her purse in the car, as she couldn't find it anywhere in the house. Entering the garage, she flipped the light switch. Panicked, she hurried across the empty cement, hastily unlocked the overhead door, raised it, and gasped with horror upon finding the driveway also vacant.

Her Mustang had been stolen.

* * * *

Denise sat on her front porch, lethargically watching the planes taking off and landing at busy O'Hare in the near distance, making out the airliners by their blinking lights. Having spent a sizable amount of money restoring it, she prayed her car would be found intact and not stripped for parts. Guilt lingered over lying to the police earlier in the day, but since she always secured her most prized possession in the garage at night, she felt that had to be where she'd last seen it when the officer asked. She didn't want him, or anyone else, to know she couldn't remember. He'd said the thief must have picked the overhead door lock since there were no signs of breaking and entering. The bastard had not only made off with her cherished Mustang, but her purse and luggage as well. She'd never had anything stolen from her, and the sense of violation went beyond words.

But that paled in comparison to having a whole day robbed from her memory.

A seven-forty-seven took off. Watching its taillights disappear into the black Chicago sky, she verbally recounted her last recollection before the lapse: "I remember leaving Los Angeles and driving down Interstate Fifteen . . . I remember seeing a truck driver getting a ticket . . . I remember a billboard advertising a restaurant ten miles ahead and deciding to eat there and . . . and . . . that's the last thing I remember."

She'd been fighting the temptation all day. Peggy would wonder why she was asking questions about things she should know the answer to, and that would arouse suspicion, which might lead to her mother finding out. The last thing she needed was that woman having an excuse to come see her, and nothing could prevent the worrywart from doing so. After retiring, none of her visits lasted less than two excruciatingly boring weeks. Now afraid she might go mad otherwise, Denise went inside and called Las Vegas. When no one answered after five rings she screamed, "Dammit, Peggy, pick up the fucking phone!"

Six rings . . . seven rings . . . eight rings . . . .

"Hello?"

"Peggy? Denise here."

"Where have you been, Denise?! I've been worried sick. I called your mother earlier, and she said you left her place two days ago. You were supposed to come see me, remember? Your mom told me you hadn't mentioned it to her so I must have misunderstood, either that or you just changed your mind, but I couldn't believe you wouldn't call and tell me. I called your cell at least a dozen times but couldn't even get your voicemail. I was about ready to file a missing persons on you, girl!"

Her stomach turned inside out with nausea as a vortex of confusion and fear whirled within her mind. She hadn't gone to Vegas, that's why she couldn't recall anything about it. But why couldn't she remember driving home from Los Angeles?

"Are you still there?"

". . . Yeah."

"Well I hope you're still coming."

Denise feared she must either be in the early stages of Alzheimer's, or slowly going insane.

"Denise? Are you still coming or not?"

"Um, no . . . I went home."

"So you're in Chicago?"

". . . Yeah."

"Well what happened? Why'd you cut your vacation short?"

She couldn't trust Peggy not to tell her mother, even if sworn to secrecy. "Um . . . I'm really sorry, just called to apologize for not making it up there."

"Girl, what's wrong; you sound horrible?"

"Must be trying to catch a cold. I did change my mind and somehow forgot to let you know until now, sorry I worried you. Listen, I have to go . . . ."

Denise started crying the moment she hung up the phone. "My god, what is happening to me? Why can't I remember?"

* * * *

Bob kept beseeching him to "get naked" ever since Denise vanished a few minutes ago. Poppy had told him it wouldn't work for them, and tried to reassure him by explaining what they were dealing with—that this wasn't a hidden paradise beneath the desert but one with it, existing in the same location, yet spiritual rather than physical in nature. The purple wall most likely formed the boundary between the two. He'd told him this beautiful countryside was a mere facsimile, a contrivance constructed just for them for reasons not yet known, so they were in no immediate danger. But Bob remained adamant and was now untying his shoes, so Poppy had to lay out the cold hard facts to save the guy from brutal embarrassment.

"Bob, listen to me. It wasn't taking off her clothes that freed Denise. Shedding her attire was simply a manifestation of faith, and the action was rewarded. This is only the beginning for her. Denise was agnostic, but now she believes, or at least is beginning to. At some point she'll have a confrontation with Christ and she'll accept Him. After that happens her belief system will grow to maturity. God called and she acted on it, even though she had no idea she was being called. However imperfect her perception of it, she acted in faith, and—"

"You're talking way over my head, Pops," Bob interrupted while unzipping his pants.

Poppy summoned a look of reassurance. "Be that as it may, I think that—"

Bob vanished.

An inexpressible feeling of aloneness enveloped him as he

stared unblinkingly at the Yankee's tennis shoes, jeans, and boxers. Nonetheless, he felt happy for him and Denise.

They were safe and sound in the real world.

It should have occurred to him that Bob could believe strongly enough simply because he'd seen it work for Denise. That was the faith of a child. And to think he'd tried to talk him out of it. If only he could make himself believe it. Unfortunately, he couldn't. Trying not to let despair overtake him, he gazed stupidly at the watch that had dropped from midair when the naked Yankee dematerialized, and said, "Goodbye, Bob."

TEN

They'd fingerprinted him, taken mug shots, and locked him up in a Los Angeles jail to await extradition—to Chicago of all places. Hell he'd never even been to Chicago, much less stolen a Mustang from there, and he must have told them so a hundred times. But Bob wasn't being extradited for grand theft auto: he'd also been charged with murder.

A loud noise had startled him awake and he'd found himself butt naked in his Skylark. The racket had come from a big-ass helicopter, spewing up dirt all over the place as it landed. Several badges jumped out and he'd tried to get dressed before anyone saw him, but couldn't find his clothes. The cops found his suitcase in the trunk, unmolested, yet except for his t-shirt—that had been stuffed under the front seat for some crazy reason—everything else he'd been wearing, along with his wallet, never turned up.

No one believed he couldn't remember driving there, had no recall of shedding his duds, or that the first time he'd laid eyes on that Mustang and Jeep was when he'd woken up to this friggin' nightmare. He'd protested until blue in the face that the last thing he remembered was heading for Las Vegas on Interstate Fifteen after leaving San Bernardino. His cousin Al could verify he'd left there in his Skylark rather than a Mustang, but he knew that wouldn't cut any ice with them. Besides, he didn't want any of his family to know he'd been arrested, certain this crazy mix up would eventually get straightened out.

He had no idea why the Mustang had his fingerprints on it, but the real kick in the ass was the Jeep. He'd been accused of whacking its owner.

* * * *

The two men standing at her door introduced themselves as Detectives John Crate and Houston Shoat. Crate, a thin blonde man with pale-pink skin and bulging eyes, cut quite a contrast to Shoat. Darkly handsome like Rock Hudson, he had a powerful build and an air of authority that exceeded the badge he held out for verification. He slipped it inside a black suit jacket and said, "Your car's been recovered, Miss Jones. May we come in and talk to you for a minute?"

Denise stepped aside so they could enter. "Is it in one piece? Please tell me it wasn't stripped for parts."

"It's probably a little dusty since it was found in the Mojave Desert, and it was hotwired so a few wires were cut, but it's intact otherwise. They found your purse and luggage as well."

"Do I have to go get it, or will they have someone drive it here?"

"I would imagine it'll depend on your auto insurance, Miss Jones."

"Denise," she insisted, grinning.

The detective donned a very disarming 'handsome' smile.

"Who stole it?"

"That's what we need to talk to you about. Do you know a Roberto Talasota from New York . . .?"

* * * *

Poppy wondered if time moved the same here as it did in the normal world. One hour in this contrived paradise might be the equivalent of a day or longer there, or vice versa, but it didn't matter. It was irrelevant here. Over twelve hours had passed since he'd relieved himself in the RV, yet his bladder and bowels were complacent, and he felt neither hunger nor thirst. Using the motorcycle for a seat with no intention of trying to ride it, he gazed idly around. The endless pastures seemed to mock him, the purple barrier dared him to find a way out.

Though the sky blazed brightly as a cloudless midday in Texas, the illumination didn't come from the sun. This place didn't have one. More proof, he felt, that this immaculate garden was merely an illusion created just for them—himself, Bob, the biker, and especially Denise.

An odd thought kept crossing his mind. He'd been trying to make it go away but it stubbornly persisted, warning that Bob had been arrested for his murder. Not only could he not shake off the strange reverie, it soon expanded into the notion that the Yankee was being extradited to Chicago.

"This is nonsense," he said aloud, again noticing his voice sounded different....

* * * *

Denise wasn't about to admit that for all she knew she *had* met a Roberto Talasota during the period of time she couldn't account for. "No, I don't know him."

"Well it appears he's your thief."

She peered at Detective Shoat through narrowed eyes, now wondering why the Chicago Police Department had sent two detectives to notify her they'd found her car. "What's going on? What are you not telling me?"

"Do you know a Paul Quinn from Evanston?"

The name Paul evoked nothing, yet Quinn mildly stimulated her. "No."

"Are you sure? You seem hesitant."

"Yes, I'm sure. Quinn slightly rings a bell, but not Paul."

"What's the first name of the Quinn you know?"

"I don't know anyone by that name, it just sounds familiar for some reason. Would you please tell me what's going on?"

"The Paul Quinn I asked you about is missing. His Jeep was found beside your car, and it appears that Mister Talasota has something to do with his absence. What we're wondering is how Talasota managed to drive his own car from New York to California, while at the same time steal yours from Chicago."

Her knees went weak. She had to tell Detective Shoat she couldn't remember or she might wind up being implicated in a murder. "I drove to Los Angeles to see my mother, and left there planning to visit a friend in Las Vegas. I remember leaving my mother's three days ago but . . . ."

"But what?" said Detective Crate.

"I can't fucking remember getting home!" She burst into tears and told them about waking up with no memory of climbing into her own bed the night before, lying to the officer about last seeing her car parked in the garage, and that the last recollection she really had of her Mustang was driving it down Interstate Fifteen, heading for Las Vegas. "The last thing I recall is seeing a sign for a restaurant and deciding to eat there. I guess that must be where he stole it."

Detective Crate scrutinized her with skeptical eyes. "And you have no idea how you got home?"

She shook her head.

"Did you have a headache when you woke up?"

"No."

"What do you do for a living?"

"I teach at Northwestern."

The detectives exchanged a knowing look.

"What?" Her heart raced with fear she was about to be arrested.

Crate's gaze turned cynical. "Paul Quinn's a professor at Northwestern as well. Some coincidence, don't you think?"

"Thought you said he was from Evanston?"

"I did," said Detective Shoat.

"Well I work in the Chicago branch, not in Evanston."

Blatantly frowning, Crate folded his arms. "Talasota's from Brooklyn, New York, and you say you don't know him. Why would he come to Chicago and steal your car?"

"I told you, he must have stolen it while I was out west. Do you think I had something to do with the disappearance of this Paul Quinn? Am I a suspect?"

Detective Shoat gave her another 'handsome' smile. "Of course not, but we need to figure out how you got home—put the pieces together. Would you help us do that?"

Though relieved to hear a negative answer to her question, she wondered if he was really telling the truth because of Crate's deportment. "I want to know worse than you do—it's been driving me crazy. I called my friend in Las Vegas and she'd been worried about me not showing up, so I know I never made it there."

He scratched his head. "I'm sorry, must be having a problem with my own memory. Would you please tell me again when your lapse ended?"

"Yesterday morning when I woke up."

"You remember everything all right since then?"

"Clear as a bell."

"Do you drink?" Detective Crate asked, smugly.

"It wasn't an alcoholic blackout."

"How can you be so sure since you don't remember?"

His arrogant expression and haughty tone angered her. She gave him a go-to-hell look. "Because I didn't wake up with a hangover, that's why."

Detective Shoat cleared his throat. "You had to have flown back or hitched a ride. Maybe you took a bus."

Still resenting Crate's insolence, she stabbed him with her eyes one last time before answering Shoat. "I've never traveled by bus before. Of course I can't swear I didn't, since I can't remember getting home."

"I'll check with the airlines," Shoat continued. "Meanwhile let's narrow down the time frame. You said the last thing you remember was planning to stop and eat. Do you recall the time?"

"Not the exact time, but it was before noon. I didn't eat breakfast and was getting hungry, so I'd guess somewhere between ten and eleven."

"What time did you wake up yesterday morning?"

"Six thirty, and I'm positive about that because my alarm woke me. I'm on vacation, so I can't imagine why I set it the night before."

"Allowing for the time you were asleep, not to mention layovers, that wouldn't seem to leave enough time to get here by bus if you left from California. It also doesn't present a very big window of opportunity for Mister Talasota to have stolen it here." He cut his eyes to Crate.

They obviously knew something they weren't saying. "Please tell me what's going on."

"It's like this," said the homely detective, wearing a look of such self importance she couldn't help comparing him to Barney Fife. "Talasota swears he's suffering from a memory lapse too, and the time frame is practically identical to yours."

Her jaw fell. Not knowing what to say, she stared blankly at Crate, whose expression clearly indicated he didn't believe her.

"He's being flown to Chicago. Maybe meeting with him will jar your memory."

"I'm not lying!"

His thin lips turned up in a deprecating smirk. "Of course not."

"Get out of my house . . .!" she stepped to the door and jerked it open.

Detective Shoat tried to charm her again with that 'handsome' smile of his, but this time she saw right through it.

"Forgive my partner, Denise. He didn't—"

"Miss Jones! My friends call me Denise, and you're not my friend, now get out."

"We'll be in touch, Miss Jones," said Crate over his shoulder while stepping across the threshold. "Meanwhile, I don't think you'd better leave town for the time being."

She slammed the door and threw herself on the couch, squalling in bitter frustration.

* * * *

Bob slapped the tabletop, reared back, and angrily raked his fingers through his hair. "Look man, I don't know any Denise Jones, and I didn't kill no Paul Quinn. I've never even laid eyes on the guy."

The bug-eyed homicide cop, who called himself Detective John Crate, sneered at him from a face that reminded him of a rabbit's. "Your fingerprints were all over her car, Roberto. Don't sit there and jerk us off by telling us you don't know her."

"How many times I gotta tell you, I go by Bob . . ." he looked up at the dreary acoustic-tile ceiling. Venting a huge sigh, he again eyeballed Crate, sitting across from him. "You say my prints are on her car so I must have touched it, but I swear I don't remember it. Look man, I know I didn't steal the damn thing because I ain't no thief, and for the last friggin' time, I don't know *anybody* named Denise Jones."

Crate's partner, Detective Shoat, had been leaning against the wall with his arms crossed, looking bored. He unfolded them and stepped to the table. "I believe you, Bob . . . I do. And I believe Denise Jones when she says she doesn't know you. What I want to know is how the two of you could wind up having this strange, identical collapse of memory. That's what I want to know. How do you figure that happened, Bob? How do you figure a thing like that could happen to two people who don't know each other, don't know Paul Quinn, and have no idea why their vehicles were parked beside his in the Mojave Desert? How does a sewer worker from New York City—"

"Brooklyn."

"Right . . . excuse me, Brooklyn. How does a sewer worker from Brooklyn and a professor from Chicago, who swear they don't know each other—yet are connected hip-and-thigh with the disappearance of a professor from Evanston—have the same fucking memory lapse? That's what I wanna know."

He gritted his teeth. "Man, for the zillionth time, I got no friggin' idea."

"Just like you have no idea why you were found naked?" said Crate, voice dripping with derision. "It's only a matter of time before they find the body, and when they do, you're going down, Bob. You want to go down alone, or do you want to cut a deal? You see, we know the two of you were in this together. Now whichever one of you tells us the truth first is going to get the most favor from the DA."

Detective Shoat dropped his hands on the table and leaned forward. "Might as well be you as her, Bob. What do you say?"

With a weary shake of his head, he once again eyed the ceiling. "I'm telling you the truth."

"Denise Jones is being escorted here as we speak. She'll be here any minute. I think the two of you should get acquainted . . . or should I say, reacquainted."

* * * *

According to his watch he'd been alone in this place for ninety minutes now. Poppy couldn't believe he'd been sitting on the motorcycle for almost that long. To him it seemed hardly any time had passed. The oddball intuition wouldn't go away. Bob had been taken to Chicago and Denise was in trouble too.

"I must be having a nervous breakdown."

"No," said a voice from behind him. "You're receiving a mental vision of something transpiring on the other side."

Poppy jerked his head around, and saw the biker.

ELEVEN

The officer motioned her inside. "Please wait here."

Denise stepped into a small room containing nothing but a bare table with two opposing metal chairs pressed against it. The young policeman closed the door, leaving her alone in the depressing enclosure. She hadn't been placed under arrest, but feared she soon would be. And why not? Who would believe her? How could she prove her innocence when she couldn't account for anything? Trying not to cry, she scooted one of the chairs back and sat down.

* * * *

The door to the men's room opened and Crate stuck his head through. "She's here."

Finished with his business, he reeled in the weasel and zipped his pants while stepping back from the urinal.

Detective Shoat, who'd escorted him there, shot him a patronizing grin. "Okay, Bob, let's go meet Denise Jones."

* * * *

Poppy couldn't see the biker's face because he still wore the helmet. "What is this place?"

"A realm of spirit, dressed in illusion to accommodate physical senses."

His answer made Poppy very suspicious of something he didn't hesitate voicing. "You're an angel, aren't you."

"The word means messenger, and I have a message. Let's

leave it at that."

Nervous about asking, but too curious to refrain, he donned a polite smile and said, "Can I see your face?"

The biker shook his head.

"Can you at least tell me your name?"

Another shake of the black helmet informed he either would not, or could not.

"Okay . . . you say I'm having a mental vision. Then Bob really is being blamed for my murder?"

"Yes."

Poppy gasped. "And Denise?"

"She'll be blamed too."

"What can I do?"

"Understand the reason for what you've seen. For that too was a vision."

"You mean the creature?"

"Yes."

"Then it *is* Abaddon, oh my!"

"It's a warning."

His heart palpitated. "I hope that doesn't mean the time has come for the unleashing of the—"

"It's a warning. More explanation at this point would only confuse you."

Queasiness overtook him, accompanied by dizzying weakness. The biker had sounded more peculiar each time he spoke. He suddenly realized why, and the revelation startled him. "Your voice, it sounds like—"

"Yours?"

"Yes . . . why?"

"It's your true voice."

Growing weaker by the moment, he thought of how the biker had no accent, yet sounded like him. "When I speak, my voice sounds odd to me. It has ever since I got here."

"It's your new voice."

"I d-don't understand . . . and I feel sick, weak . . . v-very weak." Poppy tried to get off the motorcycle but couldn't—he was too lightheaded and woozy to move.

"Faith is acting on a command," said the biker, "not on an understanding. When you are weak, then you are strong."

"The Apostle Paul's words! Oh my, is that who you are?!"

The dark shield moved back and forth.

"No?"

"No."

"What is the command?"

"Now you've asked the right question . . . ."

When the biker didn't continue, Poppy tried to implore him to do so, but a deeper wave of nausea had rendered him speechless.

* * * *

When he walked in the room her mysterious memory lapse flashed instantly away and Denise recalled everything. It flooded her with such relief and excitement, she jumped from the chair like a jack-in-the-box. The shocked expression on that Bronx ox's face conveyed his memory had just been refreshed as well.

"Bob . . .!" she hurried to him.

"Denise!" he shouted back, holding out his muscular arms to receive her.

While locked in his embrace, she noticed the two detectives gaping at each other with astonished faces. At first she felt tremendously relieved that no crimes had been committed at all, but stark fear swallowed that emotion upon realizing nobody would believe it unless Poppy showed up.

The ugly one spoke. "I knew they were both lying, but I thought they'd give us a longer run for our money than this."

"Me too," said Detective Shoat. "Okay, you two, break it up.

It's time you both started telling the truth . . . ."

* * * *

They'd really screwed up letting on they knew each other, but there was no way to put friggin' Pandora back in the box. Crate took him to another room while Shoat remained behind with Denise.

"Okay, Talasota, let's hear it—the truth for a change."

He blew out a weary sigh. "Look, I know how weird this must look, but I really didn't remember Denise until I saw her just now, I swear to God."

"How about Professor Quinn?" he said with a derisive smirk. "Remember killing him now?"

"No man, you got it all wrong. I can't explain it, but everything I couldn't remember came back to me. I do know a man named Quinn, but he goes by Poppy. I met him and Denise where the L.A. cops found me, and trust me, he ain't dead. At least he wasn't when I last saw him."

"Then where is he?"

A lump formed in his throat. He couldn't tell Crate what really happened, the dude would never believe him in a million years, and it would only make him look guiltier than he already did.

"Well?"

"Um . . ." he racked his brains but couldn't come up with a suitable lie.

An irritating grin spread on Crate's rabbit face. "You're not too smart, are you. I hope you're not counting on us never finding the body. You've dug yourself a hole with your lying mouth that you'll never be able to get out of, dirt bag. We can prove conspiracy because the two of you lied about knowing each other. And you were really stupid—as in *really* stupid—trying to fake a memory lapse for an alibi. This will go to trial even if the corpse doesn't turn up. If I were you I'd confess, own up to everything, and throw myself on the mercy of the court. Maybe then your sorry ass will be free again in twenty years or so. Otherwise, the best you can hope for is life without parole . . . ."

TWELVE

The prosecution did manage to bring the case to trial without a body. The fact that Pops was missing and presumed dead, the cops finding him naked, both their cars parked by the Jeep, their collective memory lapses, the appearance that Denise and he had conspired to cover up their involvement in Paul Quinn's murder by trying to make it look like his assailant had stolen her Mustang, had provided enough evidence.

Neither of them had hired a lawyer, knowing it would be a complete waste of money. Their only hope was Pops getting out of the garden and coming to Chicago looking for Denise, so everyone could see for themselves he hadn't been whacked. They'd gone with the same public defender, a dedicated young dude named Greg Hunn, who really seemed to care about them but had absolutely nothing to work with, because they couldn't even tell *him* what the hell really went down in the Mojave.

Like Denise, he'd confessed to the lawyer that his temporary memory lapse started right after he'd last seen Pops. But again like Denise, he couldn't admit to remembering where that took place, knowing the lawyer would never believe the garden existed. Hunn had raised his brows and asked if they'd told anyone else that, obviously finding it very difficult to swallow. When they'd answered in the negative, he'd told them to keep it that way.

Failing to get them tried separately, he'd filed a motion to keep their concurrent memory loss from the jury's ears, but the judge rejected it promptly. In his closing argument he'd concentrated on the one weakness in the state's case: no substantiated motive. He truly appreciated the attorney's valiant effort, but knew it had been pointless.

Their families didn't know anything about it, and they wanted to keep it that way, long as possible. He'd called the sewer plant, requesting a three month leave of absence, and again using his attorney's cell instead of the jailhouse payphone, told his mother he had a traveling bug and wanted to motor across America, so they wouldn't be hearing from him for a while. Denise hadn't been able to fudge with her employers because of the local news.

The jury slowly filed in. Denise sat beside him, wearing a smart-looking green dress. Her face, though pretty like always, looked so anxious and sad it broke his heart. He hated he couldn't take the rap alone. On the other side of her, Greg Hunn nervously eyeballed their dozen peers.

Bob thought about blurting out the truth, but only for a moment before nixing the idea permanently. *Hold up for just a minute, Judge! Check out the hill where you found me, then you'll fall into paradise and find your friggin' Corpus Delicti alive and kickin'... yeah, right.*

That weird section of the Mojave couldn't be trusted. Even if the cops could be persuaded to investigate it, odds were that spot on the hill where they'd fallen through had disappeared just like Creepsville and Dragon Man, and that would have garnered them both a ticket straight to the funny farm. Besides, one way or another, Pops would eventually get out of there and rescue their butts. To be such a smart dude, he'd sure been a dumbass thinking Denise's stunt wouldn't work for the two of them. Sooner or later the braniac would realize he'd out-thunk himself and give it a try.

He wanted to punch out John Crate so bad it hurt. The rabbit-face bastard had relished every second on the witness stand, coming off so high-and-mighty like he was valiantly trying to rid the world of its two most sinister villains. No doubt the dweeb was licking his chops now, sitting in back of the courtroom beside his partner, anticipating victory.

"Has the jury reached a verdict?"

"We have, Your Honor . . . ."

At the judge's request he rose to his feet but kept looking at Denise instead of the jury. She stood with eyes closed, bottom lip trembling. He'd give anything if he could somehow save her from this. A tear trickled down her cheek as the foreman said the inevitable words.

"We find the defendants, Roberto Talasota and Denise Jones, guilty . . . ."

The last thing he saw while being escorted to his cell was John Crate, wearing a shit-eating grin of satisfaction that seriously needed to be slapped off the arrogant son-of-a-bitch's face.

* * * *

Denise's knees were buckling. She had to lean against the officer for support as they walked out of the courtroom. Like Bob, she'd been remanded without bail and had been incarcerated six weeks already—most of that time passing before they ever got to court—but that did nothing to prepare her for the penitentiary.

Bob had been unbelievably strong, macho confidence never wavering, while she'd broken down numerous times during the short trial. Despite the horrid circumstances, she couldn't help feeling very proud of him.

Unable to see each other except in the courtroom, they'd never gotten a chance to recount what happened since leaving the incorporeal garden, not daring to mention the place in front of their attorney. But she knew he'd escaped the same way she had because the police had found him naked, which turned out to be a real bonus for the prosecution's case. They contended he must have burned or buried his blood-drenched attire somewhere in the desert after slaughtering Poppy and hiding the body. Then, exhausted by the ordeal, he'd decided to rest before donning other clothes and driving away, but unintentionally dozed off instead.

The prosecution proved she'd been in the Jeep because her fingerprints were found therein, so the fact she'd initially claimed not to know the victim made it appear she had to be Bob's accomplice. They maintained she lied about her car being stolen in an effort to both establish an alibi and cast suspicion on a fictitious thief as Paul Quinn's assailant, and that Bob attempted to buttress her fabrication by hotwiring it.

Detective Crate had made her very angry during his testimony when Greg Hunn had asked if he had any proof they'd ever seen each other prior to their arriving at the foot of the mountain.

"No," he'd answered through an arrogant smirk. "And since we couldn't find any other evidence tying Mister Talasota to the victim or Miss Jones, if he'd been smart enough to wear gloves to keep his prints off her car and flee the scene instead of deciding to rest first, the only way we'd have known he even existed would be for his accomplice to betray him."

The other damning evidence had been her statement to Shoat and Crate about waking at six thirty in the morning, yet not reporting the Mustang stolen until almost two that afternoon.

"No one saw Denise Jones," the lead prosecutor had said, "and no one talked to her by phone at any time prior to the call recorded in People's Exhibit Four. By her own admission she has no idea why she set her alarm in the first place, but isn't it convenient she did. She lied about knowing Professor Quinn, she lied about knowing the co-defendant, she lied about her memory loss, so what's to keep her from lying about being home at six thirty that morning? Nothing. In reality she called the police as soon as she arrived at her house, seven and a half hours *after* she claims to have woken up there.

"Although we may never know what motivated them, since the defendants refuse to enlighten us, the evidence overwhelmingly proves that Roberto Talasota and Denise Jones conspired to end the life of an innocent man. Paul Quinn was heinously and calculatedly murdered in cold blood, and since he bled so much that Mister Talasota had to do away with every item of clothing he had on while butchering his victim, the Professor must have suffered a cruel and excruciatingly painful death. You have no choice but to find the defendants guilty. The viciously spilt blood of a God-fearing man cries out for it, and justice demands it . . . ."

The cell door clanged shut. Denise numbly sat down on her bunk, wondering when she'd be transferred to prison. A disturbing thought had been haunting her for the last few days. When he left the garden, Bob hadn't wound up in his bed as she had, so where would Poppy appear in the real world when he finally got out? Would he know the Chicago authorities thought he'd been murdered? What if he were to wind up in a situation where he couldn't come for them even if he did? Until that had dawned on her, she'd felt it would only be a matter of time before they'd be released. Now she had to face the very real possibility they might never be.

Fighting back tears, she leaned forward, face in hands, wondering why all this was happening.

* * * *

The nauseous dizziness finally began to ease up. Poppy felt his strength slowly returning. "N-Now that I've asked the right question . . . what is the command?"

The biker stood motionless as a statue, saying nothing.

A glance at his watch made him gasp. He'd thought twenty minutes had passed since the strange episode started, thirty at the most, but he'd endured it for a whopping twenty-two hours.

"What just happened to me?"

No answer, or movement.

"Am . . . am I correct in assuming the only way out for me is to learn the reason for this place?"

The biker shook his head.

That unnerved him. He'd been certain his exit couldn't be obtained by any other means. "If that's not it, then how do I get out of here?"

Leather-bound thumbs hooked a belted waist as the dark faceguard tilted forward slightly. "By taking off your clothes of course . . . ."

THIRTEEN

Poppy raced down the rocky riverbed, bouncing along at one hundred miles an hour. The sand, the sky, everything was tainted a dark green by the windshield of a crash helmet. Gripping the handlebars with gloved hands, he marveled at his newfound ability to maneuver a motorcycle like a pro. The mysterious stretch of road that led to where the town once stood was no longer there. He traveled across desert sand all the way to Interstate Fifteen . . . .

Weaving in and out of heavy Las Vegas traffic like he'd been doing it all his life, he headed for the airport. Before long he was on a jet bound for Chicago.

* * * *

He had a cab take him directly to the nearest police station. Once there, Poppy explained that he was Paul Quinn of Evanston, Illinois, and very much alive. Instructed to wait for two detectives, he loitered at the precinct for over an hour before they finally showed up.

The detectives, Houston Shoat and John Crate, called the district attorney, who demanded they bring him to his office for absolute verification. Poppy complied, and after a three hour ordeal—during which the governor had been called—the Chicago authorities finally acquiesced to the fact he was alive. Arrangements were then made for the release of Bob and Denise, and the detectives escorted him back to the police station to await their arrival.

Poppy asked for a detailed account of what happened.

Detective Shoat obliged, starting from the day he'd met Denise, and ending with her being charged as Bob's accomplice. "What gets me, Professor, is why they pretended to have amnesia, then quit faking it when they saw each other. It made them look guilty as sin. Why do you think they did it?"

Having no reason to fabricate such a tale, Bob and Denise must not have been able to remember what happened in the Mojave until being reunited. In light of that making them appear guilty, the strange phenomenon could only mean The Almighty wanted them to be jailed for his murder, and then released. The three of them had been called to execute a very unique heaven-laid plan. "Do you believe in God, Detective?"

Shoat made a sour face, obviously finding the question irrelevant. "I guess so."

"Well, let's just say He works in mysterious ways."

That evoked a short laugh. "You don't know what to make of it either, do you. Just what did happen out there anyway? Where've you really been all this time, Professor Quinn?"

"Languishing in an oasis, as I told everybody."

"So you're sticking with that story, huh. Mind telling me how to get there?"

"I couldn't begin to. I found it quite by accident, and if that motorcyclist hadn't rescued me, I'd still be there."

"Excuse me . . ." the detective pulled a ringing cell phone from his sport coat and wandered off.

While waiting for Bob and Denise, he pondered the time lapse. Before taking off his clothes, he'd checked his watch. He'd spent twenty-four hours in the garden after Bob vanished, which had seemed to pass in less then sixty minutes to him, yet Bob and Denise had been incarcerated forty-two days. He found it very interesting that forty-two was twenty-four backwards.

The creature definitely symbolized Abaddon, he still felt.

Though fearsome to behold, the illusory monster had never posed any real danger because its purpose had been served by them seeing it. The biker had called it a warning, but refused to elaborate. Since he'd been told further explanation would confuse him *at that point*, logic dictated he'd understand more in due time.

Perhaps that time was now.

Forty-two profoundly brought to mind the two prophets in Revelation, who'd prophecy during the first half of the seven year tribulation. Olive Trees, they were called. Destined to testify against the antichrist, their ministry would end in martyrdom after forty-two months. Poppy shuddered with awe. If his eyes had just been opened to the truth of God's plan as he thought, then Denise's role wasn't merely to report what she'd experienced in the desert after all. She might well be the most important woman in the world at the moment.

He'd never had a vision before that strange episode about Bob, and later Denise, permeated his thoughts. If he was a betting man and a millionaire, he'd wager every cent on this also being a revelation from God.

"Yo, Pops!"

He turned to see Bob and a policeman rounding a corner. The grinning Yankee ran up and gave him a suffocating hug.

"I knew you'd finally get out."

"Not here, Bob," he muttered while pulling himself free.

"Gotcha."

Detective Crate walked over and stuck out his hand for Bob to shake. "Sorry about the misunderstanding. Just doing my job."

Bob leered at him with such vehemence, Poppy feared for Crate's safety. "You know, Bob, the man's right—he was just doing his job. Let bygones be bygones."

"Oh yeah? Well this dude might enjoy his friggin' job just a little too much."

Poppy stepped between them. "Come on, Bob, shake the man's hand, he said he was sorry."

The muscle bound Italian stood rigid and stone-faced.

"Bob, please. The wrath of man works not the righteousness of God."

The angry blaze in Bob's eyes dissipated as his wrath-tightened features slowly relaxed. "What the hell—you're always right, aren't you, Pops."

"That's the spirit." He backed away so they could shake hands, but to his horror, Bob punched the detective.

Blood spurted from Crate's mouth as he slid across the shiny floor on his back. Cautiously eyeing his attacker, he pulled a handkerchief from his jacket and daubed his rapidly swelling lips. "I guess I'd feel the same if I was in your shoes, but I wouldn't recommend decking my partner. He'll hit back."

Bob helped him to his feet, a remorseful grimace mortared to his face. "Hey look, I'm really sorry, man—I shouldn't have done that. Feel free to lay one on me, I fucking deserve it."

Crate dusted himself off and brought the handkerchief back to his mouth. "I'm too relieved you don't want more of my hide to retaliate. You ever consider boxing as a career, Talasota? That's some punch you're packing."

The compliment seemed to embarrass Bob. "Nah, got a glass jaw."

Detective Shoat ambled up, stashing his cell phone inside his coat. "Now that you've got it out of your system, I feel safe offering my own apology. John's right, we were just doing our jobs. However, he's wrong about me hitting back, but please don't prove the point."

A skeptical grin crossed Bob's face. "Yeah, right. You look about as much like the turn-the-other-cheek type as Rocky Balboa."

Poppy laughed, and so did the detectives. A moment later

Denise arrived.

She ran to him and locked her arms around his neck. “Oh, Poppy, it’s so good to see you again! Thank God you got out of—”

“Not here,” he whispered cautiously, hoping her last statement had slipped past the detectives unnoticed.

It hadn’t.

“Make it out of what?” queried Detective Shoat, brows raised.

“The desert of course.” Poppy tried to sound matter-of-fact, but noted acute suspicion in the detective’s eyes.

Denise took a step back and slapped his chest. “By the way, you liar, I happen to know you didn’t drop out of high school like you said. Why didn’t you tell me you teach at Northwestern?”

Poppy nervously cleared his throat and placed a hand on the small of her back, nudging her into motion. “Let’s get out of here and grab something to eat.”

Detective Shoat blocked their path. “Why don’t you let us treat you guys? It’s the least we can do.”

“Here, here,” said Detective Crate, still blotting his mouth.

“Thanks, but no. These two jailbirds and I have some catching up to do. Maybe some other time.”

Shoat produced a card and held it out to him. “Here’s my number. Call me anytime. I’d love to hear the real story.”

Poppy took the card. “I’m sure you’ve got better things to do, Detective Shoat.”

“Not likely, I really want to know, and please call me Houston.”

The detective’s expression held the eagerness of a hound dog chasing a trail of fresh blood, and Poppy sensed he wouldn’t quit sniffing around until he got an answer. “Tell you what, give us a few days to decompress and I’ll give you a call.”

"Speaking of that, Professor, it was the DA that called me awhile ago. He wanted me to tell you that he'll be holding a press conference tomorrow morning to explain what happened, and to offer a public apology to Miss Jones and Mister Talasota, and to you too of course."

FOURTEEN

Denise lived in a brick single-storey nestled behind a small front yard. All the houses along the street were similarly constructed, centered on narrow lots with manicured lawns cut in half by walkways leading from the sidewalk to concrete porches three steps high. Each had slender basement windows piercing the foundation a short distance above ground level, halting at a one car garage. The whole neighborhood looked serene, uncomplicated, and restful to Poppy.

Detective Shoat wouldn't hear of them taking a taxi, and had insisted on driving them. He'd also stubbornly refused to let Poppy pick up the tab for the takeout purchased at a deli Denise had suggested. When they'd gotten to her place, he'd hinted about hanging around, but Poppy had gently let him know it would be intrusive, that the three of them needed some time alone.

As the detectives drove off, Denise glanced around with a smile. "I was dreading to see how shaggy my lawn must have gotten while I was away, but someone mowed it. How sweet is that?"

"Wouldn't surprise me if it was Greg Hunn that did it," said Bob, carrying a bag containing their drinks.

Poppy, lugging the food, followed the two of them up the porch steps and into the house.

Apologizing for six weeks worth of dust in an otherwise tidy house, she led Bob and him to the kitchen, and wiped off the table with a damp paper towel. "You guys start without me, I've got some sprucing up to do . . . ."

* * * *

Denise pushed away a half-eaten order of stuffed artichokes. Bob, who'd inhaled a meatball sub, eagerly took on the burden of finishing the job she'd started.

The two of them had filled Poppy in on the trial, and the conversation turned to what happened to him after they left the garden. He recounted everything, concluding with the biker's voice, and how his own sounded different to him.

Denise squinted with recognition. "It *is* different. You sound like you're from the Midwest rather than Texas like you used to."

"She's right, Pops. So what gives?"

"I don't know, but it started when I entered the garden."

"The garden . . ." a wistful smile came to Denise. "It was all so beautiful."

Bob snickered. "True, but the most beautiful thing I saw back there was you, when you came out of your laundry."

A blush flared on her cheeks as she slapped his shoulder, giggling. "You're embarrassing me."

"Now you kids behave, or I won't tell you what's next."

Denise raised her brows. "There's more, Poppy?"

"Much more. But first I want to get out of this leather. I wonder if I could borrow a robe or something. This getup is chaffing me something fierce."

Her dark eyes twinkled with curiosity. "I couldn't believe you were dressed just like the biker. How did you get those clothes? Or did he take his off and give them to you?"

"I don't have a clue. When I left the garden I was suddenly on the hill, dressed like this, and navigating a motorcycle with perfect skill even though I'd never ridden one in my life. I found a wallet inside the jacket, and this—" he unzipped a side pocket and pulled out a wad of hundred dollar bills, which he laid on the table.

"Jeez, Pops, there must be at least five grand there!"

"That was the original amount as a matter of fact, before I had to pay for plane and cab fare. I made it all the way to Las Vegas without having to make a single stop. When I parked the motorcycle at the airport and took off the helmet I'd been wearing, they both vanished into thin air."

Eyeing the cash, Denise jostled a straw up and down its hole on the plastic lid of her soda, each stroke producing an irritating squeak. "You told us about the visions and how the biker was speaking to you in your voice, and about time being different there than here, but you never did say how you escaped."

"The same way you guys did, though I was sure it wouldn't work for me."

"I knew you'd finally wise up at some point, Pops, and pull the ol' monkey see, monkey do."

"No, Bob, I asked the biker how to get out and he told me. I wouldn't have considered it otherwise. Denise, about that robe."

"Oh, sorry . . ." she rose from the table. "My brother left some jeans here, and he's about your size. If they don't fit, you can wear my bathrobe, but I'm afraid it's a bit frilly. I also have several oversized t-shirts. I'll lay them out for you, be right back."

When Denise stepped out of the kitchen, Bob whispered, "I need your opinion about something, Pops. Back in the Mojave I didn't think it could go anywhere because we're so different, but now I'm not so sure there might not be a future for Denise and me. What do you think—have I got a snowball's chance in hell with her?"

He winked at the lucky Yankee and whispered back, "Wrong analogy. I'd say you've got a lock on her because of a mandate from heaven."

Bob's face lit up with a huge smile. "No fooling, Pops? Did

the biker tell you that?"

"No, simple logic. The Lord chose you, Denise, and me to experience the town, the garden, and all that's going to follow. I'm fifty-five, Denise can't be any older than thirty. That would make her at least twenty-five years younger than me—a huge age difference. So that leaves you to sire the progenitor of the two Olive Trees."

The smile melted. "Olive Trees? What the hell you talking about, Pops?"

"It's from the Bible. There are two prophets called Olive Trees mentioned in the book of Zechariah and Revelation. It's only a theory, but here's what I think: God's preparing the world for the end of time. If I'm right, I doubt you'll sire the actual prophets, but you and Denise are going to have two sons who will somehow set the world stage for their arrival. I believe the creature we saw represents the king of the locusts which will ascend from the bottomless pit spoken of in Revelation. I'm also convinced America is 'Babylon The Great: Mother of Harlots and Abominations of the Earth,' and will be destroyed for turning her back on God. But before that happens, your progeny will sound out a warning."

Bob grimaced. "You're talking way over my head again, Pops, and you're scaring me. You didn't lose the correct change back in paradise did you?"

"I assure you, I haven't lost my sanity. To put it in your vernacular, I still have the correct change. I know this sounds strange to you, but it won't once you've learned the truth."

"What truth?" Bob asked full throat.

"The Bible," he answered likewise.

"Sheesh, I ain't no scholar."

Poppy took a pull from the fountain drink he'd ordered along with a burger and fries at the deli. "You don't have to be a scholar to learn the truth—you just have to *want* to learn it. The eyes of the Lord roam to and fro throughout the earth, looking for a man through whom He may show Himself strong."

"Now you're preaching at me."

"No, Bob, but let me tell you one more thing: God will move heaven and earth to reveal the truth to anyone who really wants to know it, deep down in their heart."

Denise stepped into the kitchen and waved for him to follow.

She took him to a bedroom, where she'd laid out several colorful t-shirts on the bed, alongside a pair of blue jeans. "That's all the shirts I have that are too big for me, Poppy. If the jeans don't fit, my robe is hanging on the inside of the closet door. I'll leave now, so you can try them on . . . ."

He managed to get the jeans fastened, but they felt too snug and lacked an inch being long enough. The least girlish of the t-shirts was a size smaller than the others, but he chose it, grateful to be out of the leather, even if it did fit too tight for his liking. Poppy folded the leather britches, set them on the bed beside the jacket, and put the shiny black boots back on. Unlike the pants, they had a soft inner lining which shielded his skin from the cowhide like socks. They were pretty comfortable but he wished his well-broken-in ostrich quills hadn't been left behind. However, if given a choice to take one thing with him, he'd have picked his underwear instead, for he had none, a fact he hadn't wanted to advertise to Denise.

Poppy headed for the kitchen and saw the jailbirds had moved to the living room. Bob sat in a wide recliner, Denise occupied a corner of the sofa.

"Good, they fit," said Denise, patting a spot to her left. "Have a seat."

"They're a little tight, and a tad short, but I can't complain." He took the other end of the couch.

Bob grinned. "Now what was that you said to me back in

the desert? Oh yeah, you look *scrumptious*, Pops. I love that macho shirt. Orange and pink are definitely your colors."

"Oh, I'm sure," Poppy snickered.

* * * *

She'd laughed at Bob's remark, but Poppy did look scrumptious in those jeans. Finding it hard to keep from staring, Denise resettled herself at a slight angle, where she could see the silver-haired wonder without having to look directly at him.

It felt so right having them here in her house. For the first time since being pulled into that eeriness in the Mojave Desert, they could actually relax and let their hair down. All fear had passed, and so had any doubts about being in love with Poppy. She badly wanted to scoot next to him and whisper it in his ear.

Bob had been looking at her like a lovesick schoolboy ever since she'd rejoined them in the kitchen after giving the place a quick dusting. She marveled at their peculiar situation. He obviously wanted her as badly as she did the man sitting a few feet to her left. But that man's heart belonged to his God, and apparently the only desire he had was to solve the mystery that had brought them all together.

She stopped dwelling on it when it dawned on her she wasn't being much of a hostess.

* * * *

"Can I get you guys anything? Coffee? Tea?"

"Coffee sounds good to me," said Bob.

"Me too." Poppy took in Bob's yellow dress shirt, navy blue slacks, and oxfords, wondering how he'd gotten them, since he'd been brought to Chicago under custody. They were obviously new, and didn't look right on the laidback Yankee. "Did the Los Angeles police let you bring your clothes with you, Bob?"

"Ha, you kidding? Greg Hunn, the dude we told you about that got assigned to us, bought this getup for me to wear to trial. I owe him big time. My suitcase is still in the trunk of my car somewhere in L.A.—at least it better be. The cops out west wouldn't let me touch it. They put me in a chopper in the Mojave wrapped in a wool blanket, and I had to fly to Chicago wearing jailhouse garb."

Denise rose from the couch. "Greg's such a sweet man. He drove all the way out here to pick up a change of clothes for me and check my mail. I gave him temporary power of attorney so he could pay my bills, and tried to get him to take the money out of my account for what he spent on Bob's clothes and shoes, but he refused.

"I called him as soon as the officer told me you'd turned up alive and the charges had been dismissed. He was so excited for us, and said he never believed Bob and I could kill anybody, and that he'd had a hunch all along you weren't really dead. He also said he'd love to meet you. Anyway, guess I'd better get started. The coffee's not going to make itself."

When she went to the kitchen, Bob leaned forward and quietly said, "You ain't gonna embarrass me are you, Pops? With Denise I mean."

"I might have to, unintentionally, because I want to tell her the theory. If you'd like, I won't tell her with you present."

"That might be best."

"What are you guys talking so quiet about?"

Bob gawked with panic at the kitchen entrance. "You heard me, Denise?"

"Well yeah," she laughed. "I'm only in the next room."

"Oh no!" the Yankee silently mouthed.

Poppy endeavored to bail him out. "We were talking about

my theory. I told him about it when you went to get the blue jeans."

"Coffee's brewing . . ." she returned to the sofa. "Before you get to your theory, I want to know why you lied to me about dropping out of high school and all that other garbage you said back in the garden. You teach at Northwestern. They don't use high school dropouts as professors."

"I didn't lie to you. I'm no professor."

Her brows rose. "Are you saying you're not really Paul Quinn?"

"I'm Peter Quinn. My mother started calling me Poppy when I was a toddler because I loved the story about the poppy seed cakes, and constantly begged her to read it to me. I live in Texas, not Illinois—and don't even have a high school diploma, much less a degree. My Jeep had Texas tags when I met you two, but they somehow got switched to Illinois when the authorities saw it. There is no Paul Quinn from Evanston."

"He's right . . .!" Bob lunged forward, grabbing his knees. "I was on his butt the whole time we were tearing down that riverbed, and those tags said Texas, not Illinois. I'd forgotten all about it till now."

Poppy nodded. "For reasons known only to the Lord at present, He wanted the two of you arrested for my murder, then released just like it happened. I had to show my license at the airport in Las Vegas, but the one I was mysteriously furnished isn't the one I've always had. It has my picture on it, but the name says Paul Quinn, the address is in Evanston, and it's an Illinois License. A laminated card identifying me as Paul Quinn, TH.D. under the heading of Department of Religious Studies at Northwestern University, was also in the wallet I found in the jacket. I knew I had to play along to get you two out of jail."

Denise rolled her eyes with disbelief. "I guess I shouldn't be shocked with everything else that's happened, but that is so unreal."

"It is indeed."

Her expression turned from wonderment to concern. "Sooner or later they're bound to figure out you're not really Paul Quinn, and we're going to be in trouble all over again. And what happens when they discover there never was a Paul Quinn in the first place?"

"They won't be able to."

"How can you be so sure?"

"Neither my wallet, nor any of its contents made the trip with me, this one did." He pulled the driver's license and a social security card from the billfold, and handed them to Denise. "That's not my social security number. It too has changed. For all intents and purposes, I am now Paul Quinn."

She gaped at the credentials. "This is so unbelievable! Why is this happening?"

"I know part of it, the rest is conjecture. Denise, I think you're going to bear two sons in the near future who are going to radically reshape the world in such a way, that many people will think they're the two prophets spoken of in the Revelation called Olive Trees."

Shock-induced laughter accompanied a look of total incredulity. "How in the world did you come up with that, Poppy?"

"I don't think they'll actually be those prophets, but I believe they're going to set the stage for them, or be their forebears, something along those lines."

"Poppy, are you going to answer my question or not?"

"Sorry, wasn't trying to dodge it. I suspect all this because of the demon we saw. There's only one conclusion I can draw as to why the Lord made us see it before bringing the three of us together: we're nearing the end of what Bible scholars refer to as the Church Age. Jesus will soon pull His people from the earth, and The Great Tribulation will commence with the rise of the antichrist. Abaddon will release the locusts with scorpion stingers during that seven year period before Christ returns to this planet, and the two Olive Trees will fulfill their ministry during the first half of it. I believe the actual prophets will be Jewish, so more than likely your sons will just be paving the way for them. But if you have any Jewish blood in you, I wouldn't be surprised to learn the Olive Trees are coming through your line, Denise."

Her face turned pallid. "My mother's Jewish."

Poppy felt a tug in his spirit when she said that. "There you go. The two of them will prophesy for forty-two months. They'll be warning a world that thinks utopia has finally arrived, that it's a demonic despot in charge rather than the messiah." He glanced at Bob. "Got any Jewish blood flowing through those Brooklyn veins?"

"Nope. Pure Italian on both sides."

Denise, who'd been looking off into space after stating her mother's ethnicity, mumbled, "And we were in jail forty-two days."

"Exactly. That's what validates it for me as a matter of fact, since I was given the mental vision of your ordeal."

She didn't seem to hear him, and spoke as if thinking out loud: "Saul became the Apostle Paul on the road to Damascus, and now Peter has become Paul on the road to the end of time."

Chills tickled the back of his neck. He hadn't considered that. Of course it had to be mere coincidence and he started to say so, but she spoke again.

"I think you're right, Poppy—that monstrosity we saw *was* a demon. I believe that now. Something very, very strange is happening here, and since it's spiritual, I defer to your judgment."

Her acceptance impressed him, he'd expected a lengthy argument. "That's what I was explaining to Bob earlier. The creature breaking through the surface symbolizes Abaddon and the bottomless pit. I'm convinced the Biker's an angel and orchestrated the whole scenario. Three of us were pulled into the mystery, but you're the only female. That's why I think you and—" he looked at Bob to see if he wanted him to stop or continue. A nervous nod signaled him to go ahead. "You and Bob were chosen to spawn two special sons."

Her jaw dropped. "Bob?!"

He glanced at the blushing Yankee, who'd lowered his head. Bob not only looked extremely embarrassed, but deeply hurt.

"Yes, Bob," Poppy answered at length.

"I see . . ." her piercing eyes bore holes through him. "Any Jewish blood in your lineage, Mister Quinn?"

The question puzzled him at first, then shocked the fire out of him when he realized what she was intimating. He couldn't imagine why she'd consider such a possibility, but felt very flattered by it. "I don't know what my lineage is. I'm not even sure it's Irish. Legend has it my great-grandfather was Cherokee and took on the name Quinn, but that's never been confirmed."

Billowing a harsh sigh, Bob raised his eyes to Denise. "He thinks you and I are supposed to be together."

"So I gather."

"It would seem to make sense," said Poppy, wishing she'd quit staring at him. She hadn't looked away even when speaking to Bob.

"Why, because we're closer in age than you and I?"

"Well, yes. I may be wrong about the whole thing of course, but if not, I assume the three of us have received a special call. Mine is to assay all of the theological ramifications, yours is to bear the two sons, so naturally I assume that Bob's is to—"

"Sire them," she finished for him, still glaring.

"Yes."

Bob craned his head back, eyeing the ceiling. "Jeez how embarrassing . . . I'm sorry, Denise, but remember it was his idea, not mine."

"Now that's true," offered Poppy, hoping it would ease the rapidly mounting tension.

"So you don't find me desirable enough to make two babies, Mister Quinn?"

"Would you please stop calling me that? Of course I do, any man would—but I'm fifty-five and you're . . . well you're a whole lot younger than that." He wasn't about to speculate on her age, knowing he'd gotten himself in enough hot water already.

A peculiar expression came over her: rigid, far-away, coldly accepting. "You're right, I am." The look warmed into a faint smile as she got up, stepped to Bob, folded her arms beneath her breasts, and gazed down at him. "Looks like it's you and me, you Bronx ox."

Bob rose from the recliner frowning. "You better not be playing with me. Do you mean it?"

She nodded.

"Let me hear you say it."

"I mean it, now kiss me—I want Mister Quinn to see what he's missing."

When Bob didn't comply she grabbed the back of his head and planted her mouth on his. Poppy cleared his throat and said, "If you kids will excuse this old man, think I'll take a walk."

* * * *

The instant Poppy left, she pushed away from Bob.

"What the fuck?!"

"Look, you Bronx ox, I'm in love with Poppy, I just wanted to make him jealous."

"You bitch!"

"Yeah, suppose I am, but you weren't exactly cooperative, were you, so what difference does it make?"

Answering with a dejected sneer, he slumped back into the recliner.

She started for the kitchen. "Still want coffee?"

"Yeah . . . I guess . . . jeez . . . ."

* * * *

Poppy strolled down the sidewalk for fifteen minutes before heading back. He returned to find Bob in the recliner and Denise on the couch. Halfway expecting them to be in her bedroom, it surprised him they weren't even sitting next to each other. An air of hostility shrouded Bob, and Denise looked placidly indifferent.

"Want some coffee, Mister Quinn?"

He sucked in a deep breath and groaned. "All right, Denise, that's enough. What happened to you two?" She didn't answer, so he turned to Bob. "What's the matter?"

"Why don't you ask her highness over there?"

Denise folded her arms, crossed her legs, and started rocking the upper calf like a pendulum in an over-wound clock. "Oh Bob's just upset because I'm in love with someone else instead of him. He'll get over it, believe me."

If Denise was in love with someone else, she shouldn't have come on to Bob like that—what a cruel thing to do. Resisting an urge to reprimand her, he mulled over this new turn of events. It only stood to reason the man Denise loved would be the father of the two boys, so he'd obviously be included in this peculiar ministry. Having such a high call on her life, the Lord would have shielded Denise from becoming so attached otherwise. "Well he's in for the shock of his life when he learns everything you've gone through and what lies ahead for the two of you."

Denise tossed him a wry grin. "Oh, I think he'll handle it okay."

"Are you kidding me? We'd better plan this out, figure the best way to baptize him into this. For starters, what's his name?"

"His name used to be Peter, but now he goes by Paul."

"You can't mean me!" But the expression on her face made it all too clear she did. Dumbfounded at first over how she could possibly prefer him over the virile Bob, it finally dawned on him what had happened. She'd become infatuated with him because she thought he'd saved her—from the creature, and a life behind bars. God was the real hero, not him, but he had to proceed cautiously in making her see that, or he might wind up creating the nightmare scenario of a woman scorned.

"Denise, I'm very flattered, and I mean that. But I'm old enough to be your father. Heck, I may be old enough to be your grandfather for all I know. You see me as your savior—a hero—but God is the one that saved all three of us. It's Bob you belong with, not me."

"Whoa . . .!" Bob launched from the recliner. "I don't want no charity here, Pops. She's made it clear who she wants. I may not be a genius like you, but I have enough sense to know when to bow out and let the better man take over. I'll make arrangements to vacate this place soon as possible. By this time tomorrow I'll be history."

Denise scowled at the ego-bruised Italian. "You can't leave, Bob! You're in this as deep as Poppy and me. You've got to see this through, just like we do. I like you, I really do. I think you're a real hunk, and I wish I did love you instead of Poppy." She refocused on him, unblinkingly. "But you can't help who you fall in love with . . . even if they don't love you."

"Who says he don't love you, I never heard him say that. Pops, you ever say that? I sure as hell didn't hear you if you did."

Seizing the opportunity to put a wrap on this craziness, Poppy said, "No, I never said that, but it's true nonetheless."

"What, are you out of your freaking mind? You gonna stand there and tell me you don't love her after hearing how she feels about you?"

"Not in that way," he answered gingerly. "And what she feels for me is mere hero worship that'll fade away soon enough. In time she'll grow to love you."

Pain radiating from her dark orbs, Denise finally quit glaring at him and turned to Bob. "He's probably right . . . on both counts. Either way, you're not leaving here, you Bronx ox."

Bob tilted his head back, eyes raised to the ceiling, lips stretched into a lopsided sneer. Directly, an aura of raw street-toughness enveloped him. He leveled his strong chin, honed in on Denise, and hitched up his pants. "That's Brooklyn, babe, and don't you forget it."

FIFTEEN

Poppy awoke before dawn. He'd spent the night on Denise's couch, insisting Bob take the spare bedroom. He never slept naked, but since he didn't have any underwear, it was either try to sleep in the too tight jeans or nothing. Grateful for the cover of darkness, he put on the borrowed clothes and groped his way to the kitchen. Denise had prepared the coffee maker before retiring, instructing Bob and him they need only turn it on if either woke before her. He felt along the wall for the light switch and flipped it, surprised to see Denise, draped in a pink robe, sitting with knees drawn to her chest. Steam rose from a coffee cup resting on the table in front of her.

"Boo," she said softly while covering her light-assaulted eyes. "I set two cups out for you and Bob next to the coffee maker."

"Thanks . . ." he filled one and sat down opposite her.

"Been up since four, thinking. Got tired of lying in bed and decided to have coffee. Hope I didn't wake you."

"No. Thought I was the first to rise."

She lowered her hands and blinked several times as her pupils adjusted to the light. "Have you ever been married?"

The question rattled him. It wasn't hard to guess what she'd been pondering. "No."

"Why not?"

"I was never out and about enough to meet anyone, I guess. I'm pretty reclusive."

"Gee, there's a real surprise."

"Are you mad at me?"

"What do you think?" Her face didn't reflect anger

necessarily, but her eyes bore through him like a predator's scoping its prey.

"Well, I think you might be."

She brought the cup to her lips and held it there. "Well, you might be right."

"Denise, I'm sorry if I upset you, but you know I was telling the truth."

"Not about me you weren't . . ." she finally took a sip and set the cup down. "You think you know everything, don't you. Well you don't. How can someone so brilliant, be so naive? I'm in love with you, and it's not mere hero worship as you put it. I think I knew it was destined to happen the first time I saw you. Oh I'll go along with your theory. Hell, I'll marry Bob if that's what you want—he's a real good looking guy. Our two boys should turn out to be a couple of real studly heartbreakers, but let me ask you a simple question. If they're supposed to be prophets, wouldn't it make more sense for their father to be a theologian rather than a body builder, who earns his living working at a sewer plant?"

That thought hadn't occurred, and it startled him. He mused on it for a few seconds before a rebuttal presented itself. "I told you, that's where I come in. I can teach the two boys. Bloodlines don't have anything to do with truth. Truth is something we learn, not something we're born with."

"You're so full of it."

"No . . . not about that I'm not."

"Are you impotent?"

That made him chuckle. "To tell you the truth, I don't know. I darn well may be."

"Have you ever been with a woman?"

"Well of course I have."

"Ever been with a man?"

He made a sour face. "Heavens no."

"Do you think I'm pretty?"

"Why are you doing this? You know I do."

"Desirable?"

Though severely tempted to change the subject, he didn't. This needed to be settled once and for all. "Yes."

"How desirable?"

He cleared his throat. "Very."

"Then why don't you want me?"

"Denise, we've already covered that. I'm too old for you. And even if I wasn't, Bob is a big part of the equation, and I just don't see how he fits in if it's not to sire the two boys."

Before she could counter, Bob walked in. Immensely relieved for the intrusion, Poppy bade him good morning. Denise shot the Yankee a terse look, her stabbing eyes transmitting he was interrupting. Poppy winced, wishing she hadn't done it.

"Well good morning to you too, your highness . . ." Bob raked the underside of his chin in an outward motion to show his disdain, then turned to him and said, "Had a dream about the biker, Pops."

Denise pointed at the cabinet. "Your cup's by the coffee maker—and by the way, good morning."

"Yeah, right." Bob helped himself to coffee and took the chair farthest from Denise.

"Well tell us the dream," said Poppy. "It might be prophetic since the biker was in it."

"He told me to tell you that you are the Olive Tree."

"What?"

"You are the Olive Tree. That's what the dude said."

"I can't be one of the Olive Trees, so it was just a dream. But go ahead and tell me the rest of it anyway."

"Nope . . ." Bob yawned and stretched.

"Why not?"

"I don't mean nope I won't tell you, I mean nope it wasn't just a dream."

"Okay, tell it to me."

"I was in a room that had all this fog or smoke hovering on the floor, like one of those machines rock bands use. I was sitting on a chair and the biker walked in. He put his hands on my shoulders and said, 'Tell Pops he is the Olive Tree. Tell him immediately upon awaking.' That's what he said, word for word, and then I woke up."

He barely managed to keep from laughing, but couldn't hold back a grin. "The biker said Pops?"

"Yeah. Surprised me too, since I'm the only one that calls you that."

An idea struck, the dream may well have been an epiphany after all. "Do you remember what he sounded like?"

Bob frowned. "You know, now that I think about it, the dude sounded like me."

Poppy smacked the table with both hands. "That's what I thought you were going to say!"

"What does it mean, him sounding like me?"

"Maybe I need to adjust my theory a tad. Since he talked to me in my voice, and to you in your voice, and told you I was an Olive Tree, then you must be the other one."

A skeptical grunt filled the air. "I can't be no Olive Tree, Pops. What the hell do I know about being an Olive Tree?"

"As much as me."

"Come on, Pops. You got brains and you're a theologian. I got squat when it comes to either one."

"You're wrong, Bob. You're not stupid, and you can learn theology."

* * * *

Denise stared off into space, hearing their voices but not listening to what they said after Poppy told Bob he could learn theology. If those two were the Olive Trees, she wouldn't be bearing sons to either of them. Surprised to feel disappointed over not raising two little prophets, she wondered what her role was now.

There could be no more doubt about the existence of God. Too many things had happened that couldn't be explained otherwise, and she'd unknowingly become enamored with the idea of being such a prominent person in the grand scheme of things. Now it looked like she was just an extra, rather than the female lead in this extraordinary play. It suddenly dawned on her how insensitive she'd been to Bob. She'd made him feel the way she felt now—insignificant. It disgusted her, she'd acted horribly cruel, she had to make it up to him somehow.

". . . I don't see how that's possible, Pops."

"How what's possible?" She'd decided to join in but had no idea what Bob was talking about.

"Me learning the Bible."

She shrugged her shoulders. "It's a book, Bob, I used to read it. You can read a book, can't you?"

"Well, that's not exactly true," said Poppy. "It is a book, but it's not just *a* book, it's *the* book—the word of God. But having said that, there's no reason you can't learn it, Bob. And besides, I can teach you and Denise whatever you need to know. The problem is, at this point I'm just as much a novice concerning this revelation as the two of you. Whatever's happening here, we'll have to learn together, just like all the other things we've gone through."

Cutting her eyes to Bob, she took in his bulging pectorals. That was his strong point—his physical strength, that incredible body. Then she glanced at Poppy. His power lay in his superior mind and spirituality. "Bob, you're the brawn in this Olive Tree Operation. Poppy, you're the brains."

"And what are you, toots? Oh jeez, sorry I said that."

"Forget-about-it," she said with a grin, mocking his accent. "I don't know what I am in this equation."

Bob smiled. "You're the beauty."

"Beauty and the beast," said Poppy light heartedly.

"Hey!"

"Only teasing, Bob."

"I knew that."

Poppy took a sip of coffee and sighed. "Seriously, I don't think we're going to know beforehand. I've got a feeling necessity will definitely be the mother of this invention. I know Bob and I aren't *the* Olive Trees spoken of in the Revelation, so we must be more like the Olive Trees in the Old Testament book of Zechariah, which were Joshua and Zerubbabel."

Bob snorted. "Then I must be Joshua 'cause I'll never be able to remember my own name if I'm that other dude."

She chuckled along with Poppy, then quickly sobered. "So I'm not going to be a mother after all."

"I didn't say that. The term is used for those who stand before the Lord and proclaim His word, but the two Olive Trees of the Revelation are special. They'll testify against the antichrist and false prophet during the tribulation, calling down plagues upon the earth as a testimony against the falseness of the peace and prosperity the antichrist will appear to have brought to mankind. I don't want to be dogmatic, but I personally believe they'll be Jewish. You're half Jewish, and I've thought all along you were the center of this vortex that's spinning around us."

"So we're back to square one?"

Poppy sighed again. "If my theory's correct, it looks that way."

SIXTEEN

Houston arrived at Weinberg College of Northwestern University at ten o'clock in the morning. Paul Quinn troubled him and he wanted to find out more about the strange professor. He and his two cohorts were hiding something sure as hell—the faked memory lapses, Talasota being found naked, Jones reporting her car stolen, Quinn not letting anybody know he was alive for such a long time, then turning up out of nowhere, refusing to say where he'd really been. None of it added up. He didn't have permission to investigate the eccentric, but needed closure. A crime may not have been committed, but something really screwball had gone down in the Mojave Desert and he wanted to find out what. Quinn said he'd call after they 'decompressed' but Houston wouldn't make book on that.

Almost causing two innocent people to spend their lives behind bars had so mortified John, he'd refused to press assault charges against Talasota in spite of the captain demanding he do so. His partner wanted to put the whole thing behind him, so Houston had told him he had some personal business to tend to, and made the trip alone.

Two other detectives had initially investigated Quinn's disappearance. He hadn't gotten involved in the case until after Talasota had been charged in Los Angeles, so this was his first trip to the university.

A door with the dean's name on it stood a few feet behind an unoccupied desk. Houston hadn't made an appointment but opened it anyway, introducing himself and apologizing for the intrusion while entering.

"I'm Sorrel Hayden," said a scholarly gentleman with a wisp of gray hair atop an otherwise bald head. He rose from his chair and shook his hand. "Please have a seat, Detective."

Houston sat down in an armchair facing the front of the desk.

The dean reseated himself. "What can I do for you?"

"How well do you know Paul Quinn?"

"About as well as anybody, I suppose. Why do you ask? He didn't turn up dead again, did he?" A small laugh preceded the last question.

"No," he answered with a grin. "I met the man yesterday, and being a detective, I'm naturally curious."

"About what?"

"Just some loose ends I'd like to tie up."

Concern or puzzlement—Houston couldn't tell which—made the scholar's high brow furrow. "Loose ends?"

"Yeah. Are you familiar with the case?"

"Oh yes. I dare say all of us around the university have followed it very closely."

"Then you know about the two defendants' memory lapses."

"Oh my, yes. I must confess I thought those two were guilty of murdering Paul."

"Have you talked to him since he turned up alive?"

"No."

"Isn't that unusual?"

Hayden picked up a pen and started rolling it back and forth between his palms. "Not really. We're colleagues, but we don't socialize with each other. He isn't due back to the university until the fall semester starts next month, and I'd be rather surprised to hear from him before then."

"So you really don't know him that well, I take it."

"He's very reclusive, not at all outgoing. But he's a brilliant scholar, and a very nice man."

"How long have you known him?"

"Oh, for several years."

"Do you know either of the defendants?"

"No."

Houston analyzed Sorrel Hayden. There was no physical resemblance between the two, but something about the man reminded him of Quinn. He finally put it off to them both being eggheads and dismissed it. "I'd like to talk to some of his other colleagues. Who would know him best?"

"I can give you their names if you want, but I assure you they don't know him any better than I do."

"Please . . ." he pulled a small spiral notebook from his coat and wrote down each name Hayden recited, along with where they could be located on campus.

"One last question. Does Professor Quinn usually wear leather?"

"Excuse me?"

"Everything he was wearing yesterday was made of leather, and it sure looked odd on a middle-aged professor. It was the sort of attire a teenager in a motorcycle gang would wear."

The dean chuckled. "I've never seen him dressed like that. Of course I rarely see him off campus, so I really wouldn't know what he wears in his leisure time."

"I see. Well thanks for your time, and sorry once again for barging in uninvited. Have a nice day."

"You too, Detective."

* * * *

Sorrel Hayden watched Detective Shoat close the door behind him. A moment later he stepped through it himself, carrying a helmet with a dark wind guard attached to it.

* * * *

Pulling a motorcycle helmet from her head, she placed it beneath the desk, and shook out her hair.

A knock sounded on the door. "Come in."

"Professor Drummond, my name is Houston Shoat. I'm a detective with the Chicago Police Department, and I'd like to ask you a few questions about Paul Quinn . . . ."

* * * *

Professor Simpson bid Detective Shoat a good day, then opened a large drawer in his desk, from which he pulled out a crash helmet . . . .

* * * *

Houston drove back to Chicago knowing precious little more than he had before, despite having questioned six egghead friends of Quinn's besides the dean. The trip to Evanston had been a waste of time. Investigating Paul Quinn directly, rather than trying to gather information about him peripherally, was apparently the only way he'd get to the bottom of this mystery. If the professor had nothing to hide, he'd have told him everything already, so even if he did eventually call, it would only be to offer a cover story of what really went down in the Mojave.

* * * *

They took a cab to a used car lot where Poppy paid twenty-four hundred dollars for a blue Honda Civic four door. It was twelve years old with badly worn seat covers and a rebuilt engine, but the tires were new and it ran good. He drove off the lot with Denise directing him to the nearest clothing store.

Two hours later they were back at Denise's house, and

Poppy rejoiced in having a pair of men's briefs beneath his new blue jeans.

The phone rang.

"I hope that's not another reporter," said Denise as she went to answer it. Several had called asking for an interview after the district attorney issued his apology. Poppy had advised against it and she'd turned them all down. He'd also told her not to let any of them know Bob and he were staying with her, because they'd be targeted as well.

It soon became obvious she was receiving good news. ". . . That's fantastic . . . No, no need to apologize. A week's not that long . . . That's great . . . ."

She hung up with a beaming smile. "The district attorney arranged to have our cars delivered to us at the county's expense. They'll be here within a week."

Bob made a fist and swung at the air. "Yes!"

"Well, looks like I bought a car for nothing."

"I wouldn't call twenty-four hundred clams nothing, Pops."

"You know what I mean. The Jeep's had its day but I probably could have had it overhauled for half of what the Honda cost me."

"What does it hurt to have two sets of wheels, Pops? Besides, without your car we're looking at a fortune in cab fare till ours get here. At least you two are, since I'm broke."

"That's true," Denise chimed in.

"Guess I'll sell the Jeep."

Bob rubbed his hands together gleefully. "Brooklyn, here I come."

Denise gasped. "You're not going back to Brooklyn!"

"The hell I'm not. When the Lark gets here, I'll have my ma wire me some dough, then I'm settin' sail."

"No, Bob, Denise is right. We have to stick together, at least for the time being, until we know what we're supposed to do."

"Well here's what I know, Pops. I have to get back to work

so I can support my habit. All my cash and credit cards are back in that garden."

Denise gave him a firm look. "I'll help you out. You can't leave."

"I'm not taking your charity, woman."

She rolled her eyes. "Talk to him, Poppy."

He pulled out the remainder of the lucre that had accompanied him from the garden, and started counting it, planning to half it with Bob. Denise repeated her request with more insistence but he still didn't answer, due to shock.

"What are you doing, Pops?"

"Counting this money."

"What, so now you're trying to give me a hand out? Jeez."

"I started out in Vegas with five thousand dollars. I spent money on a plane ticket, cab fare, meals, clothes, and a car. I should have less than two thousand left, but count that." He handed the cash to Bob.

"I'll count it, but I ain't accepting any of it." The proud Italian thumbed through the currency and his eyes went wide. "Whoa . . . there's five thousand bucks here."

Poppy gave him a knowing smile. "If my theory's right, it'll be a good while before we return to our old jobs, if we ever do. I think we've been set on a new career path by the Most High Employment Agency."

SEVENTEEN

Houston made another trip to Evanston. This jaunt had nothing to do with the university however. He parked his car at the address of Paul Quinn, who hadn't kept his word about calling.

A man who looked very much like an eighty-year-old version of the eccentric professor answered the doorbell.

Bound to be his father.

The elder held the door cracked only wide enough to stick his face through. "Yes?"

"Hello, sir, may name is Houston Shoat. Is Paul Quinn available?"

"He's staying with a friend in Chicago."

"Denise Jones?"

The old man's face wrinkled with surprise. "You a friend of his?"

"Just an acquaintance. I was one of the investigators involved in the case concerning his disappearance. We met the day he turned back up."

"What do you want to see him about?"

"Just tying up a few loose ends. Are you his father?"

"I'm frightfully busy at the moment. Don't mean to be rude, Detective, but I must say goodbye . . . ."

Houston glared at the closed door, resisting an urge to kick the damn thing in. The rude old bastard acted like he hadn't even heard the question.

* * * *

Squinting through the peephole, he watched the detective drive away, then went into the next room and laid down.

Winona Gleason rose from her daybed in a state of mind-numbing shock. Standing stiff as a board, moving only her eyes, she surveyed her surroundings. *What am I doing in here? I was in the living room. The doorbell rang and I meant to answer it. How did I wind up lying down in the sewing room . . .?*

* * * *

Poppy had learned a few routes in Franklin Park. A week had passed since he'd bought the car, and he could now find his way to a grocery store, Denise's favorite deli, a drug store that served great old fashioned root beer floats, and a hardware store where he'd purchased a FOR SALE sign for the Jeep. Apprehensive about driving in downtown Chicago, he'd relinquished the wheel to Denise when she'd wanted to treat Bob and him to an Italian restaurant a few nights ago. Their vehicles still hadn't arrived, but the district attorney's office had called Denise earlier that morning to say they should expect them some time today.

He'd visited the deli on this trip and was on his way back with their lunch. He still didn't know what the Lord wanted them to do, but they'd made one major breakthrough: Denise finally realized she wasn't really in love with him. Her infatuation had been flattering but excruciatingly nerve wrenching. The tension had grown unbearable before she'd finally seen the light. She'd also apologized to Bob for hurting him. The wily Italian had forgiven her, but not without trying to mend his wounded pride.

During her apology he'd worn an expression of humble acceptance. But afterwards, that Brooklyn flare of savoir-faire he always exhibited when feeling his oats manifested. "No sweat, Denise, all's forgiven," the Yankee had said, smoothing the sides of his hair. "But let's clear the air here once and for all. Been thinking things over. Truth is, you were the only girl on earth there for awhile, and I'd have felt the same about any other attractive woman in that situation. We're back in the real world now, and there's too many fish in the sea to worry about one slipping off the hook. Now I don't know what's coming down the pike, whether Pops' theory is right or wrong about this Olive Tree Operation, but I do know one thing—ain't no way you and me are gonna make babies, Olive Trees or otherwise, because I don't want that. We've been through a lot together, and we'll always be friends as far as I'm concerned, but that's as far as it goes."

It had achieved the desired effect. She wouldn't have looked more cut up inside if he'd stabbed her in the gut with a bayonet. That took place several days ago, and he had to admit Bob was quite an actor. If he didn't know better, he'd think the macho Italian really *had* gotten over her. Whether or not Denise still bought into Bob's act, Poppy didn't know, but he felt grateful they were all getting along without the specter of unrequited love constantly haunting them.

* * * *

Someone rang the doorbell as they were finishing lunch. Denise wiped a dribble of mustard from the corner of her mouth and went to answer it.

It was Detective Shoat.

"Good afternoon, Miss Jones."

"Detective Shoat . . ." she looked past him, wondering where his sidekick was, and why he wore his 'handsome' smile. Anxiety started to take hold before it dawned on her the visit most likely concerned their cars.

"Please call me Houston."

"Did our cars get here?"

He frowned. "Your cars?"

His ignorance of the gesture made her extremely nervous. Why *was* he here? She hoped to God they weren't in trouble again. "The district attorney's having them transported to us as compensation."

The smile returned. "Well that's great, congratulations. Mind if I come in?"

* * * *

Jones welcomed him inside. As Houston walked past her, the smell of her natural musk, enhanced with a touch of perfume, pleasured his nostrils—but nowhere near as much as her beauty pleased his eyes. He allowed himself a lengthy glance at her shapely backside while she closed the door. Before she could catch him looking, he turned around to find Quinn and Talasota walking in from the kitchen.

"Detective Shoat," said Quinn in a neutral tone.

"Hey, what gives?" spoke Talasota. "Gonna arrest us again?" He looked nervous despite the lighthearted smirk on his face.

"Strictly a social visit." He eyeballed Quinn. "You said you'd call, remember?"

When the professor didn't answer right away, he turned to Jones. "Mind if I sit down?"

She pointed to a recliner without speaking and started wringing her hands. His presence had apparently set her on edge too.

He eased into the chair as Quinn and Talasota seated themselves on her couch.

"Excuse me," she said uneasily. "We just finished lunch and I want to tidy up. Would you like something to drink?"

"I'm all set, but thank you." Unable to keep from admiring her again, he watched her go into the kitchen, then focused on the two men.

Talasota seemed restless: scratching at his hair, frequently shifting positions.

"I'm sorry I didn't get around to calling you," said Quinn. "What is it you'd like to know?"

"The amnesia really has me baffled, Professor, and I'd like to know why you abandoned your Jeep and didn't come forward sooner. I don't buy that you got lost hiking."

"Where's your partner Harvey?" Talasota cheekily asked.

"Harvey?"

"Yeah, the big white rabbit. He's not curious like you?"

It took him a minute to make the connection that Talasota was referencing the James Stewart movie. He'd never thought about it before, but John's face did sort of look like a rabbit's. Under normal circumstances he'd have taken Talasota to task for the insult, but it wouldn't do to start a ruckus and defeat his whole purpose.

"It's not that he isn't curious. He just feels bad about the whole deal—you guys spending so much time in jail and all. He just wants to get past it. By the way, it might interest you to know he refused to press charges against you for hitting him, even though our captain *seriously* wanted him to when he heard about it. You might take that into consideration the next time you feel the urge to make fun of him."

The sewer worker's jaw fell. "He did that for me?"

"Mm hmm."

"Aw hell, what a stupid thing for me to say—a dude can't help how he looks. Me and my big mouth. Sorry, man."

The apology made him doubly glad he'd held his instinct in check. Quinn evidently wasn't going to answer his question so he addressed Talasota about something else he'd been curious about. "I noticed the other day that you and Miss Jones use different nicknames when you refer to Professor Quinn."

"He goes by Poppy, I'm the only one that calls him Pops."

"Poppy . . . that's some nickname. How'd you come by it, Professor, if you don't mind my asking?"

"Never mind the nickname," Quinn replied. "You want the truth? I'll tell you, but you won't believe it. I was trapped in another dimension—a spiritual realm that I couldn't escape from until I took off all my clothes."

Jones, who'd obviously heard their conversation from the kitchen, appeared at the entrance—eyes wide, mouth slack. Talasota gaped at Quinn like he was crazy, but the egghead remained stoic, speaking as though he actually believed his rhetoric.

"As for the amnesia, Denise and Bob were with me in that realm. Denise took off her clothes and found herself here at home. Bob later followed suit and wound up where the authorities found him. When I finally got out, I came straight to Chicago. Neither of them could remember each other, or being in that other dimension. But when they saw one another again, their memories instantly returned."

Houston took a deep breath, trying to hold back mounting anger. "There's no cause for this. I don't know why you're mocking me, I'd just like to know what really happened. This case has been strange from the start, and I'd like to get some closure, that's all."

Quinn, expression unchanged, merely shrugged and said, "Then you have closure, Detective, because every word I just told you is the gospel truth."

"Fuck me to tears . . ." he rose from the chair and went to the door, pausing after turning the knob. "Okay, have it your way. I'll be leaving now, but this isn't the end of it. I know you're hiding something about what went down in the Mojave, and if it's illegal you better pray I don't find out about it. I've got a vacation coming up and I'm going to spend every minute of it looking into this, just so you know."

"Wait, don't go!" Jones ran across the room and pressed her

back against the door. "He's telling you the truth."

She genuinely seemed to mean it. "Do you really expect me to believe that?"

Her beautiful dark eyes were pleading. "It's true. I still find it hard to believe myself, but it's the truth. You could give all three of us a polygraph test, and if those things are valid, I promise we'd pass with flying colors."

The way she ranted, and the look on her face, made him almost believe her. Almost. She'd asked him to stay, so why not? Maybe he'd get a glimmer of the truth if he could catch them off guard. He released the knob and she circled back into the interior of the room. "How long have the three of you known each other?"

Quinn was obviously the brains of the outfit because Jones and Talasota both looked at him without answering.

He nodded to Jones and she spoke. "We met early this summer."

"How did you meet each other?"

She again cut her eyes to Quinn. "Poppy?"

The strange professor turned up his palms. "Go ahead and tell him. Tell him everything . . . ."

EIGHTEEN

Driving home to his tiny apartment in Aurora, Houston kept shaking his head at the absurdity of the tale he'd been told. He didn't know which bothered him more—that he still didn't know what they were hiding, or that they'd almost convinced him they really believed their concocted horror story. There was a creature that looked like a demon, a recreational vehicle that drove itself, and a convenience store with a cast of people straight out of *Tales from the Crypt*. What topped it all was an underground Eden that could only be entered by sinking into a doorway connecting the physical with the spiritual, and couldn't be exited without donning one's birthday suit . . . .

He threw his coat over a worn armchair, stripped off his shoulder holster, and laid it on top of the morning newspaper sprawled over the coffee table. Jerking his tie loose, he unbuttoned his collar and made for the kitchen. After two hefty pulls of Old Chicago he went back to the living room, set the beer on a section of the Sun-Times, and stretched out on a couch covered with the same dull-gray fabric as the chair.

Though presently without an assignment, he and his partner wouldn't be idle long. If he was going to solve the mystery, he'd have to do it quick because the next case that came along most likely wouldn't allow time for any personal investigating.

Lying on his side, he rehashed their weird tale until the can went dry, then got up to fetch his notebook and pen. Twenty minutes later he nuked a frozen dinner, and cracked open another beer after he finished eating.

Pacing back and forth, he occasionally grabbed his notes

from the coffee table to jot down questions he either hadn't thought to ask or had forgotten to. The last entry read: *Why are Talasota and Quinn staying with Denise Jones?*

Obviously Talasota wouldn't want to leave Chicago until his car arrived, but why weren't he and Quinn staying at the professor's house in Evanston? Quinn's dad appeared to be living with him, maybe he wouldn't permit it. He could see that old bastard refusing to be hospitable all right, but that wouldn't explain why Quinn was staying there instead of his own house.

With the single exception of Jones and Talasota being arrested for murder, which had been expunged, none of them had a record. He hadn't dug into Talasota's, since he lived across the country, but Quinn and Jones both had excellent work histories, and by all appearances seemed to be upstanding citizens. All three came off as level-headed people, and two of them were smart enough to have letters attached to their names. So how could they be so stupid about this? He tossed his notes on the couch, took a swig of beer, and burped out a sigh.

"Why would a theologian, a paleontologist, and a sewer worker, with no criminal histories, make up a fairy tale not even a ten year old would believe as a cover story for whatever really happened in the Mojave?" He walked the floor, repeating the question for several minutes, then froze in his tracks.

They wouldn't.

It hit him like a shot to the head. They weren't lying. As incredibly ridiculous as it seemed, they were not lying. That left only two conclusions: it really happened, just the way they said, or someone had brainwashed all three of them into making them think it had. The latter had to be the truth. That meant he'd never know the answer until he found the culprit or culprits responsible for making two college professors and a no nonsense tough guy believe they'd actually been to another dimension.

* * * *

Denise lay in her bed, staring into the darkness. Midnight had come and gone, but she couldn't sleep. If Houston Shoat kept digging around and discovered Poppy really wasn't Paul Quinn, they were in for it. Since there was no real Paul Quinn, he'd once again be missing and presumed dead, and this time no one would be able to come forward to get the charges dropped. Poppy himself would be incarcerated along with the two of them if that scenario ever played out. They had to somehow make the detective believe they'd really experienced the supernatural in the Mojave—he obviously wasn't going to back off until satisfied he'd finally found the truth.

But how could anyone believe it? Even Poppy couldn't settle on a solid reason for it all, though he remained convinced the core purpose of their ordeal was to produce what they'd nicknamed The Olive Tree Operation. And who knew? He might just turn out to be right. After all, he'd only missed twice so far—the occupational hypothesis and how to exit Eden.

Their cars had arrived not long after Detective Shoat left. She'd driven her Mustang to the car wash with Bob following in his Buick. The trip had brought back eerie memories, but this time she'd been in the lead. Poppy had hosed down his Jeep in her driveway and parked it at the curb with a FOR SALE sign on it. The garage could only accommodate one car, and her Stang, being the head of the vehicular pecking order, rested safely within it. Bob's Skylark sat in the driveway behind Poppy's Honda.

Greg Hunn paid them a short visit at dinnertime, and hadn't questioned Poppy's oasis explanation at all, thank God.

He'd denied mowing her lawn but she didn't believe him.

Her thoughts ventured to how she'd lied to Poppy, saying she'd come to her senses and realized he'd been right about her not really being in love. The relief on his face had hurt worse than when he'd said he didn't love her. There was nothing she could do. She'd been handed one of those bitter pills from life's dispenser, and would have to learn to swallow it and move on.

She thought of the cruel way she'd treated Bob, trying in vain to make Poppy jealous. Obtaining his forgiveness had eased her conscience to a large degree, but not totally. He'd said he didn't want her anymore. She'd believed him at the time, but now felt he'd been lying through his teeth out of pride and couldn't possibly really feel that way.

Could he?

He hadn't returned the kiss when she'd pressed her lips to his. Did he somehow realize at that moment he didn't want her after all? Would she have felt anything special if he had kissed her back? She couldn't see how, since she loved him like a brother. The way he'd turned her on in the garden seemed almost incestuous thinking about it now. Her emotions had been in turmoil ever since she'd been inexplicably yanked from the interstate to that weird little town, and she'd never felt so confused. Though falling in love with Poppy at the time, passion like she'd never known had overwhelmed her upon seeing Bob's chest when he stepped out of the forest. How could such a contradiction occur?

The incident vividly sprang to her mind: the hardness of his body beneath hers, causing such a stir of erotic emotions she'd become delusional, which had led to her taking off her clothes and—

Denise bolted upright, dropping her jaw at a sudden realization. Bob had freed her from the garden. If that Bronx ox hadn't made her so hot that she'd gotten lost in a fantasy, they'd all still be trying to find a way out—none of them would have dreamed of stripping otherwise. Arousal snaked through her as she realized a mystical bond tied her to Bob.

Remembering the biker had told Poppy to take off his clothes, she tried to ignore the erotic fervor turning her steamy inside. Surely the mysterious man on the motorcycle would eventually have told the three of them how to escape if she hadn't unwittingly started the ball rolling. Besides, she loved Poppy, not Bob.

Shifting positions, winding up on her side, she tried to shed the mental image of the bare-chested hunk stepping out of those trees . . . but couldn't.

NINETEEN

Tooling around Chicago, taking in the sights, Bob had gotten lost, and had no idea how to get back to Franklin Park. He'd managed to sneak out the door without waking Pops, aching to go cruising in the Skylark, that arrived yesterday. The Sears Tower was the only landmark he recognized, the other buildings resembled the downtown scrapers of any big city in the good old U.S. of A. He'd call Denise for directions home when he was ready to head that way, meanwhile he found a parking area along the shores of Lake Michigan, and went for a walk along the beach.

The massive expanse of fresh water looked inviting and he wished he had his swimming trunks so he could go for a swim. Some shit-head cop had misplaced his suitcase. It was still on the friggin' west coast. Pops had tried to buy him a whole new wardrobe when he'd found his trunk empty, but he'd only accepted enough charity for two changes of clothes, a pair of high-tops, some boxers, and a package of t-shirts. After arguing about it for nearly half an hour, he'd finally given in and taken some spending money as well, out of which he'd bought a watch. He'd also agreed to let him pay Greg Hunn back for the dress duds when the lawyer dropped by to meet the Einstein. Greg had balked, but Pops wouldn't take no for an answer. It'd been great getting to visit with him as a free man.

It felt good to be casual again. He'd seen some dudes walking around bareback and had decided to do likewise, tucking his t-shirt in the back of his jeans, where it hung across his butt like an apron. Enjoying the soothing warmth of the sun on his chest, he moseyed along the sand.

Two drop-dead gorgeous blondes trotted towards him. They looked almost identical, but he heard one yell "Mother!" when the other gave her a playful push. Rather than being sisters, they were apparently mother and daughter. Both wore tight blue-black shorts and t-shirts with an orange *Bears* emblazoned across their immaculate bouncing breasts. Holding a flip flop in each hand, they ran barefoot along the sand on legs that put Betty Grable's to shame. Mama Bear looked almost as young as Baby Bear, making him wonder if she'd pooped her out when she was like only thirteen or what. They smiled at him big time. He reciprocated and waved, which prompted them to do the same. Both of them cut their eyes at him while jogging past, and he couldn't keep from looking back.

The rearview was as tasty as the front.

What a pair of beauts . . . .

He watched until they looked no bigger than Barbie Dolls in the distance, then turned and continued down the shore. Before long he decided to go back to his car, partly in the hope the hot chicks might reverse directions, mostly because he'd gotten hungry and planned to shell out some of Pops' mystery cash on breakfast.

Glancing at his mock Rolex, he groaned and mumbled, "Jeez, no wonder I'm starving, it's ten-thirty."

The blondes hadn't turned up again by the time he made it back to the Skylark. He wished he'd struck up a conversation with them so he could have finagled a phone number. Mad at himself for not seizing the opportunity, he snatched the t-shirt from his waist and pulled it over his head.

Someone wolf-whistled.

Looking this way and that but seeing no one, he wondered if he'd only imagined it. Shaking his head with a grin, he opened the door, slid behind the wheel, and fired up the engine. He looked rearward, preparing to back out, and there they were.

Dazzling smiles on their pretty faces, the two beauties were leaning forward, hands on his trunk, doing pushups as if trying to keep the Lark from moving. Their breasts undulated from the arm pumping, making the *Bears* insignias move as if each had a life of its own.

He killed the engine and got out of the car.

Mama Bear stepped towards him with Baby Bear in tow. "Where you headed?"

"Some place to eat."

Baby Bear giggled. "Oh what an accent, I love it!"

"New York, right?" said Mama Bear.

"That's right, Brooklyn to be exact."

"I'm Monday and this is my sister Tuesday. What's your name?"

He grinned at Mama Bear, who'd asked the question. "What a coincidence, my name is Wednesday."

The luscious duo laughed like a couple of airheads.

"Seriously, I'm Bob. What're your real names?"

"Honestly, that's what they are," Baby Bear affirmed.

"For real?"

"Mm hmm," said Mama Bear, who apparently was really Sister Bear, even though he knew he'd heard the other one call her Mother.

"You say you're sisters?"

Baby Bear, who went by Tuesday, nodded.

From the top of their bushy blonde do's to their painted toenails, they looked remarkably similar. Their eyes totally blew him away. Even their mother wouldn't be able to tell them apart if all she could see were those almond shaped orbs—dark blue and mesmerizing, filled with tantalizing invitation, and mystery.

"So where are you going to eat?" Monday asked with a flirty

grin, sexier than all get out.

He had no choice but to flip the switch: the ol' Talasota Magic-ota was now *engaged,* but only at impulse speed, which always started with the little boy pout. If things went smooth, he'd kick it up to warp one. Launching the expression, he whined, "Don't know. I got lost and don't know my way around."

"Aw . . ." they said in unison.

Monday spoke. "There's a diner a few blocks from here, but parking will be horrible. Want us to walk you there?"

So far, so good. Now it was time to see where he rated on their interest meter. "I wouldn't want to put you to the trouble. Just tell me which direction I need to go, I'm sure I'll find it okay."

"No, no trouble at all, we'd be glad to. Wouldn't we, Tuesday?"

"Yeah, Bob, let us walk you there."

They beamed as he held out an arm for each to take. *Warp one, here we come . . . .*

Bob ordered a club sandwich, French fries, and a vanilla milkshake. Monday and Tuesday only wanted orange juice. During the meal he learned Monday, ten years older than her sib, was indeed Mother. Tuesday had mentioned her age, making Monday thirty-five, yet she looked like she couldn't have been more than a couple of grades ahead of her kid sister in school.

"Dad died not long after Tuesday was born," Monday continued, "and she was only five when our mother passed away. Our parents were both orphans and met in a foster home. Mom had a horrible childhood, so when she got colon cancer and knew she wasn't going to make it, she didn't want us to go through what she did as a child. She made me promise I wouldn't let the government put us into foster care.

"She told me to lie about my age and get work as a topless

dancer. Most people would hate her for that, but I understood. I was only fifteen and didn't know how to do anything, but I was a decent dancer and had a good figure. Mom knew it was the only way I'd be able to make enough money to support us after she was gone."

Picturing the Lolita shaking her booty with that luscious rack bared, seriously provoked the weasel. Thankfully, it was hidden beneath the table.

"She told my principal we were moving out of state to keep the truant officer away when I quit school, and taught me how to look and act much older than I really was. When Tuesday reached school age, I just made out like I was her mother when I enrolled her, and no one ever caught on. After she got through school I was finally able to quit pretending to be mama."

He marveled at the change in Monday's vocal style. She'd sounded like a bimbo at the car, but now spoke like a sophisticated woman.

"Wonder why she named you two Monday and Tuesday?"

"Guess what Mom's name was?" Tuesday asked.

"You're kidding me, right? It really was Wednesday?"

"Wrong end of the week. Mom's name was Sunday."

"You guys could almost pass for twins, but I guess you get that all the time."

"Yeah, *all* the time," said Monday. "It's because we inherited our mother's eyes, though we both strongly favor her in almost every other respect as well."

Tuesday nodded. "I had to call Monday 'Mother' when we weren't alone, so no one would suspect we were orphans, and the habit became so ingrained as I grew up, I still sometimes call her that in public."

Monday pilfered one of his fries and stabbed it in the ketchup. "What's your last name?"

"Talasota."

"Oh . . ." she smiled knowingly. "So you're Italian."

The smile appeared seductive, but he couldn't be sure since both of them looked that way no matter what expressions they wore. "What's yours?"

She chewed the potato stick and washed it done with juice. "Quinn."

"So you're Irish." He managed to sound nonchalant, but the coincidence made him uneasy—so much so he felt the weasel shrink back into hibernation. The convenience store crap couldn't extend to Chicago, could it? Jeez, he hoped not.

"According to my dad we're half Cherokee, and his family arbitrarily chose the name Quinn back in the eighteen hundreds. But he was such a big bull-shitter I never knew if he was telling the truth or not. But I do know our mother was Jewish."

Almost word for word what Pops said about his dad, and Denise maintained about her mother. *No wonder they just appeared at my car, these friggin' chicks ain't human!* His guts were churning so badly he wasn't sure he could hold down the chow. He had to get out of there—warn Pops and Denise they had to bail from Chicago.

Monday squinted at him. "Are you okay, Bob? You look a little pale all of a sudden."

He glanced at his watch. "Holy cow, look at the time! Better get going. It was great meeting you both—" he grabbed the ticket from the counter. "It's on me."

Monday snatched the tab from his hand. "Don't be silly, it's our treat—but it's going to cost you, Mister Talasota."

Oh jeez, not again! Please, God, not again!

"You have to agree to let us cook dinner for you tonight. Deal?"

They seemed so harmless and sincere, he never would have suspected they were from that eerie region of hell he thought he'd left behind forever, until a few minutes ago. *Let me guess, you're planning on Roast Talasota . . . oh jeez!*

"Bob? Is it a deal?"

He wanted to run, but knew he had to be cool, not let on he knew they were twisted sisters from The Twilight Zone. Covering his mouth as a cough forced its way out, he nodded.

"Great . . ." she handed him a card. "Here's our address and phone number. Since you don't know your way around Chicago, call me and I'll give you directions."

"Um . . . okay."

"Eight sound all right?"

Afraid they'd pick up on his fear if he spoke again, because he'd sure as hell heard it in his voice, he gave them another nod.

"Great! Come on, Tuesday, let's go home . . . ."

They paid the bill and left. He suspiciously eyeballed everyone in the joint. They looked normal, but so did Monday and Tuesday. Walking slowly, cautiously to the door, he turned on the afterburners the moment he cleared the threshold.

In no time flat he was on the road.

Bob reached over and pulled his cell from the glove box. The battery was deader than a doornail, he'd forgotten to charge it. He stopped at a pay phone and called Denise, wondering where the hell were they supposed to go from here.

TWENTY

Instead of being scared out of her wits like she should have been, Denise laughed at him. "You're making too big a deal of a coincidence. Quinn is hardly a rare name, you Bronx ox. There must be dozens of them in Chicago, if not hundreds."

"This ain't funny, Denise!" He still felt queasy from the ordeal, but had calmed down some because of Pops. The wheels were spinning inside that silver head, he'd soon have the answer—he'd be able to ward off those blonde bimbos.

"What was their father's name?" Pops spoke at last. He'd been frowning with thought the last few minutes.

"I told you, Quinn."

"No, I mean his first name?"

"They didn't say and I didn't think to ask, sorry."

"That's okay. Tell it all to me again and be exhaustive, starting from when you first saw them."

* * * *

"Is Monday still working as a dancer?" Poppy asked after hearing Bob's second account of the incident.

"I don't know."

"You said she gave you a card, maybe it's her business card."

"She talked like it was her home address, but I was so freaked out I didn't look at it—just stuck it in my pocket."

"Let me see it," said Denise.

Bob pulled it out and handed it to her.

Her brows rose. "This is a swank neighborhood, and it's

definitely not a business address."

Though Poppy felt the dark power in the Mojave had only been a part of the Lord's plan, and they'd never really been in harm's way, he wasn't certain enough to risk another encounter with it. "Why don't you give them a call and ask what they do for a living and where? Then we'll check it out. Their stories won't pan out if they aren't from the real world. But I have a feeling they're legitimate and God had a specific reason for you meeting them. They said their mother was Jewish. Denise's mother is Jewish, and we know God saw to it you two met. Nothing supernatural happened, so let's hold off judgment until we learn more about them."

Bob made the call. The wary expression on the Yankee's face so humorously contradicted the cockiness in his voice, Poppy had to stifle a laugh as he watched and listened.

". . . Do you still dance or what, 'cause if you do I must see the show, if you know what I mean, and I think you do . . . So you don't dance anymore, huh . . . You own it? Far out . . . You say the place is called The Purring Panther?. . . And where would I find The Purring Panther? . . . Excuse me a sec while I write that down."

Bob looked at Denise, who produced a pen and scribbled the address on the back of the card as he recited it. Then he put his hand over the mouthpiece. "Do I need to ask for directions?"

She shook her head.

"What do I tell her about dinner, Pops?"

Poppy thought on it a moment. "Denise, do we have enough time to check out that club and get back here in time for Bob to keep his date?"

"Mm hmm."

"Tell her you'll be there."

Bob nodded and removed his hand from the receiver. "So we still on for dinner? . . . No, I don't need directions, my friend can put me on top of your place . . . ."

* * * *

They arrived at a purple brick establishment at fifteen till five. *The Purring Panther* glittered within a curvature of pink and purple neon shaped like a cat. Poppy didn't want Bob to come since one or both of the Quinn sisters might be there, and it hadn't taken any arm twisting to convince the wary Yankee to stay behind. They wouldn't know Denise or him unless they were from the other side, like the people at the convenience store.

They hoped to gather enough information to determine the validity of the Quinn sisters. Denise was going to apply for work as a dancer. Hair fluffed and slightly ratted, she had on rouge, mascara, too much eye shadow, and bright red lipstick. She looked exactly like the type of girl who worked in the field of entertaining thirsty gentlemen, and different enough from normal that the sisters wouldn't recognize her if they'd seen her picture in the paper during the trial. Poppy had asked her to use the voice she'd made fun of Bob with in the RV, and she was in perfect character.

As they neared the door, she started smacking her chewing gum. "Yo, Pops, c'mon inside wid me, I'll show youse a good time."

Poppy laughed. "It's a shame you didn't have any trampy clothes to put on, but from the shoulders up, you are one cheap-looking hussy."

"Oh, Pops, ya so sweet. Betcha say that to all the goils, don't youse?"

She went in alone. He waited a minute before making his entrance. His role was that of a liquor salesman, and since he had no idea what a liquor salesman should look like, he just came 'as is' in jeans, boots, and western shirt. Most of the patrons sat at small round tables. The chairs had a purple cat's head painted on their backs. A flashing sign stood beside an empty stage, advertising the show would begin at eight. There were cashiers at both ends of a long purple bar with stools dotting the front, most of them empty. Denise walked over and started talking to one of them, so he chose the other.

A middle-aged woman, with bags under her eyes that puffed out like marshmallows being squeezed between two graham crackers, gave him a toothy smile. "What can I get you?"

"Nothing, thank you. I'm a liquor salesman, and wonder if I might speak with the owner?"

The smile waned. "Sorry, she's not here."

"I see. Can you tell me where I might reach her?"

"No. Just leave your card, I'll see to it she gets it."

"Could you at least tell me her name, maybe she and I have done business before?" He knew it was a lame approach but didn't know how else to ask without making her suspicious.

She put a hand on her hip. "Have you ever done business here before?"

"Uh, no."

"Then you haven't done business with my boss because this is the only establishment she's ever owned. It's also the only place she's ever worked, for that matter."

"She used to work here?"

"Sure did. Started when she was just a kid. Lied to old Nick about her age and was his main attraction for years. He's the man that used to run this club. He didn't have any kids, and sort of adopted her—trained her to manage the place so he could semi-retire. Nobody had a clue he'd willed everything he owned to her. After he died, she took over, and moved me up to her old job."

"So she was the manager before you?"

"That's right."

"And you say her name was . . .?"

A frown appeared. "I didn't say her name was anything."

"I understood her name to be Monday Quinn. Is that right?"

She relaxed with a small laugh that lingered in a grin. "Well if you knew her name, why the Sam Hill did you ask me for it?" A heartbeat later her eyes narrowed. "Say, what kind of liquor do you sell anyway?"

"Uh . . . the alcoholic kind?"

"You're no liquor salesman."

"You caught me. No, ma'am, I'm not." He sighed with relief, glad to drop the charade. This type of thing was definitely not his forte. "You see, I may be related to her, but I'm not sure. Does she have a sister, about ten years younger, named Tuesday?"

"Sure does . . ." she closely scrutinized him as if memorizing every feature of his face. "So why did you pretend to be a liquor salesman? I don't get it."

He glanced around, appearing to be so distracted he hadn't heard the question. "From the look of it, this place turns a dollar or two. Are they blonde?"

"They are, and I can see some resemblance. I bet you guys *are* related. Just leave me your name and number, I'll see to it she gets it. I'm sure she'll want to get in touch with you."

"Um, I'm only in town a short while. I'm staying with a friend in Chicago and don't know the number." Though he wouldn't have given it anyway, he'd answered honestly.

"Well is your friend in the book?"

He didn't want to mention Denise by name, but didn't have to dodge the question because she came walking up, still in character, eyes telling him she'd hit pay dirt.

"Hey, Mista, can ya give a goil a lift?"

"Sure." He turned back to the woman. "Thank you, ma'am."

"My money's on you being related . . . ."

They got in her Mustang and Denise told him what happened with her cashier. "I said I was looking for an old friend of mine named Monday Quinn, that I'd heard she owned the place, and was hoping she'd hire me to dance. When she verified I had the right name, I asked if I could speak with her and was told she wasn't coming in like she usually does on Saturday nights because she met this—and I quote—'Italian hunk at the lake' and was having him over for dinner. Then she tried to steer me to the manager to set up an audition, but I told her I'd come back another time when Monday was there because I wanted to be sure I had the right woman. I told her the Monday Quinn I was looking for had a sister named Tuesday. She said that had to be her, so I asked about their mom, and she gave me a brief rundown of their history. Everything she said tallies with what those girls told Bob."

Poppy felt satisfied the Quinn sisters were normal, and likely to be part of the Lord's plan, due to the way He'd seen to it Bob hooked up with them. "Sounds like our Italian friend's in for an interesting evening."

"Does, doesn't it." Her voice sounded distant—she really seemed to be thinking it over.

"Make you jealous?"

"You know? It does a little . . . ."

* * * *

Houston spent the afternoon at the library, trying to learn about brainwashing. He found a chapter about it in a psychiatric textbook which did little to enlighten him. Cyberspace had endless sites, but most of them were the same song and dance, and no help. He personally knew very little about it, only what the average Joe on the street would know.

Patty Hearst may have been brainwashed by her abductors or she may have faked it, trying to save her ass. Either way she didn't claim to see Godzilla rise up through a street. Jim Jones may have brainwashed his followers, but not to the point where they thought they'd been pulled into another dimension. There were other cults whose members were so mesmerized they believed their leader was God, but none of them ever claimed to fall into a Garden of Eden by stomping around on a hill.

Getting nowhere with the research, he finally gave up. It wouldn't have helped with the major problem anyway. Even if he had the world's foremost expert on the subject at his disposal, the specialist wouldn't have been able to give him the information he really needed—the identity of the puppet master. That information could only be obtained from the three puppets who didn't know they were carrying it around in their heads . . . .

TWENTY ONE

When Denise Jones answered her door, Houston tried to hide his shock, but wasn't sure he succeeded. She'd teased her hair and had on way too much makeup. Then he received another surprise: instead of the troubled scowl he'd expected in response to this unannounced visit, the corners of her painted lips turned up with a smile.

She looked back over her shoulder. "Detective Shoat is here, Poppy . . . ."

* * * *

Bob followed the written instructions Denise had given him, found the address without too much trouble, and was surprised as hell to see the Quinn sisters lived in a friggin' mansion that looked like Jed Clampett's on The Beverly Hillbillies. A high block fence surrounded the estate, and two wrought iron gates blocked access to an asphalt drive. He stopped beside a short pole, capped with an intercom.

"Yes?" said a feminine voice through a blare of static after he pushed the button.

"Bob Talasota here. The Quinn sisters are expecting me."

"Great, you're right on time."

The gates swung inward and he drove through. At the end of the long drive sat a purple Lamborghini and red Ferrari, glistening under strategic outdoor lighting that illuminated the whole property. He parked beside them and got out of his Buick. It looked so humble next to those upscale hotrods.

Monday and Tuesday stood outside the front door waiting

for him. Since Pops and Denise had confirmed the Quinn sisters were normal, he strolled towards them confidently, looking forward to spending the evening with the hot, juicy babes.

Taking in the grandeur of the place, as well as the beauty of the two women, he sighed with anticipation. "You poor underprivileged girls. Let me take you away from all this."

The succulent duo giggled as each took an arm. They led him through a foyer with marble floors, into a huge room where the glistening stone gave way to luxurious carpet. Along the outer perimeter stood a well-stocked bar, grand piano, antique cabinets—housing china dolls and other delicate knick-knacks—and a huge granite fireplace. A rectangular valley, accessed by four steps continuing along three sides, occupied the center. Ritzy furniture, made for people to sit in or put things on, sat within it. An awesome entertainment center, equipped to satisfy every conceivable visual or audio need, covered the edge without stairs.

The girls seated him on a long davenport with Monday to his right, Tuesday at his left. Gleaming silver bowls and platters atop an ornate coffee table the same length as the couch, held caviar, dips, crackers, chips, mixed nuts, and numerous hors devours. Three champagne glasses rested beside an ice bucket holding an uncorked bottle of Dom Pérignon. His jeans, button-up plaid shirt, and high-tops contrasted sharply with their classy dresses and heels. Monday wore a purple tight-fitting number with a revealing top, while a red one, cut the same style as her sister's, draped Tuesday's fabulous body.

"If I'd known it was going to be formal, I would have dressed better."

Monday filled the glasses. "You're fine, Bob. We just felt dressy this evening. We'll change into something more casual if we're making you feel uncomfortable."

He scooped some caviar onto a cracker. “No, I’m fine as long as you don’t feel disrespected.”

“Oh we don’t, I promise.”

Tuesday echoed the sentiment while he chewed and swallowed.

Their perfumes differed, but mingled nicely. It surprised him they didn’t use the same brand, since they obviously had the same taste in clothes and hair styles. “You always dress alike?”

Tuesday handed him a glass of champagne and took one for herself. “We do most everything alike, and usually together.”

He took a sip. “Mmm, this is great.”

Monday’s provocative lips stretched into a teasing smile. “Should be, it’s very expensive.”

“Guess I’d better hold it down to one glass then, huh.” He’d only been joking but a mortified expression jumped on Monday’s face.

“Oh no, I didn’t mean it like that—goodness no! I wanted you to know how special we think you are. So special we’re serving our best. Please drink all you want . . . .”

As time passed, the girls were so attentive he’d started to feel self conscious despite the relaxing affects of the bubbly. They had a gleam in their eyes that made him feel a little like a Thanksgiving turkey being evaluated by ravenous thanks-givers, tired of waiting for the feast.

* * * *

Denise had not only started calling him by his first name, insisting he do likewise, she’d actually invited him to stay for dinner. Houston was awfully glad she had. Her liver and onions rivaled his mother’s, a feat he’d thought impossible. She’d given him an appreciative smile upon hearing it. They were sitting at her kitchen table having after-dinner coffee with the professor, who he now felt comfortable calling Poppy.

He told them he believed they were telling the truth, but only because someone used some form of mind control to make them think they'd actually experienced it.

"No, we weren't brainwashed," said Denise. "It all really happened. The creature was as real as that coffee cup you're holding."

Houston took a sip from it before replying. "Of course you think that. A person who's been brainwashed has no idea they have been until they get deprogrammed. If I could only do that to the two of you, you'd immediately understand that what you saw and experienced were only hallucinations that were so strong they seemed real."

The professor brought the tips of his fingers together and grinned at him, patronizingly. "Looking at it from your perspective—that we've been brainwashed—you have the following dilemma: we each had to have been brainwashed by different individuals because we never crossed paths until we met each other in the Mojave Desert, and that happened *after* each of us saw the creature."

He set the cup down. "Not if whoever brainwashed you made you forget you knew each other prior to that."

Poppy chuckled. "If that happened, we'll never know who did it to us, because if they were able to do that, they'd also be able to convince us they didn't exist."

Denise blew out a sigh of frustration. "Tell him, Poppy."

"Tell me what?"

* * * *

Poppy eyed Houston Shoat for several intense moments, deliberating. On the way back from the nightclub Denise had said she'd lain awake last night worrying about the detective finding out he really wasn't Paul Quinn. He'd told her that might be the only way to convince him they were telling the truth, and had dispelled her fear by pointing out the nosy detective wouldn't dare tell anyone else, knowing they'd think him crazy. Now she wanted him to relay it, but since Houston thought they'd been brainwashed, it would require proof, and he had none here in Chicago.

"If you'd be willing to go to Texas with me, I'm pretty sure I can make a believer out of you."

Houston furrowed his brow. "Why, what's in Texas?"

"Proof."

"Proof of what?"

"What I'm about to tell you . . . ."

* * * *

Monday refilled his glass and returned the bottle to the ice. She turned to him in a seductive manner, elbow resting on the back of the couch, slender fingers dangling near her face, scarlet nails almost touching the creamy smoothness of her cheek. With the other hand she raised her vessel and a languid rivulet of carbonated splendor flowed through her sensuously parted lips. He looked at Tuesday and saw she'd positioned herself so that she mirrored her sister. Nervous yet excited, he cleared a lump from his throat and sniffed the air as a pleasant aroma entered the room. "Is that beef I smell?"

Donning a hungry look that food could in no way satisfy, Monday set her glass on the table. Her sister followed suit, wearing the same expression. "We're having standing rib roast, and it'll be a little while before it's ready. Meanwhile, why don't you let us see that amazing chest of yours again?"

She reached for the top button of his shirt.

Before he could say anything, Tuesday worked the second, and they alternated until each pulled a plaid tail towards them, exposing his chest and abdomen. Monday grabbed his face and kissed him, thrusting her tongue between his teeth.

The savage intensity of her gorgeous mouth, and the urgency with which she probed his taste buds, sent fiery currents of desire racing through him, culminating at his thickening groin.

"My turn."

He opened his eyes to see Tuesday pulling her sister away by the hair. She glued her lips to his, setting off another electrical firestorm in his libido. A few moments later he felt her get yanked away and saw Monday holding a handful of do while planting one on her. After giving baby sister a serious face-sucking, she once again sought his.

Breaking free of the wondrous kiss, he set his champagne down and adjusted his position. As if thinking he might be attempting to bail, Monday grabbed his wrist with both hands, pressing his palm to the sofa as her sister latched onto the other.

Being much stronger than the two of them, he could easily have broken free . . . if he'd wanted to. Both girls brought their mouths to his, and a three-way tongue fest ensued. Almost simultaneously they forced his hands to their breasts. Forearms bent upwards, he groped and squeezed until the blondes pulled away and stood up. His eyes feasted and his throat went bone dry as they helped each other out of their dresses.

Neither wore any undergarments, so when the laundry fell, their flawless bodies were totally exposed. Hormones surging, he got up, tore the shirt from his shoulders, and started to unfasten his jeans, but they jerked his hands away. One untied his shoes while the other worked his pants down to his ankles. He stepped out of them and they took turns with the weasel, fondling each other while driving him wild with their tongues and lips, moaning as they sucked and licked.

He started to warn them he couldn't take much more, but didn't have to. They stood up and pushed him onto the couch. The naked sisters glared at him wantonly, eyes flaming with passion—mouths, panting blurs of smeared lipstick—breasts heaving from labored breathing.

Lying on his back, he looked up with greedy peepers. Their awesome blue orbs weren't the only genes from the family pool the Quinn sisters shared. Triangular pelts on bikini-waxed crotches announced they were true blondes. Large firm breasts sloping ever so naturally, obviously didn't owe their fullness to silicon. Tuesday's nipples turned up slightly, Monday's pointed straight out, but both sets were the same size—delectably perky, pink, and stiff as nails. With the palace-like surroundings, their porn queen inhibition made him so giddy with erotic joy, he felt like a sultan being pleasured by two amazingly beautiful belly dancers.

This was a wet dream come true.

As if receiving a telepathic message that he could now continue without popping, they made their approach. Monday straddled him, and carefully guided the rock-hard weasel inside her wet bush. Tuesday, facing her sister, buried her dripping slit on his face. Though unable to see anything but the crack of the younger Quinn's perfect ass, he could tell they were frequently locking lips by the muffling of their cries of pleasure, as each convulsed in a frenzied rhythm that increased in tempo until they, and he, exploded in raging orgasm.

* * * *

Houston scratched his head, marveling at the puppet master's evil abilities. "If you're not Paul Quinn, then who's living in his house? I was there. I talked to a man who I assumed was your father."

"My father passed away when I was a boy."

"An uncle or something then."

Poppy shrugged. "I don't know who you talked to, but he wasn't a relative of mine."

"He looked just like you, only older."

"Be that as it may, he's no relation, I promise you. I've never lived in the state of Illinois, and don't have any relatives that do."

He winced with frustration. The brainwasher had done a real bang-up job of screwing with the professor's mind. "Well, I've got to admit I've been wondering why you and Bob Talasota were staying here instead of Evanston. Where did you say he went?"

"Bob had a dinner date . . . ."

* * * *

They were lying in a giant bed in an upstairs bedroom. Everything was purple: walls, furniture, carpet, bed clothes, even the variable lighting, adjusted so they could barely see each other. They'd gotten dressed after the couch episode, eaten dinner, then the girls had led him here for a second round of raucous sex, that culminated a few minutes ago.

On his back with an arm around each of them as they rested their heads on his chest, Bob heaved a pleasured sigh. "This is a first for me."

"What is?" Monday queried from his right.

"This."

"Menage a trois?"

"Yeah. Never done it before."

"Neither have we," said Tuesday.

"Yeah, right," he chuckled.

"She's telling the truth, Bob."

"Aw c'mon. No offense, but you dolls came off like pros.

Jeez, what a rush." He eyed the ceiling with a smile.

Monday ran a hand over his stomach. "If we came off like pros it's only because of how strong our passion is for you. You brought it out in us just like we always knew you would."

"Yeah," sighed Tuesday, "did you ever."

He cut his eyes to the elder blonde. "What are you talking about, always knew I would?"

Abandoning his gut, Monday started tracing his lips with her fingers. "We knew who you were before you told us this morning."

"How?"

"The trial. Your picture was in the paper."

"Okay, so you knew who I was. That still doesn't answer my question."

"God made us for you, Bob. We've been waiting for you a long time. We're your wives."

He laughed. "Funny, I don't remember any wedding bells, or signing anything."

Tuesday pulled his face her direction. "Doesn't matter. We're still your wives."

"Would you be serious?"

"She is serious," said Monday. "I need to start from the beginning, and it may take a while. Do you have the time, or do you want me to tell you later?"

"Go ahead . . ." he fondled a tit with each hand, then slid his palms back to the sisters' shoulders. "I've got all the time in the world."

"Bob, do that again and I won't be able to talk because I'll be raping you instead."

"Same goes for me," said Tuesday. "Now you need to hear this, so please lie still and listen."

It blew his mind how responsive to his touch they were. "Okay, I'll behave. Go ahead, I'm all ears."

"I inherited this house from a man named Nicholas

Bernstein, who went by Nick," Monday continued. "He was my boss—the one who hired me when I lied about my age. Nick had a brother named Jeremiah, who claimed to be a prophet like the one in the Bible. He was always on at Nick to repent, sell his club, lead a holy life, and all that. Well, Nick always laughed at him, never took him seriously about anything. I thought Jeremiah was half crazy, but always loved the guy.

"He made me get my GED and tried to convert me. He wanted me to quit dancing and go to college, said he'd help all he could. I was always tempted every time he made the offer, but I couldn't leave Nick. He paid me very well and Jeremiah just didn't have that kind of money, and I had to support Tues and myself. Besides, I owed it to Nick, since he gave me the job.

"Anyway, Jeremiah said Nick had a special calling on his life, and one day he'd see it. Of course Nick just laughed and told him the only call he had on his life was the call of the wild. Well, Jeremiah had a heart attack and was hospitalized, which really messed with Nick's mind. Nick and I were with him when he died a few days later. Before he passed away, he said Nick was going to have a stroke within the year that would leave him paralyzed on his right side—then Nick would finally see the light, and give his life to God. He warned Nick to do exactly what God told him to when that happened. Jeremiah kept begging Nick to believe him, crying and everything. It finally got to Nick, and he winked at me while telling Jeremiah he believed him. Of course he didn't really. Jeremiah said he could now die in peace, and he did.

"Jeremiah was Nick's only family and he was devastated. Any time a guy came in the club that looked anything like his brother, Nick would break down in front of everybody. You have to understand, he was one of those guys that never cried, and couldn't stand the thought of anyone thinking he had a soft or tender side, so when he'd break down—which was happening on a regular basis—it would upset him so much that he'd cry all the more. He started drinking heavily and hardly ate anything.

"One day he fell over right there in the club. He had a stroke, and just like Jeremiah predicted, was paralyzed on the right side of his body. Nick knew he wasn't going to be around much longer, so he made out a will. I didn't know until after he died that he'd left everything to me.

"Anyway, Nick never gave his life to God like Jeremiah predicted. I was blown away that Jeremiah's prophecy about the stroke actually came to pass, and it convinced me he hadn't been just blowing holy smoke about being a man of God. But I kept wondering why the other part hadn't happened—the part about Nick being converted.

"Then one night I had the most vivid dream. Jeremiah was standing next to Jesus, and somehow I knew Jeremiah's words to Nick had really been meant for me. I was the one with the special call, and was supposed to give my life to God—and I've believed that ever since.

"Well, naturally I thought the thing God most wanted of me was to get rid of the club, and so I tried to sell it. The whole time I worked for Nick, he was always getting offers for it, but nobody ever tried to buy me out. So I put it on the market but it still didn't sell. Then a few days ago I learned why God had been blocking it. A big corporation wants that whole area, and I've been advised that I'll soon be hearing from them. I was also advised to set my price at ten times the market value, which is nine hundred thousand dollars. So it looks like I'm going to sell The Purring Panther in the near future for close to ten million."

Bob whistled through his teeth. "That's a lot of geetus."

"Yeah," said Monday. "Anyway, I started going to this church and really enjoyed it, but when they found out I was managing a dance club and used to dance myself, they let me know in no uncertain terms that I was no longer welcome there. That hurt me so badly I vowed never to set foot in a church again. Later on I learned God doesn't abide in manmade buildings anyway, but at the time it felt like God Himself was rejecting me.

"I wound up joining a home Bible study and developed a hunger to learn the Bible like the man who taught there. A prophet came to speak one night and singled me out. He told me the Lord was going to give me a most unlikely vision, and that it would be so unconventional, only a handful of believers would see it was the hand of God.

"I had no idea what he meant at the time, but believed it was from God, so I waited for my vision. Some people call it tarrying. After a while I learned that tarrying is for the birds, and decided to quit worrying about it and get on with my life, believing God would show me in His good time.

"Tuesday and I have a terrible track record with boyfriends. No matter how sincere they appeared to be in the beginning, every one of them inevitably wound up the same. Mine would secretly try to hit on Tues, and hers would come on to me behind her back. So we finally decided the only way we were ever going to have a faithful man was to have the same one. I talked to the pastor at the home fellowship about it, and he did like that church did—asked me to leave. It hurt worse than when I got kicked out of that church, because I really believed in the guy until then.

"I decided to trust God to teach me His word directly, and spent all my free time reading the Bible. Somewhere along the way I realized all we can do is ask Jesus into our hearts, and trust God to change us because we can't do it ourselves. I became alive inside, and realized I'd been spiritually dead before. Well, not only did the Lord bring my spirit to life, He opened my eyes to the real truth of all I'd been studying in His word.

"One day I was perusing Samuel and came across something that really puzzled me. King David had to flee into the wilderness because his son Absalom was trying to usurp his throne. David had left his ten concubines to tend to his house. On advice from one of his counselors, Absalom had sex with those concubines in a tent on the top of the palace so that the whole nation of Israel would know he'd slept with his father's wives.

"I read it over and over, trying to see if this went on over a period of days—because it seemed so farfetched that he'd be able to handle ten women, one after the other in a single night—but it didn't. So I thought, 'What a man—able to go ten rounds in one evening.' But the more I thought about it, that just seemed too unlikely, and I suspected they were all involved at the same time, in one setting. I read everything about multiple wives recorded in the Bible, and couldn't find anything prohibiting a man from sleeping with more than one wife at the same time. Meanwhile, I'd been sort of irked because women weren't allowed to have a male harem, but finally accepted what the Bible says about the matter—the woman was made for the man, not the other way around.

"So Tuesday and I came up with a test to determine which man we were made for. We had to be equally drawn to him, and he had to feel the same about us. Since he could easily lie about that, and actions speak louder than words anyway, we decided he couldn't make love to either of us alone until after we had a threesome. That way we'd be certain he didn't prefer one of us over the other. The last part of the test would tell us for sure. Though the man had to bowl us over completely, Tuesday and I would also have to experience erotic feelings for each other during the act.

"I'd meet someone, bring him to Tues, and she wouldn't like him for one reason or another. She'd do likewise, and the same thing would happen. Mind you, none of those men knew what was going on. I saw your picture in the paper and read how you'd been accused of murdering a man with the same last name as ours. The Lord quickened to my spirit that you were innocent. I showed it to Tues, and she flipped like I did. We both felt like you were the one we were made for. Only problem was, it looked like you were going to spend the rest of your life in jail, so we figured the Lord was showing us our man was someone that looked a lot like you."

He burst out laughing, no longer able to keep a straight face at hearing this goofy talk.

Monday started giggling, then stopped suddenly. "Are you laughing with me, or at me?"

"With you, don't take offense." He gave her a peck on the forehead for reassurance, but it was becoming pretty damn evident she didn't have the correct change and had apparently fouled up Tuesday's piggy bank as well with her crazy notions.

"When we heard about you being cleared of the charges," Monday resumed, "that convinced us beyond doubt that we were made for you, rather than some look alike. Then we had another problem, how to meet you. The papers said you were from Brooklyn, so naturally we assumed you went back there after you were released. We tried to call you, but every Roberto Talasota we talked to was the wrong one."

The thought of getting a phone call from them made him chuckle inside. Not knowing the lunatic minds on the other end of the line were housed in the bodies of goddesses with devilish libidos, he'd have hung up not long after hello. "I'm listed as Bob Talasota. Of course I wouldn't have been there."

"We didn't know that's what you went by then. Anyway, because of the club I can't leave town for more than a day or two, so we were planning to fly out and find you after it sold. But lo and behold, who do we run into on the beach but a man who looked an awful lot like the picture of you in the newspaper.

"We were sure you couldn't be our Roberto, but I got a definite hit in my spirit when we passed by, and when I mentioned it to Tues, she said the same thing happened to her. The longer we talked about it, the more we agreed that maybe we'd just jogged right past Mister Right, and weren't supposed to be with the man who'd been charged for the murder of Paul Quinn after all. So we went to the parking area and prayed that if you were the one for us, God would see to it you'd show up there within half an hour.

"Sure enough you did. We ducked down behind your trunk, and I couldn't help whistling, just to freak you out, then we sprang up as if from out of nowhere."

"How did you know it was my car?" He thought back on how frightened he'd been at the diner when thinking they'd miraculously appeared.

"We didn't. We just happened to be standing beside it. When we saw you coming, we lowered our heads and watched you through the windows. Before you could spot us we ducked, and slipped around to the back. I was peeking around the corner of the trunk when you put your shirt on. We thought you'd walk past, and we were going to sneak around the car so you couldn't see us, then follow you. But you opened the door instead.

"When I heard your New York accent I flipped, because I knew right then it was more than likely Roberto Talasota himself we were talking to. I take the fact that we unwittingly choose your car to hide behind as another sign from God that the three of us were meant to be together.

"We'd planned to get to know you and try to explain things a little at a time, but we weren't able to keep our hands off you. We didn't plan on this being our wedding night, but praise God it is, and my vision has finally been fulfilled."

"Whoa . . .!" he jerked himself into a sitting position. "Ladies, this was great fun, but I ain't married to nobody. I like you both a lot, and that was the best sex I ever had. Maybe it's the best sex I ever will have, but give me a break, that don't mean we're married."

Monday looked shocked and hurt, as if she'd been slapped in the face while being slandered. She threw her legs over the edge of the bed, jumped to her feet, and spun his direction—her voluptuous body a heavenly vision bathed in quiet purple light. Sexy fingers clenching her narrow waist, she cast her angry eyes on her sister. "Can you believe he doesn't believe us?!"

Tuesday sat up and put a hand on his shoulder. "Give the boy time, he'll come around to our way of thinking."

He let out a deep moan and rubbed his temples. "Sheesh, this has got to be the freakiest summer anybody ever had. I went through a friggin' nightmare out in the desert, got my butt thrown in the hoosegow over killing a man that never died, and now here you come—saying we're married just because we did the big nasty."

Monday started crying. "Oh, Bob, we love you . . . don't you understand? And you made us so hot we went after each other like two shameless lesbians—something that's never happened before—so it firmly validates my vision. Please, you've got to believe us!"

Vacating the bed, Bob looked for his clothes the sisters tossed when they'd practically torn them off him. He located his boxers atop one of the dresses crumpled on the floor, and bent over to fetch them. Tuesday came up from behind, reached around him with both hands, and massaged his crotch, eagerly.

Oh jeez . . . .

Monday, still sniffling, stepped in front of him when he raised up. The sisters pressed their bodies against him, and the weasel sprang to life, refusing to be denied.

For the third time that evening, he found himself soaring

to heights of unbelievable ecstasy, and once more wound up lying on his back afterwards with a wacky Venus on either side, each declaring her undying love for him . . . .

TWENTY TWO

Denise listened, and responded when Poppy or Houston spoke to her, but her mind wasn't on their conversation. She'd grown increasingly frustrated over Bob. As the hour grew later, her jealousy waxed stronger.

It's almost midnight, what's taking him so fucking long?!

She kept thinking about how he'd looked without a shirt on, the emotions that had surged through her when lying on top of him, the swelling in his jeans, how reluctant she'd been to get off of him. That stupid lopsided sneer he wore when feeling full of himself had always irritated her, yet even the thought of it now stirred her insides. A rude awakening had occurred: what she felt for that muscular Italian with the oh-so-pretty face, wasn't brotherly love anymore, if it had ever really been that in the first place. Having never experienced such intense physical yearning for any man, she didn't have a clue how a chauvinistic sewer worker had induced it, but she needed him desperately. Nobody else could quench the inferno of her flaming lust, growing hotter minute by minute.

Bob had called the Quinn Sisters BBB. When she'd asked what that meant, he'd said, "Beautiful Beyond Belief." It had taken awhile to face the reality of the situation. She'd tried hard to fight it, but the rising anxiety over him spending so much time with those two women made it impossible to deny any longer. The truth had finally surfaced, washing away all confusion. She might not ever grow to love him in her mind and soul, like she did Poppy, but her body belonged to that Bronx ox, and every fiber of its being demanded he take immediate possession of it.

* * * *

Poppy chuckled inside over Denise—still pretending to listen, but unable to conceal her distraction anymore. She'd started the evening with a cheerful demeanor, but when Bob hadn't returned by eleven, she'd been increasingly incapable of hiding her foul mood. Houston had noticed it too. Not knowing it to be jealousy over Bob, he'd misread it as Denise growing bored with the discussion, and politely offered to leave.

But Poppy didn't want the detective going anywhere until convinced they weren't brainwashed, because during the course of the evening he'd become aware that Houston Shoat was somehow a part of whatever The Almighty had in store for them. God had unmistakably alerted him to that fact deep in his spirit. He talked him into staying, and the three of them moved to the living room. Before he could try another tactic in persuading Houston they weren't victims of mind control, Bob came bounding through the door.

"You're not gonna believe what got laid on me tonight by the Quinn sisters!"

Poppy motioned for him to hold his news.

Houston glanced at his watch. "Guess I'd better head home, it's after midnight."

While walking Houston to the door, he noticed Denise glaring at Bob from the sofa. The Yankee didn't see her expression as he headed into the kitchen.

"Goodnight, Denise," said Houston, smilingly.

Denise muttered a goodnight but didn't look away from the kitchen entrance, even though Bob had already passed through it. She sat with arms folded, legs crossed, upper calf rocking.

He gave Houston an apologetic smile and said, "Have a safe trip home. Call or come by tomorrow, and we'll continue our discussion."

"Why don't we reconvene over at my place tomorrow? I'll spring for dinner."

He'd obviously made the offer for Denise's sake, not wanting to put her through another boring evening. The detective had no way of knowing she was anything but bored. "Unless you live within earshot, I'd never be brave enough to tackle the big city traffic, I'm afraid."

"Not a problem, I'll pick you up if you're game."

That would give Bob and Denise some time to sort things out without him being in the way, so he agreed.

"Great. I'll pick you up at six if that suits you."

"That'll be fine."

Bob bopped into the living room with a glass of milk and a saucer stacked with peanut butter cookies Denise had baked for dessert while preparing dinner. She'd left a platter-full on the table for Houston and him to enjoy during their discussion. Judging by the size of the pile Bob placed on an end table, that serving dish was most likely now empty. Plopping into the recliner, he gobbled one in two bites, washed it down, dried his upper lip with the back of his hand, and grinned at Houston. "Bet you got an earful. There's never a dull moment around these two."

"Well, we did have quite an interesting discussion after a wonderful dinner." Houston aimed a polite smile at Denise. "Are you okay?"

"I'm fine, drive safely." No longer hiding her frustration, her voice reflected what her body language had been radiating.

Poppy wished Houston would leave before she exploded. Bob being oblivious to her mood as he gorged himself on her cookies was making matters worse. He could see the detective feared he'd somehow offended her and wanted to make amends, but that would only exacerbate the already volatile situation. He whispered, "Best get while the gettin's good. It's nothing you did. She's irritated at Bob."

Responding with arched brows and mouth forming an O, the detective made his exit.

"You look like you must have had a grand evening," said Denise, the second Houston closed the door behind him.

Still unaware of her mounting hostility, Bob took a big swig of milk and wiped off a white moustache. "Just wait till you hear."

"Are you sure you want to hear?" Poppy asked while making for the couch.

She glowered at Bob. "Why, I wouldn't miss this for the world. Tell us about your evening, Talasota, and you damn well better not leave anything out."

Bob frowned at Denise, then glanced at him. "What's with her?"

Ignoring Bob for the moment, he asked Denise if she wanted him to leave.

"Not on your life." She kept her eyes focused on the object of her irritation. "Come on, Talasota, tell us about your evening."

He finished off the milk, set his glass by the empty saucer, and leaned forward with elbows on knees. "First off, they're rich. You would not *believe* the castle those girls live in. And talk about chow! Champagne, caviar, the works for appetizers, and standing rib roast for the main course."

"I'm not interested in the real estate or the cuisine, Talasota," Denise ejaculated, increasing the frequency of her calf pumping. "I want to hear about the Quinn sisters."

Bob shot her an angry scowl. "What the hell's up with you, toots?"

Poppy winced. *Oh, Bob, of all things to say!*

In one rapid motion Denise's arms and legs uncrossed. She leaned forward as if ready to pounce across the room and scratch the unwitting Yankee's eyes out. "What did I tell you about calling me that, you son-of-a-bitch?!"

"Whoa! My mom ain't no bitch, you take that back, Denise!"

"Take back your toots and I will."

"Jeez . . . ."

"Take back your toots!"

"Alright already, I'm sorry I called you that."

"Then I'm sorry I called you a son-of-a-bitch, you fucking bastard."

Bob detonated. "I don't get it! Am I missing something here, Pops? Feel free to clue me in and rescue my ass if I am. When I left here this evening everything was peaches. Now Denise is acting like I keyed her Mustang or something."

As he'd watched her jealousy mount while Bob was at the Quinn's, it had excited him, because it buttressed his theory that she and Bob were going to produce the progenitors of the Olive Trees, if not the prophets themselves. But now things were getting out of hand. "Denise, that's enough. That kind of talk is stupid, and basal, and juvenile, to say the least. You're not some foul mouth teenager, you're a grown woman with dignity, and respect for others. Now apologize to Bob and let's learn what happened tonight."

A glittering tear leaked out, dangled on a thickened lash a moment, then dropped to Denise's cheekbone. Before it made its way past her nose, the dam burst. "I don't know what's happening to me . . . I've always been so in control of my emotions . . . That fucking desert! . . . Why did I wind up there? Why did we all wind up there? . . . If God's got a plan, why won't He show us what it is? And why does it have to involve us anyway? Why didn't He choose three other people instead? I haven't been myself since I saw that fucking monster . . . ."

Mascara streamed down her cheeks. The rouge and bright lipstick made her look like a sobbing clown. She rubbed her eyes and saw it on her hands. "Oh my god, I forgot to take off the makeup! Poppy, why didn't you remind me?!"

She yanked a handful of tissues from a box on the coffee table, scrubbed the lipstick off, and wiped her face. Then she seemed to remember what brought on the outburst in the first place, and turned to Bob. "Can you ever forgive me?"

* * * *

". . . Bob, I mean it, stop toying with her!" Pops' voice sounded menacing, and he marveled at the strength behind it. It never occurred to him the preacher could be a tough guy—willing to get down and rumble—but if his tone wasn't just bark with no bite, Pops had a serious set of cojones. He'd come to love the dude like a father, so to disrespect him in any form or fashion was unthinkable. No way he hadn't planned on forgiving Denise, but he'd wanted to drag it out—make her sweat the possibility he might not. But Pops wasn't willing to wait, and he didn't want to buck him.

Wondering what the hell had made her so mad in the first place, he got up and started towards her, gesturing for a hug. "All's forgiven."

She rushed to him and squeezed tightly. Pressing the side of her face against his—the side Pops couldn't see from his vantage point—she whispered, "I want you to fuck me."

When he regained his composure after the shock of her statement, he flipped his face to the other side of hers to keep Pops from hearing, and whispered back, "You're not going to use me to make Pops jealous this time, thank you very much."

Denise switched sides again. "I'm not trying to make him jealous. After he goes to sleep, come to my room."

"That's enough apologizing," said Pops in his usual voice. "I want to hear what happened. Now the bell has rung. You two break and go to your neutral corners . . . ."

He told them everything except for the sex, which made

the part where Monday informed him they were his wives sound sillier than all get out. Not long after he'd started recounting the night, it dawned on him what had been wrong with Denise earlier. She was jealous of the Quinn sisters. That gave him a sense of satisfaction, but he knew she didn't love him. For some crazy reason she'd gotten horny for him because of the two blondes, and that didn't figure to last long.

She'd said Pops had turned out to be right about her feelings for him being merely hero worship, and she'd seen the light. Yeah, right. And if Pops really believed that, there was a bridge in dear old Brooklyn he'd like to sell him. All she'd done was try to save face like him when he'd lied out his ass, saying he'd come to realize they were never meant to be anything more than friends. He still loved her, and knew he always would, but she could forget about him being her expendable stud for a one night stand to satisfy a temporary case of the hots. Especially since he had those two incredible bimbos to take care of his own sexual appetites. As crazy as they were—and those chicks were loons, no doubt about it—he liked them, and wanted them to continue using him as their boy toy as many times as they wanted, and time would allow.

He kept avoiding Denise's stare because her eyes burned with the same fire the Quinn's had earlier. The blaze in those dark brown orbs left no doubt she meant what she'd whispered in his ear. Ironically, there was a time when that would have been exactly how he'd have wanted the cards dealt: no commitment, no syrupy speeches, no flowers and expensive dinners, just no-holds-barred animalistic sex.

Pops' wheels were spinning, and he couldn't wait to hear his take on Monday's crazy talk. He started to speak to him, but checked himself. Poppy Quinn would always be Pops to him, but now it seemed inappropriate to call him that, and he felt he'd been rude for not using his proper name all along.

From now on, he would. "What do you think, Poppy?"

"You say they made a reference to King David?"

"Yeah, Monday did."

"Tell me what she said in detail."

"Aw, Poppy, she was talking a lot of Bible stuff that went right over my head. I couldn't get it half right."

"Try."

"Well, like I said, she was talking about King David having troubles with his son. For some reason the son screwed his old man's concubines, and she came to the conclusion he did them all at once, like it was an orgy. Don't ask me how, but that confirmed to her that she and her sister needed to come up with a test to see who they were supposed to marry. They both think it's me. Crazy, right? One thing I forgot to tell you is that she really likes to study her Bible. Guess she's sort of like you in that respect, Poppy."

"Bob," Pops said with a frown like he'd pissed him off, "why are you calling me Poppy?"

"Because that's your name."

"Call me Pops—it sounds weird hearing Poppy come out of your mouth."

Relieved that was the only thing bugging the Einstein, he grinned. "Why?"

"Don't know, it just does."

"Okay, Pops. Glad you feel that way because it sounded funny to me too."

"Than why'd you change?"

"It just suddenly hit me that it might sound disrespectful. Of course I never meant it that way."

"And I never took it that way, though I'll confess it bothered me a little the first time you said it. Glad we got that cleared up."

* * * *

Poppy managed to extrapolate the gist of what Monday Quinn had meant from what Bob could recall. "Interesting. I've always glossed over all the references to David's multiple wives and concubines, but what Monday said makes sense. However, I must take exception on her belief that she and her sister are your wives, because in Leviticus the command is given that a man can't marry his wife's sister during the wife's lifetime. Since both sisters are alive, they can't both be your wife."

"Well no man should have more than one wife anyway," said Denise indignantly.

"Multiple wives are never forbidden. It's just as viable an option for a man today as it was when Moses wrote the Pentateuch."

Bob frowned. "The what?"

"The first five books of the Bible were written by Moses, and collectively they're referred to as the Pentateuch, meaning five books. Parts of it deal with marital regulations, and though there are restrictions on which woman a man might take as a wife, there's none prohibiting multiple wives."

Denise tossed him a playful grin. "Good, think I'll have ten husbands then."

Poppy grinned back. "Think again, Denise. Women aren't allowed more than one husband."

She slapped her leg and crossed her arms beneath her breasts, features blazing with outrage. "That's the biggest load of bull I've ever heard, Poppy! What's good for the goose is good for the gander."

"Not in this case it's not."

"Are you serious? The Bible really says a man can have all the wives he wants, but a woman can only have one husband?"

"Yes, and here's why: woman was made for man. Adam was created for God, Eve was created for Adam. But having said that, a man can't have all the wives he wants, there are certain restrictions. For instance, besides not being able to have sisters at the same time, he can't have a wife that's immediately related to him, such as his sister or aunt."

"What about his cousin?" Bob inquired.

"No restriction there that I can recall."

"What about a man marrying a man?" asked Denise.

"Forbidden. Homosexuality is an abomination before the Lord, no matter what man thinks about it."

She scowled at him as if he'd just made the most repugnantly unjust declaration imaginable. "That just can't be right, the Bible's wrong on that one. A man can't be blamed for being born with a sexual preference for men."

One of Satan's most masterful lies, Poppy thought sadly. "The Bible's not wrong about anything, and as for being born homosexual, that's the load of bull. Men become homosexual the same way they become drug addicts. They dabble into something their own conscience forbids, and before they know it they get hooked. Now I'm not saying some men aren't naturally effeminate, but no man's born homosexual.

"The Apostle Paul explained the process perfectly when he said, 'And even as they did not like to retain God in their knowledge, God gave them over to a reprobate mind.' The meaning is simple: keep tuning Him out in order to numb your conscience over sinful activity, and God will turn you over to a reprobate mind, where you no longer have the ability to discern the thing you're doing is actually wrong.

"No one who claims to believe the Bible can call homosexuality sinless, because it clearly states, 'Thou shalt not lie with mankind as with womankind: it is abomination.' No one's born with a particular sexual preference, it develops later on. The way things are going in this wicked day and age, pedophilia will be regarded as an alternative lifestyle eventually."

"Humph! Well I don't agree with that at all, Poppy, no

matter what the Bible says. Some men prefer boys, and some women prefer girls, and that's just the way it is, and always will be."

A puzzled look crawled over Bob's face. "What about menage a trois, Pops?"

"That I don't know about," he answered, noting Denise still frowning at him. Her mind was made up, and he could see there'd be no changing it. "What Monday said about the ten concubines certainly seems possible. The term means a lesser or secondary wife, much like a man having a mistress besides his wife in modern times. A mistress is usually there strictly for pleasure, rather than bearing a man's children, doing his laundry, keeping the house clean, and so on. David was never rebuked for having them. Solomon had three hundred wives and seven hundred concubines. God chastised him for being led astray by some of them, but he was never reprimanded for having so many women. Having said that, if it is allowed, the man has to be married to the two women involved—otherwise it's just another form of adultery or fornication."

"I've been thinking about the claim you made concerning the sisters," said Denise with an insightful smirk. "Care to back up on that, Poppy?"

"No. The Quinn sisters may think they're supposed to be Bob's wives, but they're not."

"I don't mean them. I mean the injunction in the Bible you spoke of."

"Yes?" He couldn't imagine why she failed to understand such a clear commandment.

"Well, you said the Bible's never wrong."

"Right."

"And you're sure about that?"

"Yes, I am."

"Well it certainly contradicts itself."

"How so?"

"Correct me if I'm wrong, but didn't Jacob marry two sisters?"

"Yes, but there's no real contradiction, only an apparent one."

"Oh really?" She smiled victoriously, clearly relishing the idea of one-upping him.

"Really. You're right, Jacob married two sisters. Not only that, his grandfather Abraham married his half sister, another marital no-no in the law. But the law was not yet given. Had Jacob married Rachel and Leah after the law, it would have been a transgression. But where there is no law, there is no transgression." Something stabbed at the back of his mind and quickly came to the forefront. "Sorry, Denise, I'm incorrect. I just recalled a scripture in Genesis where God was telling Isaac he was blessing him because his father Abraham kept His laws. So even though the law wasn't recorded until Moses, it was certainly known by Abraham.

"I'm so glad you said something, because you've just made an old dog learn something new. Since Abraham knew the law, and married his half sister, the ordinance in Leviticus has to be talking about illicit sex rather than marriage. However, Jacob marrying two sisters would have been unlawful had he done it intentionally—but he only married Leah because her father hoodwinked him into it. Her sister Rachel was the one he wanted and struck a deal for."

"Jeez, this is all so complicated," said Bob, scratching his chin. "I'll tell Monday she's wrong, but I know she won't believe me. If you could put me on top of that scripture, Pops, I'd appreciate it. At least I can show her what the Bible says."

"I know it's in Leviticus, but I'll have to find the chapter and verse. When are you supposed to see her again?"

"Told her I'd give her a call tomorrow."

"Do you have a Bible, Denise?"

"Yes, but it's late and we all need to get to bed."

"You're right. But would you be kind enough to bring it to me now, so I can look it up for Bob first thing in the morning?"

She nodded and went to get it . . . .

* * * *

Bob awoke with a start. Something was moving under the covers. "Whoa!"

"Shush, it's just me, you Bronx ox. Thought I'd fall asleep and forget about it, didn't you. Well I didn't. It's time we got to *really* know each other."

She pressed her firm body against him and hissed in whisper, "I want you . . . Oh, Bob, I want you so bad."

He totally freaked—she didn't have a stitch of clothes on. Despite leaving it all on the playing field with the Quinn sisters, when Denise pulled his hands to her tender breasts and fastened her pretty lips to his, the weasel turned to steel. The kiss was *so* magical—felt so very, very right—it killed him inside that she didn't love him . . . .

Thrashing like a wild animal beneath him as she started climaxing, he tried to hold out until she reached the end of her rainbow, but she kept thrusting her hips so violently he eventually couldn't hold back. When his semen gushed inside her, Denise bit his neck so hard it had to have left teeth marks. They weren't going to be easy to explain to Pops, and he wasn't going to like the idea of them doing the big nasty outside of wedlock one bit.

TWENTY THREE

Bob and Denise were still asleep, at least he assumed they were since both bedroom doors were closed. Poppy brushed his teeth quietly as possible, tiptoed from the hall bathroom to the kitchen, turned on the coffee maker, and set down at the table. The dribbling coffee cast a rich scent that made him impatient for his first cup of the day. While waiting, he pondered last night's developments.

Two sisters believed they were Bob's wives. Denise felt more for Bob than she'd been willing to admit. Houston Shoat thought they'd been brainwashed, and needed to be convinced otherwise, then hopefully his role in The Olive Tree Operation would become clear. Poppy still didn't know exactly what his own function was, other than being a harbinger of the truth.

Though both Quinn's couldn't be Bob's, one of them might be, and he wondered if Denise would be able to accept the fact she'd have to share him if that wound up being the case. The nation of Israel sprang from four women. Maybe the Olive Trees, or the progenitors thereof, would come from two: Denise and a Quinn. God only knew. Having no desire to be married to even one woman, he couldn't imagine having to handle two—especially when one of them was a spitfire, who had to have every 'i' dotted and every 't' crossed.

Monday and Tuesday Quinn popping into Bob's life the way they had couldn't be coincidental, and he wondered if he might be related to them. It certainly seemed possible with the surname, Cherokee similarity, and the lady at The Purring Panther thinking it likely. He needed to meet them and do a little digging into their family history. A morbid chill suddenly flooded his entrails: the memories of his own seemed to be immersed in a gray haze. Incidents were more identifiable with the telling than their origins. Though keenly aware he'd relayed both correctly to Bob and Denise, he couldn't recall actually being told how he'd acquired his nickname or hearing his father speak about the Cherokee legend.

Where had he bought the Jeep? When did he purchase it? Was it new or used when he acquired it? What destination had he hoped to reach when driving it through the Mojave Desert? Who taught him Hebrew, Greek, Italian, Russian, German, and all those other foreign languages he could speak so fluently? How many of them did he actually know? What was his mother's maiden name, his father's first name, what town did he live in, was it really in Texas . . . where was he born? He had no recollection of any of those things.

Merciful God, what is happening to me?!

The biker turned to face him, the helmet's dark mask concealing his face. Poppy knelt before him, wearing something white. He was dreaming, that's why he couldn't remember. His brain had been anaesthetized, and the biker's thoughts echoed in his ears. The words were strange. Bob *was* married to the Quinn sisters. God had ordained it even though it appeared to contradict scripture. He tried to tell the biker that couldn't be, but the leather clad messenger telepathically communicated: *"The verse you seek is Leviticus eighteen-eighteen. Read it, and your eyes will be opened."*

Poppy woke up with the warm smell of freshly brewed coffee filling his nose. He was sitting at the table, wearing a white towel wrapped around his waist. Since he hadn't put his clothes on right away as usual, he had to have been walking in his sleep.

He hurried to the living room, quickly got dressed, returned the towel, and picked up Denise's Bible on the way back to the kitchen. It had taken her a while to find it last night, and she'd confessed it hadn't been opened since her high school days, when she'd begun to question God's existence.

Looking up from Leviticus, the eighteenth verse of chapter eighteen, Poppy smiled with wonderment. *Neither shalt though take a wife to her sister, to vex her, to uncover her nakedness, beside the other in her life time,* it read. Monday Quinn hadn't been mistaken after all.

"Morning, Pops," said Bob, waddling in, stiff-legged from just waking. He fetched coffee and joined him at the table, eyeing the open Bible. "Find it for me?"

He nodded, and frowned. "Bob, that's the same shirt you wore last night. Why don't you let me buy you some more clothes? You shouldn't have to wear the same shirt all the time."

"In case you forgot, I did let you buy me two. Anyway, I may never wear another one again."

"Why?"

"Because this, my man, is my lucky shirt."

Denise walked in with a peaceful, satisfied look on her face, dressed only in an oversized t-shirt that hung to the middle of her thighs. She wasn't wearing a bra, and her protruding nipples embarrassed Poppy.

"Good morning, gentlemen." She let out a deep yawn and stretched lazily.

"Good morning." He made a mental note to locate a motel later. Bob and he needed to find other accommodations. Denise was becoming too relaxed around them, and he feared she'd be walking around in her underwear before long.

Recalling the dream, he realized Bob didn't require a motel room. He was married to the Quinn sisters so a castle, as the Yankee called it, awaited him. Maybe he and his two brides would let him sleep in the dungeon, Poppy mused with an inward grin.

"Morning, sunshine," Bob said to Denise, a warm smile on his face.

She beamed at the sleepy-eyed Italian, and ambled to the cabinet for coffee.

Bob turned his head her direction, and Poppy spotted tooth marks on his neck, surrounding a painful looking hickey. They weren't there when he came home last night. He and Denise had made love, that's why he'd called his shirt lucky. They'd unwittingly consummated their inevitable marriage, as he'd thought would happen all along, though neither of them knew it at the moment.

"Did you find the scripture for him, Poppy?" Denise asked sweetly.

"I dreamed about the biker, and he told me to read Leviticus eighteen-eighteen, so I did—and darned if it isn't the exact scripture I was going to look up for Bob."

She pulled a cup from the cabinet. "That doesn't surprise me."

"Would you write it down for me, Pops, so I can have Monday look it up?"

"No need." Unable to resist the urge to have a little fun with this, he shot the Yankee an obnoxious grin. "Monday's right."

"Huh?"

"Yeah. Congratulations, you lucky dog, you're a married man with two wives. Or should I say three?"

Something shattered on the floor. He turned to see Denise had dropped her cup.

"Not to worry, Denise. You're wife number three."

Mouth ajar, arms hanging limp at her sides, she gawked at him fretfully, as if he was holding her at gunpoint

Bob had turned pale. "So Monday's not mistaken after all?"

"No."

"Holy shit . . .!" he whisked his hair back and planted his

hands on his crown. "Polygamy's illegal in this country, Pops."

"God doesn't need the government to bind what He brings together, Bob. Christ said, 'What God has joined together, let not man put asunder,' yet the state-issued marriage license becomes null and void by a divorce decree, making it a meaningless piece of paper. And as for multiple wives, why that's what American men have been doing for years. Shuffling from wife to wife, from chapel to divorce court and back again, sneaking behind wife number two's back to have sex with wife number one because she suddenly becomes attractive again when she's forbidden fruit. And often there's a wife number three, and so on.

"What's really disgusting is that in this country a man can marry and divorce as many times as he wants, yet is forbidden to have more than one wife at the same time. The Bible says in Malachi that God hates divorce, yet multiple wives are something God never condemns, as long as the proper criterion is met. Christ made it clear that divorce was never part of God's plan. He said a man is committing adultery against his wife if he divorces her and marries another woman, so that proves God doesn't acknowledge the separation. They strain at the gnat of multiple wives, and swallow the camel of divorce and remarriage. The highest earthly estate is treated like a joke in America and most of the western world."

"Wow," Bob muttered, looking stupefied.

Denise swept up the pieces of her broken cup, filled another, and joined them at the table. "Well if you don't need a marriage license, how *do* you get married?"

"When Abraham's servant brought Rebecca to Isaac, he took her to his mother's tent and she became his wife. No ritual, no license, no fanfare of any kind. The two of you became man and wife when you made love last night. Let me be the first to congratulate you."

The same astonished expression captured both their faces.

"How did you know?" Denise asked at length, red-faced with embarrassment.

He gave her a teasing smile for an answer.

"Oh jeez!"

"What's the matter, Bob?"

"I'll tell you later, Pops."

It hadn't occurred to him until that moment, but now he knew why Monday thought they were already married. Bob had made love to the Quinn sisters. Denise would go ballistic if she found out.

Gazing absently at the salt and pepper shakers, lightly massaging her temples, she looked numb—like a woman refusing to let some form of earth shattering news sink in. "You said a man couldn't be married to two sisters while both were alive, Poppy."

"I know, but I was wrong. Listen to what that scripture says: he read it aloud, and closed her Bible. "It says a man can't *vex* his wife with her sister. The same Hebrew word used for wife in this passage can also mean woman. What the verse forbids is a man angering or upsetting his wife, or any other woman, by uncovering the nakedness of her sister in her presence. If the woman doesn't mind, she can hardly be vexed. It's referring more to coital relations than marriage, in fact the whole chapter is. A man can be married to two sisters, but only if the sisters are in agreement about it.

"And Abraham marrying his half-sister Sarah gives us another clue. It was forbidden for a man to have premarital sex with his half sister, but nowhere does it say he couldn't marry her. King David lived long after the law was given, yet his daughter told his son—her half-brother—she was sure David would give her to him as a wife when she was begging him not to rape her. Being David's daughter, she'd have known the law, so that can only mean the marriage would have been valid. Incidentally, she was Absalom's full sister, and her being raped by said half-brother set the wheels in motion that eventually led to Absalom's revolt against David, Monday Quinn spoke about. The eighteenth chapter of Leviticus is more about forbidden sex than forbidden marriage."

Denise finally quit staring at the spices and eyed him. "Then Jacob could have legally married the two sisters even after the law was written."

"Right. But if you've ever read the story about Rachel and Leah, you know darn well those two sisters would never want to be with Jacob at the same time. That's not the case with the Quinn sisters, according to Bob."

"So Bob and I are married, that's what you're saying?"

"Unless you want to call it fornication, yes. You can't have it both ways. The Bible says the marriage bed is undefiled, but whoremongers and adulterers God will judge. That's a very serious warning."

Bob nervously rubbed the teeth marks on his neck as if trying to wipe them off. "And I'm also married to the Quinn sisters?"

"Only if you want to be, but the same restriction applies. If you sleep with them without considering them wives, then it'll be sin." He hoped it was enough to hold Denise's temper at bay.

She turned to the amorous Italian, eyes threatening, yet worried. "Do you want them, Bob?"

"Jeez . . . ."

"Well do you?"

Poppy intervened. "I need to talk to the Quinn sisters. Why don't you give them a call, Bob, and ask if they'll meet with us? Here or there, whichever they prefer."

"I'll give them a call after breakfast. What's on the menu this morning, Denise?"

"Not so fast, Talasota, you didn't answer me."

The Yankee gave his neck one last massage and dropped his hand. "Listen, they say they love me, and I know you don't. And since we all know God is doing something really, really crazy with the three of us, I'm at a loss. I can't say I don't want them because the hound in me does, and that's as honest as I can be about it."

Denise screwed her eyelids together for a long moment. When she opened them, two sweltering orbs of defiance and resolve appeared. "According to Poppy we're married, and I'm not about to share my husband with other women."

Bob whacked the table, causing a splash of coffee to surge upwards and collapse back into his cup like a tiny brown geyser. "Look, this has gone far enough! I ain't married to you, and I ain't married to the two days of the week. Now Pops, no disrespect here, but you're wrong on this one. I ain't married to nobody, and don't wanna be. If I'm a whoremonger then I'm a whoremonger, so friggin' be it. Now all I want right now is to eat some breakfast, is that too much to ask?"

He started to challenge Bob but couldn't speak. His bowels constricted, causing his stomach to launch an acidic dry heave that flooded his oral cavity with a putrid tang as the room started spinning. Head bobbing with dizziness, he grimaced as pain reverberated throughout his musculature, sucking away all his energy, depleting his strength. Pulled to the brink of unconsciousness, he fought hard to stay awake despite the compelling promise of shock-induced anesthesia, fearing he wouldn't be seeing this world again if he closed his eyes.

Denise gasped with alarm. "Poppy, what's wrong?!"

Fiercely determined not to faint, he gritted his teeth and knotted his hands into fists—eardrums vibrating with the hyperactive pulse of a heart pounding rapidly as machinegun fire, innards compressing and twisting with nauseous agony, torturing sensations knifing through his flesh as if he'd been impaled on a bed of nails. Too many thoughts were forming at the same time—a storm of ideas and possibilities whirled like a tornado within his reeling mind, expanding so rapidly he envisioned his cortex exploding into a trillion particles of gray jelly.

Then, suddenly as it started, it ended.

"My god, Poppy, you turned a sickly shade of gray all of a sudden, and your eyes looked like they were going to pop out of their sockets. We better get you to the emergency room."

"No . . . I'm fine now. I apparently walked in my sleep before you guys got up—something I've never done before to my knowledge—so something's out of whack. But I don't think it's anything serious. It was probably just the result of a combination of frayed nerves and a temporary chemical imbalance brought on by a spike or drop in my blood sugar. I bet some breakfast will fix everything. I agree with Bob. Let's eat."

She leaned forward and felt his forehead with the back of her hand, studying him skeptically for several moments before relenting. "Well, you may be right. You don't feel feverish and your color's back to normal."

Bob looked petrified.

He gave the Yankee a reassuring grin. "I'm okay, Bob."

"Jeez . . . I hope so, Pops."

"Anyway, Denise, back to the topic at hand. I believe I'm right and Bob is wrong, but either way, we need to meet these girls and see what we think about them."

"Go ahead if you want to, Poppy, but you'll do it without me."

"Denise, be reasonable. I understand your reluctance, but it's much better to face the inevitable rather than put it off, which is all you'll be doing."

"Inevitable? Ha! Not likely, my friend—I'm not ever going over there, and they're not setting foot in my house." She shifted her livid glare from him to Bob. “Look, it’s me or them, you’ll have to choose. I’ll give you twenty-four hours to make up your mind.”

Bob heaved a sigh. “It’s a no-brainer, Denise. All you want me for is my body.”

“You fucking bastard . . .!”

TWENTY FOUR

After breakfast, Bob called Monday Quinn and arranged a meeting at her place that afternoon. Poppy again tried to talk Denise into going with them but she wouldn't even discuss it. Nor would she speak to Bob.

At one o'clock Bob backed out of the drive and waited on the street as he moved his Honda to the curb so the Mustang wouldn't be blocked in. He got in the Buick and they headed for the Quinn residence.

It took an hour to get there.

Bob's description of the women's beauty and the splendor of their home certainly hadn't been overstated: the Quinn's were total knockouts, the grounds of the estate luxuriant, the mansion opulent, its interior palatial. Houston Shoat was supposed to pick him up at Denise's at six, and they'd have to leave by five to get there in time—so after being given a grand tour, Poppy had a little over two hours to interview the girls.

They were having iced tea on a beautiful veranda beneath the shade of a large tree, the name of which Poppy knew in Hebrew but couldn't recall in English for some reason. Monday and Tuesday wore identical apparel, all of it white: v-neck shirts made of stretchy material that clung tightly to each swell and curve of their upper bodies, tight shorts barely covering their shapely hips, and sneakers with ankle-high socks. He sat across from Monday at a round patio table made of chrome and glass. Bob sat to his left, facing Tuesday. Pleasantries had been exchanged, now it was time for small talk to end.

Poppy started the ball rolling with, “Bob tells me that one of your forebears was Cherokee and took on the name Quinn.”

Monday nodded. “That’s what Dad told me, but he was famous for telling tall tales, so I don’t know for sure. And he was orphaned at a very young age, so even if he wasn’t lying, he may not have been remembering correctly.”

He liked the serene boldness in her eyes when she spoke. Monday was an exceptionally beautiful woman, shrouded with an intangible magnetism—a spiritual quintessence stemming from within that had nothing to do with her amazing physical attributes. If Denise ever saw her, she’d immediately understand Bob’s reluctance to give her up. Tuesday didn’t strike him as being quite the same caliber, but she seemed nervous and preoccupied, obviously not trying to make her best impression. Being a decade younger, perhaps she’d acquire that certain something her sister possessed with time and experience. “My great-grandfather is alleged to have done the same thing, traded in his Cherokee name for Quinn.”

Monday’s pretty lips spread into a smile of pleasant surprise. “Wouldn’t it be something if we’re related? Where are you from?”

“Texas.”

“That’s where Dad was born.”

“What was his name?”

“Stewart.”

“No Stewart Quinn’s in my family that I know of. I guess it’s just one of those odd coincidences that sometimes happen.” But in light of the situation, he found it difficult to believe in one of this magnitude.

She eyed him for a thoughtful moment. “You look very familiar. I swear I’ve seen you somewhere before.”

He’d been thinking the same thing, but didn’t mention it. “It’s doubtful you saw me here in Chicago. Ever been to Texas?”

"No."

"Hmm . . ." he took a sip of sweetened tea and noticed Tuesday looking at him. She seemed to be loosening up. He wondered if she'd sensed his influence on Bob and found it threatening. If so, she'd apparently concluded he wasn't trying to keep her away from the Yankee.

Still perusing him, she finally spoke. "I've seen you before too."

He gave her a friendly smile, hoping to ease her mind if Bob seeing him as an authority figure *had* been the reason she'd been ill at ease. She struck the same chord of déjà vu in him as her sister. "That's interesting. You and Monday seem familiar to me as well. I can't imagine we saw each other here, since I'm seldom out and about, so I'm at a loss to explain it."

Monday laughed. "Maybe we saw someone that looked like you, and you saw someone that looked like us."

"Maybe so," he chuckled back, glad to hear a cheerful giggle emerge from Tuesday.

"The papers said you teach theology at Northwestern," Monday said with a tone of admiration, a similar expression on her face. "That must be very rewarding. I read the Bible a lot. I'm no theologian, but I consider myself pretty knowledgeable about it. Did Bob tell you that Tues and I believe we're his wives?"

He'd been trying to find a tactful way to bring it up. Her directness really impressed him. "Yes, and I'd like to talk to you about that."

"Oh, I already know what you're going to say. 'You have to obey the law of the land, and the law of the land prohibits a man from having two wives,' but I say the law of God supersedes the law of man."

Her defensive tone, and the way she'd obviously braced herself for an onslaught of dogmatism from him, made him relish her shocked expression when he said, "I couldn't agree more."

"You couldn't?"

"That's right. However, you should know that he has another wife as well."

The sisters focused on the totally surprised Yankee. Their countenances evoked the image of two lionesses robbed of their cubs.

"Is that true, Bob?" the elder sister interrogated.

Bob's sagging jaw tightened with a sneer. "What is this, Pops, kick my butt day? Sheesh."

"Is it true or not?" demanded Tuesday.

"Forgive me, Bob, but we need to get everything out in the open." Poppy glanced at each sister. "You two weren't the only ones to marry him last night. He also formed a union with Denise Jones, the woman who was accused of being his accomplice in my murder."

"Come on, Pops, stop it already, will ya?"

Monday stiffened in her seat, visage growing more intimidating by the second. "What's he talking about, Bob?"

Hissing a sigh of frustration, Bob threw his hands in the air. "Look, I don't know what's going on. I never married nobody last night—not you, not Tuesday, and not Denise—jeez!"

She jumped to her feet. "You most certainly did marry us!"

Poppy felt horrible. He'd really mishandled the situation and Bob was having to suffer the consequences of his ineptitude. "Monday, please don't be angry with Bob. That's why we're all here, to straighten this whole thing out. Let's all calm down and discuss this calmly and rationally."

Her hands flew to her hips. "I think Denise Jones should be here too, don't you?"

"I wanted her to come, but she's just not up to it right now."

A wind gust sent napkins flying off the table and a wave of blonde hair across Monday's angry eyes. "You're right," she hollered through the stiff breeze, "we need to discuss this calmly! Where do we start?!"

The air suddenly became still, as if her question had stopped the wind. Poppy adjusted the right side of his collar that had flapped up against his neck. "Why don't we start with why you think you and Tuesday are supposed to be Bob's wives?"

Returning to her chair, she took a quick gulp of tea and explained her position, with Tuesday occasionally interjecting. ". . . and when we found out it wasn't just a guy that looked like him, we were completely blown away, because we knew God had made him cross our paths. And then, last night—"

"You made love," Poppy finished for her. "And you believe your marriage was consummated."

"Right."

Bob's eyes shot wide. "How did you know that, Pops?"

"I managed to put two and two together this morning from your reaction after I explained to Denise how Isaac and Rebecca became man and wife. You said you'd tell me later. Remember?"

"Yeah . . . I'd planned to, but didn't get around to it."

Monday eyed the Yankee with a quizzical frown. "What's that on your neck?"

Bob quickly covered the bite marks with his right hand.

"Did we do that to you?"

"Um . . . not sure . . . ."

She looked at her sister. "Did you bite him, Tues?"

Moisture welled up in the younger Quinn's eyes as she shook her head.

Face turning scarlet, Monday again rose to her feet. "You bastard! You fucked her, didn't you!"

Tuesday lunged forward. The long red nails on her arching fingers clicked against the opaque glass like menacing claws when her palms landed on it. Elbows locked, she jutted her face towards the astonished Yankee, tears streaming from her fuming blue eyes. "Bob! How could you?!"

Bob screwed his eyelids together, creating a network of wrinkles above his high cheekbones. He gritted his teeth as his bottom lip started quivering. Though clearly trying to hold everything in, his resolve faltered, and the floodgates flew open. A loud groan preceded a deluge. The macho Italian broke down bawling, and it devastated Poppy. Watching those broad shoulders heaving, he realized he loved that brash New Yorker as much or more than a father could love a son.

The poor guy had been wrenched from the real world, forced to witness a terrifying demon, abducted by a haunted recreational vehicle, threatened with cannibalism, and finally found his way back to reality, only to be accused of theft and murder, for which he'd spent forty-two days behind bars. Unlike Denise, Bob had never vented as the weight of horrific emotional stress accumulated from one ordeal to the next, at least not in front of him. And being such a tough guy, Poppy doubted he'd ever done so in private either. Now he had to battle a tumultuous conflict in his very soul: his love for Denise, desire for the Quinn's, and fear of plural matrimony. The two sisters were hurt and angry, Denise was mad at him, and apparently having to deal with three women's wrath at the same time became the straw that broke the camel's back.

"Jeez . . . I never meant for any of this to happen. Yeah, I balled Denise, but it wasn't my idea . . . She crawled in bed with me and woke me up . . . And you may as well know right now that I love her . . . She don't love me, but I love her. It's the first and only time we did it, I swear . . . Even though I love her, I still want the two of you, but dammit to hell, I'm not married to anyone. Pops . . .?"

Poppy would almost rather be facing the creature in the Mojave than have to be in the middle of this mess he'd created with his big mouth, though he'd only been trying to ascertain the truth of the situation. Bob kept sobbing, cupping his hands over his face. The Quinn sisters were hugging each other, crying hysterically. Yet he could only sit there, dry-eyed, feeling like the biggest fool who ever walked the planet. He knew he had to say something, and hoped it wouldn't make matters worse.

"This . . . this is very complicated. There are things that have happened to Bob, Denise Jones, and I that you'd find very hard to believe. But it's all interconnected, and somehow has something to do with God's will for mankind at this particular point in time. Now God has brought the two of you into the mix, along with a detective.

"Since Bob maintains at the moment that he's still single, let's assume that neither Denise Jones, nor the two of you are married to him yet. You must, therefore, keep your relationship with him platonic until we're either sure Bob's mistaken and is in fact your husband, or he decides he is. There is no middle ground—you can't be a little bit married any more than a little bit pregnant. What happened last night is in the past, nothing can change it, but let's keep this pure from here on out. If we can agree on that, then we've taken a solid step towards discovering the truth here."

* * * *

Houston didn't answer. Poppy hung up the phone and asked Bob for Denise's number. She didn't answer either.

TWENTY FIVE

Denise was driving aimlessly around with no destination, feeling like a whore for using Bob like a shameless bitch in heat. Of course she hadn't felt that way at the time, when uncontrollable lust had driven her to him. Why had she wanted that Bronx ox so badly last night?

He certainly hadn't disappointed her after she'd crawled in bed with him. He'd been every bit the macho super-lover her abnormal passion anticipated, and had given her a very special gift—an experience she'd previously believed to be pure fiction: multiple orgasms. They'd been so intense she'd bitten him, something she'd never done to a man before. She'd never known such carnal ecstasy, but couldn't savor the memory because she'd used him. Last night would forever be stained with shame, tainted with the filth of guilt, a mortifying portrait of an unforgivable selfish act.

The wonderful mood she'd awakened with that morning had been obliterated by Poppy's analysis of the situation. But what really bothered her about the whole thing was her insane jealousy over a man she didn't even love. How could she want Bob so much, yet not love him? Would she love him if Poppy didn't exist? And why was she so in love with Poppy anyway?

As the day progressed she'd gone further downhill, and now felt totally despondent. Her eyes were red and itchy from crying. She'd adjusted the rearview mirror so she couldn't see them when she had to use it, for they disgusted her—not because they were bloodshot and puffy, but because they lacked integrity.

A tempting thought crossed her mind while driving past a bar. She made a block and returned to it. Taking one last look at the deceiving bloodshot windows to her soul, she freshened her makeup, and went inside . . . .

It took a couple of minutes to acclimate to the dark atmosphere. Spotting a table in an empty corner, she made her way to it. A skinny girl with thin white hair that barely succeeded in covering a pink scalp came over.

"What can I get you, ma'am?"

"I'll have a bottle of Budweiser and a tequila shooter. Better make that two shooters. Oh, and do you have a cigarette machine . . .?"

Back at the table after garnering a package of Kools and a butane lighter, she stared at an unlit cigarette she'd pulled from the pack. "Ten years . . . oh well, what the hell."

The first drag made her cough but she persisted. By the time it was half smoked the cigarette tasted marvelous, making her wonder why she'd been such a goof as to quit in the first place.

"Here you go, ma'am," said the waitress. "That'll be eighteen even."

Denise wrestled a twenty from her purse and handed it to her. "Keep the change, and don't let me go dry."

The waitress thanked her and scurried off.

She licked salt and bit into a wedge of lime, grimacing while raising the glass to her lips. Tequila burned her throat on the way down, and she cooled it with a chase of beer. A second later she repeated the process and the first shooter was gone. After a few more swigs of ice cold Bud, she attacked her second glass. Holding up two fingers, she waved, and the waitress soon delivered two more shots and a cut up lime . . . .

Smiling now, she felt marvelous, thinking of how much fun it was to sit in a bar smoking cigarettes and getting plastered on a Sunday afternoon in Chicago. She savored the moment because such two-fold pleasures wouldn't be possible in an establishment like this after the smoking ban went into effect at the end of the year.

A man came over and tried to hit on her. "Mind if I join you?"

Giggling, she responded by singing the first line of *My Kind Of Town.*

He gave her a puzzled look. "Do I take that as a yes?"

"Hell no . . . beat it, pal, I'm not in the mood for company."

After he wandered off like a whipped puppy, she got up and looked around. Finally locating the jukebox, she threaded her way to it. The damn thing wasn't on there.

"What kind of Chicago bar doesn't have ol' Blue Eyes in the juke box?" she muttered under her breath. "What a gyp."

Lumbering back to her table, she heard a familiar voice shout, "Denise!"

She turned and saw Houston Shoat waving at her from the bar.

* * * *

What is she doing here? Houston liked the place and haunted it often, but it was little more than a dive, definitely not the type of joint he'd ever expect to see Denise Jones patronize. He'd decided to have a few rounds of Old Chicago from the tap before heading to her house to get Poppy.

"Over here," she said with a wave, walking towards a table. "Join me over here."

Was that a cigarette in her hand?

Houston grabbed his mug and arrived at the table shortly after she did. Denise was smoking all right, and well on the way to getting drunk. Two empty shot glasses and a couple of squeezed out lime chunks told him she was doing tequila shooters. He could tell by the way she looked, this wasn't her first round. Apparently a Monday morning hangover lay in store for the dark-eyed beauty.

"What are you doing here, Detective? Here to arrest me?" An inebriated giggle followed.

"This is my home away from home. I didn't know you smoked."

"I don't, quit ten years ago . . . Just seemed like the thing to do . . . I like 'em, want one?"

"No thanks. That's one bad habit I managed to avoid in my wayward youth."

Taking a deep drag, she turned her head to keep from spraying him with a cloud of smoke as she exhaled. "And just what bad habits did you not avoid?"

"You name it, I probably did it—at least once or twice—but not cigarettes."

She took a swill of beer and sat the bottle down hard, almost spilling it. "Wanna to do a shooter with me?"

"Uh, no. Are you sure you need another one?"

An incensed frown swathed her pretty face. "I'm here for one purpose, Detective, to get drunk. Drink my blues away. Maybe you'd be good enough to drive me home when I'm ready, and bring Bob or Poppy back here to fetch my Stang. I really don't think I should be driving it in the condition I plan to descend to."

"Be happy to as long as it's within the next couple of hours. I'm supposed to pick up Poppy at six. We're planning to continue last night's discussion at my place."

She ground out the cigarette. "That's right . . . I remember now. And just why wasn't I invited, Detective?"

"Consider yourself invited." He knew she was only mouthing, and wouldn't want to endure another evening of hearing Poppy and him debate the brainwashing issue.

"No way, you kidding? Let Poppy see me drunk?"

"I don't see how you're going to avoid that, do you?" He

took a tiny sip of beer and wiped his mouth.

"Sure. I'll stay here and get drunk while you and Poppy do your thing, and when you take him home, bring Bob back with you so he can drive my car. Bob and I will hang here until after Poppy's bedtime, and no one will be the wiser. Clever, huh?" A loud burp erupted and she giggled. "Excuse me. How rude was that?"

"Okay, I'll bring him back here, but make sure he stays sober."

She unstably shook her head. "No good. Poppy won't go to sleep until after I get home because he sleeps on the couch, so that won't work after all. You come up with a plan, Detective. You figure out how to save my honor."

Her gorgeous eyes were already bloodshot, and he knew she didn't need to drink anymore. But he didn't want to cause a scene, and that's what would surely happen if he tried to hinder her aspirations for inebriation. Denise Jones wasn't the type of woman to be ordered around. "Unless you sober up before going home, or spend the night somewhere else, I don't see how you can dodge this bullet."

Face brightening, she snapped her fingers. "I've got it! Invite him to crash at your place, that's what you do."

"My place is a dump. I wouldn't insult the man by asking him to stay there. Besides, I only have the one bedroom. He'd have to sleep on my sofa, and that thing resents being slept on, believe me. It's taken its aggression out on my back more times than I can count when I've fallen asleep on it watching TV."

"Oh poo, I bet it's a wonderful place."

He grinned. "For a troll maybe."

"If it's so bad, why not move?"

"I will one day. Plan to do just like you did, get a nice house somewhere in the burbs. Been saving up for it, that's why I live in a dump. Cheaper rent."

"Who's the lucky girl?"

"Excuse me?"

"I assume you're planning on building a love nest with your significant other. Who is she?"

Houston looked down at his beer. "No one."

"You're kidding! A good looking man like you without a woman? Unthinkable. You are straight, right?"

The compliment elated him. "Yeah, of course I am."

"Will I do? Want to marry me? Hey waitress!" She held up two fingers.

"Sure," he laughingly answered, "just name the time and place."

"How about right now?" She had a silly grin on her face—the kind a pig-tailed second grader wears while making a fool out of the class chump by pretending she likes him, until finagling the toy he has that she covets.

"Hmm, let me check our itineraries. Whoops can't do it, conflicting agendas. You're scheduled to get drunk, and I have to pick up Poppy pretty soon."

"Oh, that's right, I forgot . . ." she took a long swig of beer.

The waitress brought the tequila. Denise handed her a fifty. "I'll need the change this time, honey, but keep two dollars for yourself."

She raised a shot glass to her lips as the waitress walked off, chased it with beer, and said, "Okay, I have to get drunk today, so we can do it tomorrow. Tomorrow sound good to you?"

"Sure, always wanted to get married on a Monday."

"Me too . . ." she let out a boozy cackle. "You're not drinking very damn fast, Detective."

"Three's my limit when I have to drive."

"So is that your third one or what? Trying to make it last?"

"Yes on both counts." It was really his first, but he hoped his snail pace might encourage her to slow down.

"Well I have no limit." As if to illustrate the fact, Denise downed a mouthful of Bud. "You know, I haven't tied one on in a long, long time. Too long. Hate it you can't drink with me, Detective."

"I thought we agreed on Houston."

"We did, but not today. Today your name is Detective. I like the sound of that—DETECTIVE—Mrs. Denise Detective. Hah! Ha-ha-ha-ha . . .!"

Her makeup was conservative again, like it had been every time he'd seen her with the exception of last night. She'd looked like a tramp, albeit a very good looking one. He'd been curious about it but refrained from asking, since she might have thought him rude. Now, two sheets heading for three in the wind, maybe she wouldn't take offense. He decided to risk it.

"I couldn't help noticing your hair and makeup were much different last night than at any other time I've seen you. Hope you don't mind my mentioning it, but was there some special occasion or something?"

"Hah, that . . ." a stream of giggles flew out of her mouth. "Poppy made me do it."

"Poppy?"

"Yeah." Denise leaned across the table, looking this way and that, as if she were a spy about to relay some top secret information to her contact, making sure no one would overhear. Then she fixed her eyes on his, and just above a whisper said, "I had to apply for the noble position of a topless dancer."

"What?"

"You heard me."

"You're a college professor. Why would you do that?"

"Quiet! You want everyone to hear?" She raised the bottle to her mouth but started laughing too hard to take a drink. At length she succeeded, set the beer down, and folded her arms beneath her breasts. "What, you don't think I have the bod for it?"

Denise would sorely regret this embarrassing fabrication when she woke up with a hangover tomorrow. He decided not to answer, hoping the tequila would float her thoughts to some other topic before she realized he hadn't. His curiosity about the excessive makeup was apparently going to remain unsatisfied.

"Well, Detective?"

"I'm sorry. What was the question?"

"Don't be coy with me, young man. Do you think I have the body for it or not? I want to know—inquiring minds want to know . . ." another bout of liquor-induced laughter ensued.

"Yeah, you've got it all right. Just remember, you asked."

"Good, glad we got that cleared up. And may I say, you would make a fine dancer yourself, Detective. You're a good looking guy, you know that? Ever consider a career at Chippendales?"

He snorted a short laugh. "Oh yeah, I obsess about it all the time."

"Obsess . . . now there's a word. I'm obsessed with Poppy, who's obsessed with God, and Bob is obsessed with me. Who are you obsessed with, Detective?"

So she had a thing for Poppy. For the life of him he couldn't imagine why. Though very disappointing to hear, he was glad she'd said it. Now he didn't have to wonder if she'd go out with him. He knew the answer without having to suffer the blow of rejection.

Denise Jones was perplexing, intelligent, and beautiful, even with those bloodshot eyes. The scarlet rivulets flooding the whites couldn't diminish the conveyance that fools would not be suffered gladly, while at the same time retaining an alluring vulnerability. Talasota hid his feelings for her well. Every time he'd seen them together the two came off like brother and sister. Of course she'd been equally adept at disguising her own for Poppy. If she hadn't told him, he'd never have suspected it.

"Answer me, young man. Who is your obsession?"

"Nobody at the moment. So you like Poppy, huh." He tried to sound neutral about the matter.

"Think he's too old for me, don't you. Well he's not. He's a genius and has the nicest butt—of course I've never seen it uncovered. And I just adore his hair. Poppy Quinn is the most incredible man I've ever met."

He forced a smile. "Sounds like obsession to me, all right."

"You know it, Detective . . ." she looked off into space. "And he doesn't even know I'm alive."

If Poppy didn't want her, it had to be because of the age difference. Either that or he just didn't want a woman period. She was right about him being smart, but he didn't figure the man for a genius. Of course he barely knew him. The egghead certainly qualified as one of the strangest people he'd ever encountered. He'd never come across anyone like him.

"It's almost five, Denise. If I'm going to help get your car home I need the plan, because I'll have to bail soon. So what's it going to be?"

"You're the detective, Detective. You tell me."

"I'll call Poppy and cancel our dinner plans. What's your phone number?" He pulled out his cell phone.

She snickered. "Why, Detective Shoat, I'm shocked you don't have my number. There's no need to bother, he won't be there. Neither will Bob for that matter. They're having a boys day out together."

He called his partner instead, noticing before dialing he'd missed a call from a Monday Quinn. The name bothered him. Though unable to put his finger on the reason, he knew it was more than just the coincidence of the caller having the same last name as Poppy.

TWENTY SIX

Houston drove Denise's Mustang to her house and waited for John, who'd agreed to drive him back to the bar so he could get his car. Wondering how he'd missed the call, he saw the ringer had been inadvertently turned off. He switched it back on, highlighted the name, and speed-dialed Monday Quinn. A sexy female voice uttered hello after two rings.

"Hello, this is Houston—"

"It's him," he heard the lady say before he could tell her his last name.

"Houston? It's me, Poppy."

"Poppy?" So the professor lied about not having any family in Illinois.

"Yeah, I called earlier to ask if you could meet with me here instead of Denise's, but you didn't answer."

"My ID says Monday Quinn," he said without bothering to hide his irritation. "Thought you didn't have any relatives nearby."

"No, just a coincidence—we're not related. Do you mind if we have dinner here instead of your place? I've been informed my hostess is a great cook."

He wondered what Poppy was trying to pull. "Thought we were going to continue our discussion from last night?"

"Oh we are, I assure you. I know this sounds confusing, but I want to include two ladies in it. I'll explain everything when you get here. Would you mind?"

The egghead sounded sincere so it didn't figure to be a snow job. "Okay, I'm game."

"And I wonder if I could impose on you to do me a favor

when you head this way?"

A favor? Paul Quinn was full of surprises this afternoon. "Um, sure. What is it?"

"Denise isn't home. I've called several times and have no idea where she is. Bob and I don't know her cell phone number, so we can't get hold of her. Would you mind stopping by her place and leaving a note if she hasn't come home by then, telling her she'll be alone for supper? Tell her Bob and I will be eating with the Quinn sisters, and will be back by midnight at the latest."

"I'll see to it she gets the message."

Houston hung up and started to stash his phone, then it dawned on him he'd forgotten to get Monday Quinn's address. John pulled up, so he decided to call Poppy back after he returned to the bar . . . .

He'd told John about running into Denise, and explained her situation to him, requesting he keep it to himself should he ever see Poppy or Talasota again. Still mum about his surreptitious investigation, he didn't have to come up with an excuse to dissuade his chauffeur from going inside with him when they pulled into the parking lot. The teetotaler wouldn't set foot in a bar unless it was in the line of duty.

He found Denise sitting at the same table, sucking on a freshly lit cigarette. She gave him a drunken smile and exhaled smoke as he sat down.

"I'm going to order a bite. Can I interest you in anything solid?" He wasn't hungry, but hoped to get some food in her.

"N-Nachos. Some nice ch-cheesy nachos." She raised a shaky hand to signal for the waitress.

"Don't bother, I'll order it at the bar . . . ."

After requesting a jumbo size nacho platter, he pressed Monday Quinn's number again.

* * * *

Denise still didn't answer. Poppy was too worried about her to continue the evening. It had been half an hour since he'd received a call from Houston Shoat telling him that she hadn't been there when he'd dropped by her house. The detective had also asked for a rain check on dinner because something came up he needed to deal with.

He asked Bob if he wanted to stay, reminding him he couldn't sleep with the Quinn sisters since the lover boy claimed not to be married to them. The women begged their paramour to spend the night, even if he did have to use the guestroom, promising to fix his favorite food for supper, no matter how expensive or difficult to prepare. Bob offered to let him take his Buick, but Poppy called a cab. He didn't want to drive through the heavy Chicago traffic regardless of how stiff the cab fare might be. The fee didn't matter anyway. His mysterious roll of cash never went more than twenty-four hours without somehow replenishing itself to the exact sum of five thousand dollars.

As the silent cab driver braved the six o'clock traffic, Poppy analyzed Bob's situation, pondering why God would want him to have three wives. Whatever The Almighty's reasons, it appeared He did, and evidently wasn't willing to share them with him at the moment.

* * * *

Sitting in the kitchen, perched on a stool at the end of a long wooden island, Bob watched the women work. They were so beautiful he felt like the luckiest man in the world, and damn well may have been. Tuesday was chopping veggies for a salad while Monday manned the stove, boiling potatoes and frying pork chops. They'd done the big nasty right after Pops left, and except for the bib aprons they wore, the girls were still naked. Wearing only his boxer's, he sat with elbows resting on the counter, reveling with pride. The blondes couldn't get enough of him, and he felt likewise.

To hell with Denise, and to hell with Pops' marital theories. He wasn't married to the twisted sisters but had no intentions of leaving them alone either. Denise would never love him, so she could go her own way—he'd had it. It was time to move on and move in with the Quinn's—live the good life, enjoy the sweet ride as long as those two nymphos allowed him to. What more could a man ask for than to have two rich women, pretty beyond belief, built like brick shit-houses, be gaga for him? No more lowly sewer for him, big bad Bob Talasota had just moved up in the world. Hands folded under his chin, he smiled, recalling their conversation earlier.

Monday had waltzed into the living room after seeing Pops to the door. "You don't think we have to wait, do you, Bob? Don't you feel, down in your heart, that we're married?"

He'd decided right then to go along with their delusion. Hell, he knew he was still single, but what harm did it do to lie just to make them feel good? Answering by unzipping his jeans and pulling out the weasel, he'd told them the lonesome fella needed some attention.

The girls had fastened their hungry eyes on it as Monday warned, "Bob, we can't do this unless you believe we're married, or Poppy's right—it's fornication."

"You're right," he'd lied with a smile. "We're married, just like you said. You, Tuesday, and me—happily ever after. Deep inside, I think I knew it all along . . . ."

Gazing at their wondrous asses, Bob sniffed deeply, relishing the savory smell of battered pork simmering in hot fat. Then he sighed with contentment. Tomorrow he'd go back to Denise's for the last time, pack up his few clothes, tell her c'est la vie, say so long to Pops, and return to paradise . . . .

* * * *

Houston had eaten a grilled cheese sandwich and Denise's leftover nachos about three hours ago. She'd quit doing shooters after eating, but was still drinking beer. Though refusing to talk about the Mojave mystery, she'd blabbed endlessly about Poppy, and had gotten maudlin.

"It's time to call it a night," he said with a firm look, meant to convey she had no option in the matter.

She sniffled. "N-No, it's still ear-early yet."

"You can either let me take you home now or call a cab later, because I'm out of here."

"Well, s-since you put it that way . . . ."

TWENTY SEVEN

It was almost midnight and Denise still hadn't come home. Her Mustang was in the drive, so she'd obviously left with somebody. The day their cars arrived, she'd made Bob and him a copy of her house key for occasions such as this, but Poppy wished she'd had the courtesy to leave a note. Though she certainly didn't have to account to him, the three of them needed to keep each other informed of their respective whereabouts. For who knew what hazards the forces of darkness might place in their way to thwart God's plan? Bob had been foolish sneaking out without telling anybody when he'd wound up meeting the Quinn sisters. If they *had* been from the other side as the Yankee first suspected, it might have cost him his life.

The phone rang. He ran to it and jerked the receiver off the hook.

"Hello?"

"Poppy?"

"Is that you, Houston?"

"Yeah. Just calling to make sure Denise made it home okay."

"She's still not here and I'm worried about her."

"Um . . . she's okay, but when she gets home you might pretend to be asleep for her sake, and never let on you knew when she came in."

Poppy noticed a change in the detective's tone. "What are you talking about?"

"Listen, she didn't want you to know—and she'll kill me if she finds out I told you—but I don't want you worrying

needlessly. Denise is downtown at a bar getting drunk."

"What . . .?!" he took a step back, reeling with shock. Other than a glass of wine with her meal at the Italian restaurant she'd taken Bob and him to, he'd never seen her drink anything stronger than coffee.

"I happened to be there this afternoon when she stopped in. I drove her car home and had my partner drive me back to the bar. I tried to get her to leave with me an hour ago, and warned her she was going to have to hail a cab if she didn't, but she told me to buzz off. Anyway, she'll be home before too long since she'll have to leave when they close the place."

"Tell me how to get there."

"Not on your life. She'll be fine, but I'd appreciate it if you wouldn't tell her I told you any of this."

"What's the name of the bar?"

"Sorry, Poppy, can't tell you because I know you'll go there, and Denise will have my head. She'll be fine, don't worry."

"I'm going to have your head if you don't tell me where she is! Denise will be the least of your worries." He heard a noise outside that sounded like a car door slamming shut. "That may be her now, hold on . . . ."

Poppy hastily opened the front door and saw a cab drive off. Bobbing from side to side as if trying to skate without wheels, Denise waddled towards the house, head bent down, eyes on the cement walk. She was drunk all right. He went back to the phone. "She's here . . . ."

* * * *

Houston hung up his landline phone and vented a weary sigh. He could only imagine the scene taking place over in Franklin Park. Denise had been adamant about Poppy not knowing she'd tied one on, and the way the egghead sounded over the phone, he obviously wasn't going to cooperate with his request to pretend to be snoozing when she walked in.

He downed a glass of water and stripped for bed . . . .

Beating his pillow to death in the process, Houston tossed and turned for over half an hour before finally giving up. He couldn't sleep. Something kept bugging him about the name Monday Quinn. Hoping her address might jolt his memory, he vacated the useless bed and went to the living room. Blinding brightness stabbed his dilated pupils when he turned on the light. Once they acclimated, he opened the phone book.

A queasy uneasiness came over him when saw where she lived. Something had happened in that area a few years ago, but he still didn't know why the name troubled him. He put his clothes back on and headed for his car . . . .

Though sure of the street, he didn't know if the numbers were right. If he could only recall the name on the case file, he could verify it with a quick phone call to headquarters. Since his brain refused to cooperate, he'd have to check out the address or go crazy worrying about it. He remembered the house looked like The Beverly Hillbillies' mansion, but the identity of the deceased owner eluded him. Hoping it wouldn't be the same residence, he drove through the Chicago night.

The name finally came to him before he turned onto the avenue that coursed through a very posh neighborhood. Pulling up to the gates, he looked down the drive, and winced.

It was Nicholas Bernstein's estate all right.

A friend of Bernstein's had accused his mistress, the deceased's sole beneficiary, of poisoning him in such a way as to make it look like he'd died of natural causes. The case got closed when the coroner verified that a stroke brought on by age and hard living had killed Bernstein. But John and he became concerned a month later when the accuser turned up dead from what also appeared to be a naturally occurring blood clot in the brain. They suspected they were dealing with a Black Widow, who'd discovered an undetectable toxin. Their suspicion hadn't flown with the district attorney, and the matter got quashed. They'd wanted to dig into it on their own but were assigned another homicide, and their caseload had only gotten heavier from there. So much time had passed, Houston hadn't been able to make the connection at first, but now he finally knew what had been subconsciously nagging him. When Bernstein's name finally surfaced in his brain, so had that of the mistress accused of murdering the rich man: Monday Quinn.

Looking across the grounds at the Black Widow's lair, he eyed Talasota's Buick, envisioning the sewer worker paralyzed within a silk cocoon, hanging from the ceiling on a spider's woven rope. Recalling him telling Poppy and Denise they weren't going to believe what the Quinn sisters laid on him, Houston realized they must have been who Talasota had dinner with last night. He'd spoke like the professor wasn't even acquainted with them, much less related.

Could Monday Quinn be the mesmerist that had brainwashed the Quinn trio? If she didn't possess such capabilities herself, she certainly had the resources to pay off someone who did. Poppy had sounded eager to get him over here. Maybe the professor had told her about a certain homicide detective thinking he'd been brainwashed, and she'd decided to lure him here through her silver-haired pawn in order to silence him with her voodoo.

Houston felt compelled to pay Bernstein's mistress a surprise visit to catch her off guard, and make sure Talasota was safe. He buzzed the gate. When no one answered, he kept pushing the button until an angry female voice blared through the intercom.

"Who is it?"

"A friend of Bob Talasota's."

"Do you have any idea what time it is?"

"I know it's late, but could I speak to Bob Talasota please? I can see his car from here. Is he there?"

"He's asleep. Come back tomorrow."

"Is this Monday I'm talking to?"

"Yes. Have we met?"

"Some time ago. I'm Detective Shoat. My partner and I interviewed you after Nicolas Bernstein died."

A load buzz sounded and the gates moved . . . .

The Black Widow opened the door, wearing a purple robe and a sleepy expression of irritation. He'd forgotten what a looker she was.

"Come in," she said with a tone reflecting her aggravation.

She led him to a large kitchen and beckoned him to have a seat on a stool, situated by a large butcher-block island with numerous copper skillets hanging above, orderly descending in size. Stepping to a cabinet, she briskly slapped a filter inside the upper compartment of a fancy coffee maker, scooped some coffee in it, filled the back with water, pressed a switch, retraced her path, and sat down across from him.

"I don't want to wake Bob. Why are you looking for him this time of night?"

"I wanted to talk to him about something. I didn't know he was planning on spending the night, so I figured he was still up when I saw his car."

"How did you know he was here?"

"A little bird told me."

She frowned. "Am I under investigation again?"

"No, I'm off duty. Just a coincidence we happen to have a mutual friend in Bob."

"Some coincidence," she said cynically.

"More than you know. I'm the one who arrested him."

"And he considers you a friend?"

Houston smiled, watching her closely. "He didn't at first. But you know the old saying, all's well that ends well."

"And is this going to end well?" Her features portrayed no

sense of insecurity or nervousness, just fatigue, irritation, and impatience.

"Just wanted to talk to him, that's all."

She pursed her sexy lips for a drawn out moment and said, "If you're a friend of Bob's, you must know my Uncle Poppy then."

So Quinn *was* lying after all. "Yeah, I know him."

"What does he look like?"

"Tall and wiry, silver hair. So you're his niece, huh."

"No, I was just testing you, we're not related. I just met him earlier today as a matter of fact. Since you know Poppy, you must be telling the truth about Bob."

He snickered inside. Paul Quinn, who claimed to be Peter Quinn, was one slippery son-of-a-bitch. Just when he thought he had one fact about the eccentric professor finally nailed down, a new piece of information loosened the whole thing up again. "Yeah. I'm the guy who called here this evening after missing his call."

Her face brightened with a smile of surprise. "Oh, you must be Houston, the detective Poppy invited over! Why didn't you say so? If I'd known it was you, I wouldn't have been such a bitch. Please forgive me."

"Nothing to forgive."

"Oh yes there is. If you knew what I was thinking."

"What were you thinking?"

She narrowed her eyes. "That you might be thinking what that nitwit was thinking."

He knew exactly who she was referring to but said, "What nitwit is that?"

"You know—the one who thought I poisoned Nick."

"No. Just came to see Bob."

"At four in the morning." The face she made left little doubt she knew he was lying.

"Like I said, I didn't know he was staying the night, so I

assumed he was still here and awake, since he didn't come back to his place."

"His place? I thought he was staying with Poppy at the Jones woman's house."

"You mean Denise. Yes, that's where he's staying, that's what I meant."

She studied him for at least half a minute, obviously weighing his statement against her suspicions. Evidently the bluff won out because she lightened up. "Okay, if you need to talk to him that badly, I'll go wake him."

"No need . . ." he rose from the stool. Whether or not she poisoned Bernstein, she had no plans to harm Talasota, and definitely wasn't the puppet master. "It can wait. Let him sleep, and I'll let you get back to bed as well."

"I'm wide awake now and the coffee's almost ready, so if you're not sleepy, let's visit awhile."

"Well, if you're sure you don't mind, I could sure use a cup."

"How do you take it?" she asked on the way to the coffee maker.

He eased back down on the stool. "Black."

A minute later she set two steaming china cups on the counter and repositioned herself across from him.

The coffee smelled wonderful, and tasted uniquely robust and flavorful. "Man, this is some great brew."

Her sultry lips turned up at the corners, appreciatively. "It's a special blend. Comes from Holland, I think. They weigh it out into a bag at the store, so there's no label to say where it's made."

"Where do you get it . . .?" he savored another swallow.

"Schubert's is the only place I've been able to find it."

"I'm not familiar with the name."

"Schubert's Import Emporium. You have to be a member to shop there."

"Oh, must be pretty expensive then."

"Yeah. You could buy ten pounds of any regular brand for what a pound of this costs. It's called Dutch Blend, that's why I assume it's imported from Holland."

"That'd be my guess."

Monday took a sip of it, scrutinizing him over the rim of her cup, and squinted while setting it down. "You know, you sort of look like Bob."

"Yeah . . ." he grinned. "We both have black hair."

"No, it's more than that. Your features are somewhat similar too."

Discharging an indignant chuckle, he grimaced as if being insulted, but really found her comparison flattering. "I don't see it. I think I'm far better looking."

"In your dreams, Detective."

"Thanks for bursting my bubble." Her remark actually didn't bother him at all. He knew he wasn't as handsome as Talasota. Few men were. The sewer worker would make a great Elvis impersonator.

"So you met Bob when you arrested him?"

"He was arrested out west and extradited here. I handled his case afterwards, along with my partner."

"I kept up with the trial, but somehow missed your name if it was mentioned. Meeting Bob was almost like meeting a celebrity. So was meeting Poppy."

"And Denise Jones?"

"Haven't met her." The look on Monday's face and tone of voice were hostile.

She clearly didn't like Denise. Jealousy over Bob could be the only reason, since she didn't know her. Certain the drunk paleontologist had only spilled the beans because of a tequila-loosened tongue, he didn't mention her perceived competitor wanted Poppy.

"So tell me about her. Is she as pretty in person?"

Realizing he'd just wandered into a mine field, Houston knew he'd better weigh his words carefully in order to get out of it unscathed. "Yeah, she's a pretty woman."

"As pretty as me?"

So that's why she'd invited him to stay for coffee—to interrogate him about the competition. He wondered how long it would have taken her to bring up Denise if he hadn't. Monday's steady gaze silently warned him not to even think of prevaricating, but her last question had airlifted him to safety because he had the truth on his side. "I don't know that I've ever seen any woman as pretty as you."

A light blush filled her cheeks, and her eyes glistened with satisfaction. "Are you just trying to avoid a direct answer?"

"I mean it, it's the truth."

"Then you're saying she's not as pretty as me?"

"That's what I'm saying."

Obviously pleased, she took another sip of coffee.

Now it was his turn to see if Monday could provide him with some information. "Has Bob told you what happened to the three of them out west?"

"No. Poppy was going to, but he wanted to wait until you got here for some reason. He also wanted Tues and I to meet Denise Jones."

"Tues?"

"My sister Tuesday."

He couldn't hold back a laugh.

"I know," she laughed back. "We get it all the time. Our mother's name was Sunday, believe it or not."

"Now that's one I've never heard before—Sunday, Monday, and Tuesday. Since Monday comes before Tuesday, I'm guessing you're the older sister."

"That's right. By ten years."

John and he hadn't met or asked about any member of her family during the short investigation. He wondered if Tuesday was as well favored. "That's quite a gap. Any other siblings?"

"Nope, just me and Tuesday. You know, I think I'm starting to like you. You're not the bastard I had you pegged for when you and your partner drilled me after Nick died."

He admired the way she spoke her mind and made direct eye contact while doing so. His instincts told him the DA had been right in not pursuing her, that this woman couldn't murder anybody. He knew John would agree if he could see this side of her. It was a shame she had a thing for Talasota, or he'd risk asking her out.

The irony of the situation amazed him. He hadn't wanted to be with a woman in years. Now, within a mere span of hours, he'd found himself chewing the fat with two he liked, and both were linked to the sinewy professor and bulked-up sewer worker. Spending the evening with Denise woke up something that grief had forced into hibernation, making him realize how lonely he'd been. And now this blonde heartbreaker made him even more painfully aware of the long dry spell he'd endured.

He'd been in love with a wonderful girl named Clara and they had plans to marry. She'd gone on vacation with her family and happened to be visiting a famous New York City landmark on a fateful September day in two-thousand-one. Her life had been taken away by some mindless terrorists. Though he knew he'd never totally get over losing her, he realized the time had finally come to allow another into his heart. He needed someone to fill the void, now making its presence known as tangibly as hunger pangs radiating from an empty stomach.

Monday walked across the kitchen to get the coffee pot. Watching the smooth movements of her body beneath shiny purple satin, he began to wonder if maybe it was his libido rather than his heart that so stringently ached for a woman. Suddenly feeling self conscious, he looked away, pretending to be gazing at a window when she came back to refill their cups. He didn't lay eyes on her again until she sat back down.

She spoke of her life, repeating some of the things he'd learned while investigating her. At her dying mother's behest she'd found work as a topless dancer at Bernstein's club, supporting herself and her kid sister, and worked her way up to manager before inheriting it. Soon the club would be sold and she was never going back to that way of life. Despite what Bernstein's friend had accused, not only did she not murder her benefactor, she'd never even kissed him on the lips, much less been his mistress.

Though totally convinced she had nothing to do with Bernstein's demise, he couldn't understand why the man would leave her everything if she wasn't playing house with him. That part of the story didn't add up, and he didn't buy it any more now than he had when she'd said it during the investigation. Of course he hadn't told her that, just nodded sympathetically as if he'd believed her claim they'd never been lovers.

But he found what she was wrapping up now even harder to swallow. ". . . and when we saw Bob on the beach, we knew at long last we'd finally found our husband."

* * * *

He'd managed to pour a pot of coffee into Denise and she'd sobered quite a bit. Poppy had never gotten drunk in his life. It amazed him that people thought it such fun to dull their senses and stupefy their minds with alcohol. She'd cried a river, ranting about how ashamed, humiliated, degraded, overwhelmed, mortified, devastated, and debased she felt for him to see her in such a condition—profusely apologizing throughout. With each penance Poppy assured he wasn't judging her, and yet she bawled all the more.

Finally the tears subsided, the sniffles ceased, and she could talk without breaking down. She wanted to know why he didn't love her. He told her he did in fact love her.

"I don't mean like that, not the same way you love Bob. Why don't you love me the way I love you—the way a man loves a woman? You do like women, don't you? You really have had sex with one before, right?"

It was happening again, but this time in real life. Poppy remembered saying he'd been with a woman, but couldn't recall a single time. He tried to call other things to mind, but just like in the dream, he had no recollection of anything he'd spoken about actually happening. The Mojave Desert stormed its way into his deteriorating thought processes. Why did he find that stretch of barren waste so unnerving?

And they had a king over them . . . .

"Poppy?"

Denise's voice stirred his insides, rippling through the confusion of his troubled mental state as if trying to free him from this strange place, where his essence seemed to be imprisoned in a corner of his mind—a nook where not a single memory of his entire existence was permitted entrance except . . . the Mojave.

Too many thoughts were forming again: concepts, ideas, spiritual comprehension of things unexplainable by mere words—impossibly complex yet irresistibly compelling. Somehow, through it all, his mind's eye remained focused on the Mojave Desert.

* * * *

"Poppy, what's wrong?!" Denise cried frantically. Poppy's face was ashen, his eyes bulged with pain, and he kept grabbing at his stomach as if he'd just swallowed strychnine. "Do I need to call nine-one-one?! Dammit, Poppy, answer me!"

* * * *

"Poppy?!" He heard Denise crying out from a distance, though he couldn't answer. Then, suddenly, everything came back to him—all became clear.

"Poppy?!" she shouted again, voice trembling with fear . . . and then he heard her scream, "NNNNOOOOOOOOO!!!"

TWENTY EIGHT

Talasota stepped into the kitchen wearing nothing but his birthday suit.

"Whoa . . .!" his hands flew over his crotch.

Houston tried not to laugh but Monday's hysterical reaction demolished his resolve. "Sorry about that."

"Jeez, what are you doing here?"

"Came to see you."

Monday managed to quit guffawing, and wiped tears of laughter from her cheeks. "We've been chatting over coffee, honey. Why don't you put some clothes on and join us?"

Shaking his head with bewilderment, Talasota walked away.

"Now *that* was funny," Monday giggled out.

Her mirth made him cut loose again.

By the time Talasota returned, they were finally able to talk without one of them cracking up, sending the other into a laughing frenzy.

The sewer worker gave Monday a kiss on the lips, then leaned across the counter on his forearms. "So what brings you out here to see me at such an ungodly hour?"

He couldn't tell him the real reason, so he said, "I talked to Poppy on the phone a little after midnight and he said he was at Denise's alone. I figured you must have stayed here, and there might be a party going on. I couldn't sleep, so I dropped by."

Talasota yawned. "He was really worried about her. Do you know if she ever made it back home?"

"Yeah, she pulled up while I was talking to him."

"Good."

Houston glanced at his watch. "My gosh, it'll be daylight soon. Sorry I kept you up all night. I'd better be going."

"That's okay," said Monday brightly. "I enjoyed it. Take some coffee with you."

"Thanks anyway, but I'd probably only wind up spilling it, and I'd hate it if I accidentally broke your cup."

"No, not made coffee, silly . . ." she headed for the opposite end of the kitchen, entered a walk-in pantry, came back with a white bag, and handed it to him.

"Thank you so much. I love this coffee."

"You're welcome." She tossed him a knowing smile. "So you were hoping to crash a party, huh."

Relieved she'd bought the bogus excuse, he looked down at the bag, grinning. "Guilty as charged."

"Well you had to know there wasn't one going on when we spoke over the intercom. Were you just lonely for someone to talk to or what?"

"Guilty again."

"Hey, I'll take some made coffee," said Talasota through another yawn. "I'll drink a cup, then I'm off to Denise's to get my stuff."

"Get your stuff?"

"Yeah. I'm moving in with the Quinn's, where I'll be in like Flynn."

That flabbergasted him. Apparently Talasota agreed with Monday's contention that she and her sister were his brides.

* * * *

Bob ate Monday for breakfast and she went back to bed after gobbling the weasel. They'd done the sixty-nine on the divan where he'd feasted on Tuesday's bush while Monday was screwing him the first time. He yawned while pulling out of the estate, turned right, and headed for Franklin Park. The first rays of dawn were breaking over the horizon, bringing on this bittersweet day. It wouldn't take more than a minute to collect his duds, then he'd be saying his last goodbye to Denise and Pops. He planned to forget she existed, and damn sure didn't want to hear any more of Pops' marital shit. Fuck that stupid Olive Tree Operation—he didn't want to be a part of it even if Pops was right. The thought of never seeing the braniac again made him sad, but he'd get over it after a while. Preoccupied with reliving the wild time he'd had with the sisters last night, he didn't see the semi until the trucker's horn snapped him back from fantasyland.

* * * *

Houston had called his partner and told him he'd lost a battle with insomnia and would be showing up late for work. But instead of going to Aurora for a nap after leaving Monday's place, he'd driven to Franklin Park. Denise would definitely be sacked out, but Poppy might be up. He wanted to find out why the egghead planned to tell the Quinn sisters about the Mojave.

Lights behind the living room curtains indicated he was awake, so Houston rang the bell, even though it was only seven. To his surprise Denise answered the door, wearing the same outfit she had on when he'd left her at the bar. She obviously hadn't been to bed. Staring at him through swollen red eyes, soaked with tears, she let him in without saying a word.

Something was dreadfully wrong. Though she walked like a zombie, her gait didn't appear to be caused by a hangover. A gut feeling told him the heaviness that hung in the air had nothing to do with her Sunday escapade.

He followed her into the kitchen.

She motioned for him to take a seat at the table, brought him a cup of coffee, and sat down. "You're here to see Poppy, aren't you."

"Yes," he answered, feeling very uneasy.

"Well, Detective, I'm afraid you're a bit too late . . ." she kept moving her lips as if trying to continue, but no words came forth. Then a shrill wail shot out of her mouth and she started bawling, hysterically.

He sat motionless, watching her cry, wondering what the hell was going on.

"Poppy's gone," she managed at last, voice now drained of emotion.

"Gone where?"

"Just gone."

"I don't understand. Just gone where?"

"Back to the place he was from."

"He went back to Texas?"

Denise closed her eyes and took a deep breath. When she finally exhaled, he could smell traces of booze and nicotine. Her lids slowly parted, and heavier waves of agony radiated from her tear-drenched orbs. "He wasn't from Texas."

"That's what he told me."

"That's what he told all of us!" she shouted with venom.

Startled, he reared back in the chair, lifting the front legs so far off the floor he had to grab the table to keep from falling backwards. A loud and disturbing *CLOP!* rang out as they regained contact with her decorative linoleum after he pulled himself forward. He sat there quietly, afraid he'd upset Denise more by asking her to explain, and patiently waited until she finally spoke again.

"Remember what we told you about the Mojave? Remember the biker?"

"Yes."

"Well it turns out he *was* the biker. Poppy is an angel."

He heaved a deep groan. "Denise, you're so exhausted and hung over your mind's playing tricks on you. You need to go to bed—get a nice recuperative sleep."

She stared absently into space. "I wouldn't believe it either if I hadn't seen it. He was standing in my living room and suddenly got confused and looked very ill, then started having convulsions. I watched him . . . saw the whole fucking thing go down. Poppy was wearing a western shirt and jeans like he always wore, but I saw them transform into leather, and suddenly he was wearing a helmet, just like the biker wore, and I couldn't see his face anymore. Then his whole body exploded into the brightest, whitest light you've ever seen, and I had to look away to keep from going blind. And then I heard his voice from within my mind, saying it was time for him to return because everything was now put into place—and though I didn't understand it now, in time I would, and rejoice. Then, when I looked again, the light was gone. Even the suitcase and clothes he bought after he got here are gone. Everything he owned is gone."

"Well his Jeep's still here, it's parked at the curb."

"No it's not. I looked. His Honda's gone too."

He shook his head and expelled a sigh of exasperation. "Denise, I know you believe what you're saying, but you were hallucinating. Remember, you had an awful lot to drink."

"Think whatever you want, I don't give a damn." She looked numb now, and her tone reflected it. "I know he was an angel and became a man, and at the same time, somehow made himself forget he was an angel. He always said the biker's voice sounded like his own. He was able to be a man and the biker at the same time. You still don't believe we were ever in the garden, so you can't fathom what I'm saying. But we believe, we were there. Bob will believe me, that's all that matters. If you want proof all you have to do is try to find out where he lived in Texas, or try to locate any of his relatives.

You'll find nothing, I promise you. Peter Quinn of Texas, like Paul Quinn of Evanston, never really existed."

Houston was fuming inside, wishing he could get his hands on whomever brainwashed this beautiful woman. "Denise, Paul Quinn of Evanston does exist. Poppy is Paul Quinn of Evanston. I spoke to his father or some other relative. We need to find out who brainwashed the three of you and undo it. I know you believe what you're saying, but Poppy is still here in our world. Remember me telling you I've got a vacation coming up? Well I'm going to spend every minute of it trying to solve this thing. I promise you—no I swear to you—I *will* solve it, and you guys will be free of this nightmare forever."

She shook her head. "No you won't, there's nothing *to* solve. I told you the answer and you refuse to believe it. I have to take this one day at a time, and somewhere down the line the meaning of all this will become clear to me. I believe that because Poppy said I'd come to understand it. I'm going to ask you to leave now. I'll call you when I'm ready to talk about it again, but right now I just want to be alone . . . ."

Houston left as she requested, and didn't see the Jeep or Honda when he stepped outside. Somebody must have moved them while he'd been talking to her, he was certain they'd been there when he pulled up. His anger over the puppet master now extended to Poppy. Brainwashed or no, he didn't have the right to play such head tricks on Denise.

He drove to headquarters to check in, and see about taking his vacation a few weeks early.

John greeted him when he got to his desk. "That's too bad about Bob Talasota."

"What's too bad?"

"Oh, figured you'd already heard. He got killed in a car wreck this morning. Ran into a truck . . . ."

TWENTY NINE

Having booked the roundtrip flight a week prior, to coincide with the first day of his vacation, Houston landed at Dallas-Fort Worth International Airport shortly after noon. He rented a car and checked his atlas for the shortest route to Decatur, Texas. Though this figured to be little more than a wild goose chase, he had no other leads to follow. Every Peter Quinn with a listed phone number in the whole state of Texas had gotten a call from him, but only the one in Decatur had anything to do with theology. More importantly, he also went by the nickname Poppy. He'd made an appointment with the preacher over the phone from Chicago.

Poppy believed he was Peter Quinn from Texas, so whoever brainwashed him into thinking that, might have known the Peter Quinn of Decatur. He hoped to find a trail that would lead him to the mind manipulator, but in no way expected to crack the case on this visit to The Lone Star State. The man on the phone had sounded like such a *good old boy,* Houston found it hard to believe he could be involved in the conspiracy.

The day after Talasota died he'd gone back to Evanston, trying to find Poppy, or any information leading to his whereabouts. When no one answered the door at the house the egghead swore wasn't his, he'd driven to Northwestern to see if anyone there had heard from him. Dean Hayden said Paul Quinn had resigned and moved overseas without leaving a forwarding address. Houston hadn't been surprised to learn the professor had called it quits less then twenty-four hours after Denise thought she'd seen him transform into an angel and disappear.

Even though the puppet master had obviously made him do it, Houston couldn't help still feeling somewhat angry with Poppy, and wondered if he knew Talasota had met his fate not long after he'd so cruelly abandoned Denise.

She'd flown to Brooklyn for the funeral, on the same plane that carried Talasota's body. As far he knew, she was still there. He'd driven straight to her house after John told him about the accident, hoping she hadn't heard about it on the news. She hadn't, and after he broke it to her gently as he could, an awful scene followed.

Face paled with shock and total disbelief, she'd gaped at him blankly for several minutes before her dark eyes closed and she fell to her knees. Arms flailing helplessly, screaming herself hoarse, she'd demanded—in language so foul it would have made a sailor blush—that God tell her why the two most important men in her life had been taken from her. When she finally stopped crying and rose from the floor, her drained features had seemed void of emotion. Almost robotically, she'd once again told him to leave, promising to call when she was ready to talk, warning him not to come back beforehand.

Despite her admonition he'd checked on her the next day. She'd scolded him for not staying away, then told him about arranging to accompany Talasota's remains, and that she didn't know when she'd be back. He hadn't talked to her since.

After telling Denise about the accident, he'd gone to see Monday Quinn. She and her younger sister didn't know their lover had been killed, and both had gone into hysterics when he told them. Unlike Denise, they couldn't seem to talk enough, and he'd visited them several times since. They'd wanted to go to the funeral, and he'd cautioned them not to share their beliefs with anyone, because even though they were convinced they were the widows of Roberto Talasota, his family wasn't going to see it that way. Once Monday learned

Denise would be there, she'd nixed the idea totally.

Today marked three weeks since the accident. He found it ironic that Talasota had died on a Monday while in route to pick up his things to move in with a Monday.

He located the farmhouse and parked the rental. When Peter Quinn opened the front door, Houston couldn't believe his eyes. The silver haired man standing before him was the spitting image of Paul Quinn of Evanston, Illinois.

"You must be Houston Shoat . . . ."

During the evening he'd spent with Poppy and Denise while Bob had been on his dinner date with the Quinn sisters, the two of them claimed the accent Poppy had then, wasn't the same one he used to have. Denise had said, "When I met Poppy he spoke with a Texas drawl, but when Bob and I saw him in Chicago, he had the Midwestern accent you hear now."

Houston had put it off to more proof they'd been brainwashed.

Unless Paul Quinn had professional vocal and acting skills capable of winning an academy award, the man now speaking couldn't be him pretending. The baritone voice had a very unique resonance that would be difficult to mimic, and the personality behind it was nothing like the Poppy's he knew.

"Got a fresh pot of coffee on the stove, come on in and make yourself at home."

Houston followed him through a modestly furnished living room into a country kitchen that struck a nostalgic chord. Blue-and-white checkered curtains, tied back at a window above the sink, matched the tablecloth and seat-covers of an old fashioned dinette set. Steam rose from a percolator resting on a gas stove that couldn't have been manufactured any later that the fifties, with its uniquely shaped knobs and rounded edges. Besides the aromatic smell of percolated coffee grounds, a pleasant aroma haunted the air, hinting that endless batches of biscuits and cornbread had been baked in its oven, innumerable chickens fried, and countless cabbages boiled on its burners.

"Take a load off."

"Thank you for seeing me, Mister Quinn." He sat down on one of four wooden chairs adorning the table.

"Glad to oblige. You got my curiosity up when you called. You say you know a Peter Quinn that goes by the handle Poppy up yonder in Chicago, huh. Well that's a topper. And speaking of that, call me Poppy. I don't much cotton to any of that Mister stuff. And I'll call you Houston if it's all the same to you."

"Please do."

"Need sugar or cream?"

"No." Still amazed at the resemblance, he watched his host fill two white mugs and bring them to the table.

"Now then, what can I do for you? Must be important since you flew all the way down here from Chicago just to talk to me in person."

"To start off, may I ask how you got the nickname Poppy?"

"When I was knee-high to a grasshopper I used to drive my mama crazy, begging her to read me the story about the poppy seed cakes. One day she started calling me Poppy because of it, and it stuck. Been going by that handle ever since. How'd your friend come by his?"

"I asked but he never told me. You said over the phone you consider yourself a theologian. Is that how you make your living?"

"I'm a non-denominational preacher that earns his living farming." He took a sip of coffee. "Tell me some more about your Poppy if you don't mind."

"The Poppy I know is quite a mystery to me. I met him as a result of the most oddball case I've ever been a part of. He was reported missing, and when his Jeep was found abandoned in the Mojave Desert, some peculiar circumstances led to him being presumed dead. But it turned out he wasn't."

"Heck you say. I used to drive a Jeep, a white hard top."

His pulse quickened. "That's what his was."

"Well I'll be . . ." he took another pull from his mug.

Houston scrutinized him closely. Every feature perfectly matched the professor's. The physical resemblance was far too great to be coincidental. They had to be twin brothers, and must have been separated at birth since the preacher had told him over the phone he didn't have any siblings. The puppet master *had* to know this Poppy Quinn too.

"What happened to your Jeep?"

"Sold it a few months back."

"Do you mind if I ask who bought it?"

"Don't mind at all. He was a Yankee just passing through. Had an Italian sounding name. Sarasota, Borasetta, something like that."

"Could it have been Talasota?"

"Could have been."

"What did he look like?"

"Brawny, black hair like yours, a real handsome cuss."

A cold chill shot through him at the possibility he might be on the verge of finding a hot trail. "Did he say where he was from?"

"Sure did. Brooklyn, New York." The preacher tilted his head with a humorless grin. "That must mean something to you, judging by that look on your face. I remember his first name was Bob if that's any help."

Feeling an adrenaline rush, Houston had to stifle a shout of excitement. For the first time since learning the Quinn trio had been brainwashed, he felt genuine hope of finding the evil mastermind that did it. "I hate to impose on your hospitality, but could I have a look at the receipt?"

He shrugged. "Don't have one. I just signed the title over and was done with it."

Though confused about the puppet master's motive in engineering the transaction, he felt it had to be Talasota that bought the Jeep. But he needed proof. Denise would never believe him otherwise. A diabolical genius was at work here—manipulating Talasota into buying the Jeep and handing it over to Poppy, then making them both forget they knew each other until after he'd convinced them they'd seen a monster. Such a feat required a very powerful form of mind control.

"Was this Bob alone or with someone?"

"Just him."

"How did you sell it? Did you put an ad in the paper or what?"

He let out a short laugh. "That was a real funny deal because I hadn't even thought about selling it. He saw it parked in the drive and came a-knocking, asking if he could buy it."

"What did he give for it, if you don't mind my asking?"

"Told him just what I told you—that I hadn't thought about selling it, but he said he just had to have it, and asked what I'd take for it. Told him to make me an offer, and he paid me five thousand dollars cash. Heck, that wore out jalopy wasn't worth a quarter that much. I was real tickled to sell it to him for that because that's how I got the pickup you saw in my driveway."

"Why did he want it so badly?"

"No idea, he didn't say."

"Did he say where he was going?"

"Not that I recall."

"Did he talk about family, friends, or anything like that?"

"No. Just wanted the Jeep and I sold it to him."

"Can you remember the date you sold it?"

"Let's see . . ." he lowered his eyes while thinking on it, and heaved a sigh when he raised them. "Sorry. Seems like it was last May or June but that's about all I can say for certain."

"Did you deposit the money in the bank?"

"Now there you go, I sure did." He rose from the table. "Hang on a second. Let me check my bank statements and I'll tell you exactly what day it was. I went straight to the bank after going with him to city hall to sign it over."

Houston sipped coffee and waited. The preacher returned several minutes later.

"June seventh."

"Thanks . . ." he pulled out his notebook and scribbled it down.

"Care for a warm up?"

"Please."

Quinn fetched the percolator. "Can I ask why you're so curious? Must be more to the story than just meeting a man that goes by the same handle as me. You told me on the phone that you're a homicide detective. Did someone get murdered?"

"No, nothing like that—I'm on vacation, and this is strictly personal. I just got curious about him."

"Mind if I ask why?"

He gave him a brief rundown of the case.

"And you think this Bob Talasota may have been the man that bought my Jeep?"

"Yeah. The Poppy I knew said he hailed from Texas, and I was hoping to locate his family, learn more about him. We were becoming friends and he just left without a word."

The preacher frowned sympathetically. "That's too bad. Well he's no relation to me, I can tell you that much."

"You know, that's really weird, because you two could pass for twin brothers."

"Heck you say," he responded with an incredulous grin.

Houston had seen that exact expression on the professor's face two or three times during their debate. "Yeah, I'm not exaggerating. You'd swear you were looking in a mirror if you saw him. Have you always lived in Decatur?"

"Born and raised right here in this house."

He thought about Poppy telling him he could prove he was Peter Quinn if he'd go to Texas with him. If only the egghead had accompanied him on this trip, the shock of seeing the real Peter Quinn might have snapped him back to reality, at least enough to know he needed deprogramming.

But why did the puppet master want Paul Quinn to think he was the man sitting across from him? "Do you have any relatives in the Chicago area?"

"You asked me that over the phone. Unless they're some distant kin I've never met, no."

"Any in or around Brooklyn, New York?"

"Nary a one."

"What about Los Angeles?"

"Nope."

Houston took a sip of coffee and smiled. "Hope this doesn't sound like I'm interrogating you."

"Not at all. Glad to answer any questions you want to ask. Sorry my answers aren't much help."

"How about Las Vegas?"

"With the single exception of a cousin who moved to Maine a few years ago, all my relations live in the south . . . ."

After Houston ran out of questions to ask, the preacher showed him around the farm, and invited him to stay for supper. He enjoyed Peter Quinn's hospitality until seven, then had to get back to DFW in time to catch his return flight.

* * * *

Poppy's voice kept echoing in his mind, telling him the same thing over and over. Houston couldn't see the professor, only endless fields of green grass and an amazing array of flowers on either side of a beautiful river . . . .

* * * *

Wishing he still had some of Monday's Dutch Blend left, Houston nuked a cup of instant coffee in the microwave, and sipped it in the living room. Yesterday's trip to Texas occupied his thoughts until he recalled having an odd dream last night, that fled from his memory the second he tried to recall it in detail. He shrugged it off and headed out the door for a late breakfast at his favorite café . . . .

THIRTY

Looking through the window of an American Airlines jet, Denise watched the city disappear behind a haze of December snow clouds. She'd spent the last three months in New York, and was heading back to Chicago, carrying Bob's child in her womb.

At some point she'd have to tell his family. The Talasota's were forward, self-centered, assuming people, and she'd left the cemetery hoping never to see any of them again. But she hadn't known about the baby then. She owed it to Bob, and their son had a right to know both sides of his lineage.

She'd spent the bulk of her stay in a special school located in a rough Brooklyn neighborhood, backed by a non-profit organization. Teaching only the Bible, it was tuition free but room and board cost fifty dollars a week. No more than twelve people could enroll for each twelve-week session, and then only after passing a battery of tests. One of the pallbearer's was an alumnus, and Bob's mother had taken him to task over it, calling the organization sacrilegious because it wasn't Catholic. Denise had gotten intrigued and decided to check it out.

The purpose of the symposium was to help preachers, with little or no seminary training, better understand the primary tool of their profession. Despite not being a pastor, when none of the other applicants scored high enough on their exams to occupy the twelfth slot, she'd managed to get into a group scheduled to start the next day. Forty-one such classes had preceded hers, and she hoped Poppy had looked down from heaven long enough to see her receive a certificate proclaiming her a graduate of the forty-second.

One morning during the seventh week, she had to leave class due to an onset of severe nausea. Having never skipped a period before, and seldom late more than two days, she'd known right then it had to be morning sickness. Before the attack, she'd thought the stress of losing Poppy and Bob had affected her cycle. Knowing the exact date she'd forced herself on the gifted lady's man, she'd told the gynecologist that had to be when conception took place. He'd counted forty weeks from there and set June second as her due date.

"You're at least a month away from an ultrasound being able to determine the baby's gender," the doctor had said.

"I'm pretty confident it's a boy," she'd answered with a smile, while thinking: *If you only knew, this baby is not only a male child—he's either an Olive Tree, or going to be the father or ancestor of one.*

* * * *

About to enjoy some Chinese takeout he'd just spread out on the coffee table, Houston grimaced with irritation when his cell started ringing. Stabbing his chopsticks into a carton of chow mein, he grabbed the nagging phone.

"Yeah?"

"Houston?"

The voice sounded familiar. He swung the phone to the front of his face to check the ID, and dropped his jaw when he saw the name on it. "Denise?"

"So you didn't forget me."

"Hardly, what a pleasant surprise. I gave up hope of ever hearing from you again."

"Just got back from Brooklyn last night."

"What's it been, four months?"

"A little over three."

"Were you teaching up there?"

"No, but I was *in school. I've been learning the Bible."*

"Oh . . . ."

"Don't worry, I'm not out to convert you."

He laughed. "I probably need converting."

"Oh, no doubt," she said humorously. *"Want to come over and visit a while?"*

"Sure. When?"

"Is now convenient?"

"I assume you're still at the same address?"

"Same ol', same ol' . . . ."

All he'd been able to confirm during his vacation was that whoever brainwashed the Quinn trio either knew Poppy Quinn of Decatur personally, or had somehow learned all about him. He still couldn't think of a logical reason for the puppet master wanting the Northwestern professor to believe he was the Texas preacher. His partner would most likely say something like, "It's some sort of government experiment being tested on a section of an unwitting populace." But John never said it, because he still hadn't told him about trying to solve the Quinn mystery.

The vehicular records in Texas verified that Roberto Talasota purchased a Jeep from Peter Quinn at Decatur for the sum of five thousand dollars. And if he was alive, Talasota would have no memory of ever having done it, just as he hadn't remembered knowing Poppy and Denise prior to the Mojave experience all three firmly believed they shared.

An old lady named Winona Gleason lived in Paul Quinn's house now, and said she'd never heard of him. The woman had serious memory problems, as she'd claimed to have lived there for several years. Knowing she really believed it, he hadn't had the heart to tell the poor dear that couldn't be true, because an obvious relative of Poppy's had answered the door only a matter of weeks before.

The Quinn sisters gave him a call every now and then, just to say hello. Monday had sold her night club, and they'd taken a year-long vacation to see the world. They'd phoned from Jerusalem, Madrid, Rome, London, Sydney, Tokyo, and were in Paris the last time he'd spoken to them.

He'd quit trying to get hold of Denise over a month ago, and had given up the investigation when it looked like he'd never see her again. With no leads or clues, beyond what he'd gathered from his trip to Texas, he'd been forced to throw in the towel, because without being able to probe the mind of any member of the Quinn trio, he wasn't apt to find any more.

But now Denise had made contact, and since he could prove to her that Poppy and Talasota had to have known each other prior to the Mojave experience, maybe she'd finally believe him and seek help. If he could only get her deprogrammed, he felt sure she'd be able to point the finger at the evil bastard or bastards responsible. Then the mystery would be solved, and justice—however inadequate the penalty, since such a heinous act should be dealt with as harshly as kidnapping in his opinion—would be served.

Entering Franklin Park, he smiled inside at that possibility, and really looked forward to seeing her pretty face again.

* * * *

Denise understood now, whereas before she'd been confused and self-condemning. God had seen to it she couldn't control her lust for Bob, for if she'd been able to, she wouldn't be pregnant with his child. One of the more interesting things she'd learned in her Bible studies was how passionate some of the Old Testament passages were, and that every God-given desire had the potential to be fulfilled. Evil lust was merely passion gone awry, but true desire couldn't be denied. When the fiery urge to merge her body with Bob's had reached its peak, she could no more have resisted it than a falling rock could defy gravity. She'd felt like a cheap whore the day after, and had tried to bury the memory. Now she often relived it in her mind with pure joy, and felt extremely grateful to be carrying that Bronx ox's child.

Houston being at the bar that day hadn't been a coincidence, God had seen to that too. She'd been kicking against the goads, thinking something wicked and filthy lurked within her, but now knew it to be a legitimate craving, placed there by God. Whoever coined the phrase *God works in mysterious ways* would flip if they could see how mysteriously He was working in her life. Now the time had come to embrace God's will instead of fighting it, as she'd done when Poppy said she belonged with Bob.

She heard a car pull into the drive . . . .

Houston was forcing a black fedora to stay on his head when she opened the door. A cold wind threatened to blow it off. She turned sideways to allow him past, and closed it. He wore a gray trench coat and his 'handsome' smile.

* * * *

A sensuous air hung about Denise like the sweet essence of her perfume, stemming from a glow of alpha femininity. She'd let her hair grow past her shoulders, and he wanted to run his fingers through the lush brown mane. The last time he'd seen them they'd been puffy and bloodshot from crying, but now her eyes were clear and inquisitive—beautiful and probing. Her swelling breasts strained against a pink blouse as if yearning to be caressed, squeezed, and fondled. Serenity had replaced the sorrow and confusion she'd worn on her face when he'd last been here, but her pouting lips hinted at being aroused.

Houston longed to kiss them.

Taking his coat and hat, she bade him to have a seat in her recliner. "I was about to have some hot chocolate, would you like a cup?"

His lack of discretion while ogling her had put a discerning half-smile on her face that made him feel self conscious. He nodded and sat down. She stored his things in a hall closet, and went in the kitchen. A few minutes later she came back with two steins and handed him one.

"Thanks." Steam rose from a cluster of mini marshmallows floating atop the cocoa. The mixture smelt richly sweet, and very hot.

Placing her cup on the coffee table, Denise centered herself on the sofa, and stretched her arms along the back while crossing her legs. "It's good to see you, Houston."

"Same here. Figured I'd never hear from you again."

"You figured wrong, didn't you." She said it with a knowing smile that seemed to hold a secret behind it. Then she looked towards her living room window. The curtains were pulled to the sides, allowing an ample view of her front yard. "It's beginning to snow."

He glanced at the large pane. Snowflakes were flying across it, driven by a biting, twenty degree wind. "Weatherman missed again. We weren't supposed to have snow until tomorrow."

"Is that right? Didn't catch the weather today." She kept eyeing the window, but it was obvious her thoughts weren't on the fluffy crystals swirling in the turbulence. Denise looked contemplative, and had started rocking her raised calf as if bored. He feared she might be having second thoughts about him being there.

Say something witty, stupid, he warned himself. Unable to think of anything, he decided to recite the weather forecast for the week, but thankfully she broke the silence.

"The last time we saw each other, Houston, you told me

you'd met the Quinn sisters. What do you think of them?"

So that's what she'd been brooding over. "They're both nice ladies."

"I need to meet them."

That stunned him. "Why?"

"Bob."

Did she know they thought they were Talasota's wives? *Tread lightly here, bub.*

"I'd like for you to introduce me to them if you don't mind."

"Can't, the last time I heard from them they were in France."

"When was that?"

"About a week ago."

She finally took her eyes off the misty portal to her front yard, and put them on him. "Maybe they're back by now. Why don't you give them a call and set up a meeting?"

"They're on a world tour."

Her face dropped with disappointment. "Can you contact them?"

"No. I have no idea where they are."

Reaching for her hot chocolate, she blew across the top and took a small sip. "I have something to tell you, but first I want to know if you still think I was brainwashed."

He wasn't about to touch that issue with a ten foot pole at this juncture, not after finally getting to see her again and starting off on such shaky ground by gawking at her like he'd never seen a woman before. She'd get angry, or sad, or just weird, and ask him to leave, as she'd done the morning after Poppy abandoned her—and again, when he'd broken the news about Talasota. Prudence dictated dishonesty. "No."

"You took too long to answer. You're lying, Detective."

Relieved she didn't seem distressed about it, he wondered what she thought could have changed his mind on the matter, but wasn't about to ask. "Okay, you caught me. I didn't want to upset you. What did you want to tell me?"

"I'm pregnant with Bob's child."

The statement hit him like a giant fist slamming into his stomach. Stupefied, he could only gape at her, wondering why she'd slept with Talasota when she'd professed to love Poppy.

"Cat got your tongue?"

"I uh, thought it was Poppy you cared for."

She gazed at him with eyes that had gathered moisture, but weren't releasing tears. "What I told you about my feelings for Poppy were true at the time. When you saw me at that bar, I was feeling like shit because I'd practically raped Bob the night before, even though I was in love with Poppy. That's why I got drunk. Something came over me that night he was with the Quinn sisters—an insane jealousy that made me want him so badly I couldn't stand it. I now know why, and that's what I want to talk to you about.

"That was the only time we made love. God saw to it that it happened. I believe Bob also had sex with the Quinn sisters before he came home that night, and I think one of them is also pregnant. If he didn't do it that night, he did it the next, when he stayed over there the night before he . . . the night before the accident."

He shook his head with bewilderment. "Denise, I'm really confused."

"Did you know they thought they were Bob's wives?"

"Yes, Monday told me. I was wondering if you knew. You don't agree with that craziness do you?"

To his surprise she nodded. "I don't have the option not to because I was also his wife."

Fuck me to tears . . . .

"Houston, are you all right?"

"Yeah, just totally blown away, that's all. I don't savvy any of this. You think you were Bob's wife too?"

"Yes, Poppy explained it. I had no intention of marrying Bob when I slept with him, because I was still in love with Poppy. I'd hoped to make Poppy fall in love with me, but now I know that would have been impossible, since he's an angel. Did you ever do the background check on him?"

"I checked out Peter Quinn, if that's what you mean."

"Well?"

"I went to see him on his farm in Decatur, Texas. He looks like Poppy's twin and even goes by the same nickname."

Her eyes went wide. "Are you sure it wasn't Poppy you saw?"

"Positive . . ." he told her how he'd called every Peter Quinn listed in Texas, and why he'd decided to go see the one in Decatur. Still feeling it wasn't the right time to present his evidence, he kept mum about the Jeep.

"But you didn't find any of my Poppy's family, did you? You weren't able to find where he lived, or went to school, or anything like that, were you?"

Stalling for time because he didn't want to go there, he tried some of the cocoa. "This is great hot chocolate."

"Thanks. You didn't, did you?"

"Denise . . . I didn't bother with that because I know he's really Paul Quinn. I went to Northwestern and the dean said he'd moved out of the country. I know you think you saw him vanish but—" his cell phone rang from the inside pocket of his blazer. "Excuse me."

"Hello?"

"Hey there, how are you?"

"Fine, how are you, Monday?"

"Homesick, that's how I am. Tuesday too. We cut the tour short, but decided to do Vegas before coming home. That's where I'm calling from."

"You're in Las Vegas? When did you get back to the states?"

"Two days ago. We're flying back tonight."

"Tonight?"

"Mm hmm. I wonder if you'd mind picking us up at the airport."

"Sure, what time?"

"We'll be arriving at eleven-thirty . . ." she relayed her flight information. *"Will that be a problem, picking us up so late?"*

"No problem at all."

"Great. Tues says hello. See you tonight."

"Tell her hello from me."

"Will do. Bye."

Denise became animated. "Are they flying in from Las Vegas tonight? That's what it sounded like."

"Yeah, they cut the tour short. They want me to pick them up at the airport at eleven-thirty."

"Can I go with you?"

The shit was about to hit the fan, or as John humorously put it: *the defecation is in all probability about to collide with the oscillator.* When Monday told him she and Tuesday were Talasota's wives, she'd also said he'd confessed to being in love with Denise. Monday had then sworn, "That bitch will rue the day she was born, if we ever cross paths."

Now 'that bitch' wanted to meet her. It would only lead to a catfight if he let her go with him, but Denise Jones wasn't a woman to be easily dissuaded, so he had no option but candor. "When I spoke with Monday before Bob . . . before the accident, she was pretty jealous of you. Seems he told her he was in love with you. I think I'd better go alone."

She took another sip of hot chocolate and crossed her arms, holding the stein a short angle from her left breast. "That's all right, I'm jealous of her too, but we need to meet. Go ahead and go, I'll stay here, but let me write a note for you to give her. Will you at least do that?"

"Sure."

"I'll go write it, enjoy your cocoa."

Before he'd reduced the contents of his stein more than two inches, Denise returned with a sealed envelope.

"Give this to her, and I'll leave the rest in God's hands."

He accepted the letter. "Why do you think one of the Quinn's is pregnant? It's possible they used some form of birth control, you know."

"It's possible, but I know they didn't."

"How do you know?"

She smiled at him like a mother responding to a child who'd asked a question requiring an answer incomprehensible to a young mind. "I just do."

A change of subject matter seemed in order, so he asked about her stay in Brooklyn. She spoke very briefly about Talasota's family and said she didn't much care for any of them. Though she'd enjoyed her time at the school, she hated not being able to retain all she'd learned. Some of the concepts had either been too lofty for her, or were errantly interpreted by her instructors, she felt. Either way, there was much about the Bible she couldn't fathom, even though she'd been taken through all sixty-six books, one verse at a time.

"Have you given up teaching?"

"No, I'm going back to work when the next semester starts in January, even though my heart isn't really in it. Paleontology just doesn't intrigue me the way it used to, especially now that I've gotten so enchanted by theology. What Poppy and I told you really happened, we weren't brainwashed into thinking it did. Soon you'll believe it happened too."

He frowned at her. "What makes you say that?"

"Because Poppy said you were called to this along with the three of us . . . ."

They talked until eleven and he told her goodnight. She reminded him to give Monday the note. He assured her he would, and headed for O'Hare . . . .

THIRTY ONE

By the time they got to the mansion, snow was falling so hard Houston could scarcely see more than ten feet in front of him. Along the way Monday and Tuesday had talked incessantly about their adventure overseas. Getting to see the Jordan River in person had been their sightseeing high point, followed by the pyramids, canals of Venice, and the Eiffel Tower. Rome won out as their favorite city, Tokyo occupied the bottom of their list because they'd felt so disoriented there.

Chocolate mousse, Quiche Lorraine, and Catalonian meatballs over rice served with ratatouille, took the cake in France. The Tortilla de Patatas and Gazpacho of Spain were to die for, and they implored him to try a stuffed cabbage called Holishkes, should he ever go to Israel. They'd laughed about being so excited to eat an actual Italian pizza, only to have the waiter bring a circle of baked dough topped with nothing but seasoned tomato paste.

He'd asked if they'd had to fight the men off on their various stops. Tuesday had giggled out "Only everywhere" and told him a renowned Parisian artist had begged to let him paint them in the nude. They'd respectfully declined, permitting only a facial portrait, which he'd decided to keep for his personal collection even though, according to him, it would easily have sold for at least a thousand Euros at any gallery.

Their bodies were hidden behind full length mink coats when he picked them up at O'Hare. Houston slyly took note as they came out of them, after all the luggage had been hauled into the foyer, where Monday decided to leave it for the time being. Wearing jeans and snug-fitting striped sweaters, their midsections were flat and shapely. They sure hadn't started showing yet if either was pregnant, but then neither had Denise.

He followed them to the kitchen and everyone took a seat at the island where he'd first gotten to know Monday. The sisters were hungry and had asked him to stop at a twenty-four hour takeout joint near the airport. Monday doled out the disposable dishes and cutlery accompanying the order, insisting he help himself to their bounty.

The smell of fried chicken had been making his mouth water since they'd left the restaurant, so he was more than happy to oblige. While reaching for a quart container of potato salad, he noted the butcher-block gleamed like the kitchen floor. "This place sure looks spic and span for the two of you being away so long. You guys have a maid or what?"

Tuesday nodded while spooning out a portion of coleslaw. "A sweet little Portuguese man and his four daughters come in twice a week to clean it for us."

"Must be nice," he snickered while raising a crispy thigh to his mouth.

She grinned sheepishly. "Oh it is, believe me . . . ."

If the snow didn't let up he'd have to spend the night but hadn't mentioned it yet, hoping they'd ask him to stay. He feared a self invite might be mistaken as a hint for more than a warm place to sleep.

Finishing off a wing, he set the bones on his plate, and wiped chicken fat from his lips and fingers with a paper napkin. "That was delicious, thanks."

Monday started clearing the counter. "Want a nightcap?"

"If you're having one."

"What's your pleasure? We have everything."

"A brandy sounds good."

"Brandy it is. Let's retire to the party room, shall we?"

"The party room?"

Tuesday rose from her stool. "It's where we unwind. I think you'll like it . . . ."

He followed them into a cavernous enclosure composed of three levels, each about half the depth of the one preceding it. Billiard tables, pinball machines, and video games occupied the first. Two steps, stretching from wall to wall, led to the second, where a horseshoe-shaped bar surrounded glass shelves stocked with fine liquors, liqueurs, and mixes. A lighted dance floor lay beneath a battery of speakers hanging from the ceiling. Besides barstools to sit on, swiveling armchairs sat around a long oval table at least ten feet wide, looking somewhat like a space-age boardroom. Accessed by a short flight of oval-shaped stairs at the center, the third floor was equipped with a massive hot tub, and all the accessories.

Tuesday led him to one of the chairs. Monday pulled up a section of counter, and stepped behind the bar.

"Brandy for the detective," she mused aloud, while opening a new bottle of very expensive cognac. "Rum and cola for me. Tues?"

"I'll have a martini."

"A martini for the lady . . . ."

Tuesday brought the brandy to him and took the chair to his left, cupping her glass with the stem centered between her lithe fingers. She gave him a seductive smile, then clicked her drink against his before sampling it.

A moment later Monday sat down on the other side of him. "I guess you know you're our guest tonight. You can't possibly be thinking of trying to brave that storm."

"Thank you. If it doesn't let up I'm afraid I won't have any choice."

Removing a toothpick-impaled olive from her martini, Tuesday placed the green ball deep in her mouth in a deliberate motion, as if preparing to give it oral satisfaction.

Pulling the wooden shaft through her moist, puckered lips, she chewed provocatively, swallowed, and smiled. "Then let's hope it doesn't let up."

"At least not until morning," said Monday.

They were staring at him with bedroom eyes. He didn't know what prompted their shift in attitude, but felt more than a little nervous about it. If they were planning on an orgy, they'd picked the wrong guy. The day he'd gone back to tell Monday about the accident, both sisters had emphatically declared—with grief-stricken certainty—that no one could ever replace Talasota.

"Bob made every other man I've been with seem like a clumsy high school kid in comparison," Monday had said, which prompted Tuesday to assert, "There is no comparison. Being with Bob was like finally getting to eat a t-bone steak served with the world's finest wine, after a lifetime of stale baloney sandwiches and Ripple. No one will ever be able to make me feel the way he did."

Houston didn't consider himself a slouch in bed, but wasn't about to compete with the ghost of the super-stud they thought they'd been married to. Besides, it had been so long his first performance would likely be substandard. They might not give him the chance to redeem himself. Pretending not to notice their seductive stares, he tasted his drink. "Good brandy."

"We settle for only the best—" Tuesday placed a hand on his thigh "—of everything."

"What she said is so true, Houston. Only the best will suffice for us."

Throat tightening, he downed some liquor to loosen it, and contemplated driving through the blizzard after all. Then he remembered Denise's note.

"I almost forgot, I've got something for you." He stood and reached inside his blazer for the envelope. "Denise Jones asked me to give you this."

Monday opened it and pulled out the letter. The licentious radiance on her face evaporated as she perused it.

"What's it say, Mon?"

"Let me read it to you. 'Dear Monday. You don't know me but I know you've heard of me. My name is Denise Jones and I would like to meet with you and your sister to discuss some things concerning Bob Talasota. Please contact me at your earliest convenience. Thank you. Sincerely. Denise Jones.' Then she goes on to add her phone number and address."

Pulling the sweater sleeve back from her left wrist, Monday glanced at a diamond studded watch. "It's one-thirty. Do you think she'll mind if I call this late?"

He marveled at her reaction. Not only had the note not made her angry as he'd expected, she actually seemed eager to talk to Denise.

And so did her sister, who said, "Call her, Monday. It's a Saturday night, maybe she's still awake."

Houston shook his head. "Correction, it's early Sunday morning. She's most likely asleep by now. I wouldn't do it."

"You're probably right, but I'm too curious to wait . . . ."

* * * *

The phone woke her. Denise squinted at the alarm clock, wondering who'd have the audacity to call at such an hour.

She yanked the receiver off the hook. "Hello?"

"Is this Denise?"

"Yes. Who's this?"

"Monday Quinn. I just got your note asking me to contact you. Hope I didn't wake you. I probably should have waited until tomorrow to call, but since this is about Bob, I wanted to talk to you soon as possible."

Hearing how sexy Monday Quinn sounded made her all

the more jealous. She drew a deep breath and sat up. "I understand."

"What is it you wanted to discuss about him?"

"I need to ask you a personal question if you don't mind."

"Like what?"

"Are you pregnant?"

Monday laughed and said, *"She wants to know if I'm pregnant,"* to someone on the other end, before sarcastically answering, *"No, I most certainly am not."*

The bitchy way she answered pissed her off, but Denise ate it, for the time being. "Is your sister?"

"No."

"I see."

"Why are you asking such a thing?"

"Because I'm carrying Bob's baby."

"Are you sure Bob's the father?" Monday finally responded after a lengthy pause, now sounding hurt and intimidated.

"Yes."

"Did someone tell you I was pregnant?"

"No."

"Then why did you ask if I was?"

"Because . . . I thought one of you would be."

"Why?"

"You did make love with him, didn't you?"

"I don't see how that's any of your business!"

Denise bit her lip, trying not to get madder. "And your sister did as well, didn't she?"

"That's none of your business, bitch!"

"Call me anything you want, but please answer my question. I know you and your sister think you were his wives. I believe you were too if you slept with him . . . that's why I need to know. You did sleep with him, didn't you? Please tell me."

A muffled sob filled her ear, followed by a stream of

sniffles.

Minutes went by.

"I'm sorry I called you a bitch . . . I shouldn't have snapped at you like that."

A hot tear slid down her face. "It's okay."

"Are you sure it's Bob's baby you're carrying?"

"Positive. Did you make love that night he first came to see you or not? Please . . . I need to know."

"Yes."

"And your sister did too, right?"

"Yes."

"Okay. See, the thing is, I made love with Bob the same night, but after the two of you did. It was the only time we did it, and before you get upset with him, it wasn't his idea. I made him do it."

Monday wailed, then started crying. *". . . I-I'm sorry to break down like this, but it hurts . . . I already knew you'd slept with him . . . we found out the day he came over with Poppy . . . but hearing it from you just went all over me. Couldn't . . . couldn't it be someone else's? H-How can you be so sure, if you only did it that one time?"*

"He's the only man I've been with in well over a year."

"Why did you think one of us would be pregnant?"

"Not over the phone. When can we meet?"

"Tonight's no good. Not with the storm and all."

"I'm free tomorrow, can we meet then?"

"Weather permitting. Where do you want to meet?"

"You choose the place . . . ."

* * * *

There were no windows in the Quinn party room, so Houston went outside to check the conditions. The snow had stopped and he could see a few stars. He went back inside.

When he'd heard Monday tell Denise they couldn't meet tonight because of the snowstorm, something made him think they could, that the blizzard would cease just so they could. Though baffled by the odd intuition, he'd found it impossible to resist.

He put a hand on the weeping Quinn's shoulder. "Monday, it's not snowing anymore. You can meet with her tonight if you want . . . ."

THIRTY TWO

Because of the possibility of recurring snow, everyone agreed the meeting should take place at Denise's house, so he could do the driving. As they'd done when leaving the airport, Monday sat up front, Tuesday in back as he chauffeured them to Franklin Park.

"Remember saying Denise Jones wasn't as pretty as me?"

"Mm hmm."

"Did you mean it?"

He cut his eyes to Monday and grinned. "Is someone feeling apprehensive?"

"Maybe . . . ."

* * * *

Denise checked her makeup one last time, making sure she looked her very best. First impressions were the strongest, and she wanted the Quinn sisters to feel at least a little unsettled, taste some of her jealousy when they laid eyes on her for the first time. Her nerves were already on edge and she knew they'd only get worse when Monday and Tuesday arrived. She rehearsed the meeting in her mind—what she planned to tell them, how they would react, how she'd counter if they responded the wrong way. If only Poppy were here to supervise this.

But he wasn't, the ball lay totally in her hands.

She modeled her body in the mirror. Wearing her best dress would be too obvious, she'd have to accentuate her attributes within the limitations of casual attire. Thankfully she wasn't showing yet, and her favorite skin-tight jeans still fit. The blue-and-white striped sweater she had on clung to her nicely, enhancing her bust, so she decided to go with it. After agonizing over footwear, she finally chose comfort over glamour, and slipped on a pair of blue sneakers with slightly raised heels.

The doorbell rang. They were here . . . .

Houston removed his fedora while stepping inside. The Quinn sisters took off their coats and handed them to him as if he was their valet. They were absolutely stunning—she felt like an eighth grader, just beginning to bloom, trying to compete with two gorgeous seniors. Though the blondes looked very much alike, the older one possessed a certain jena se qua that made her the more intimidating of the two. Despite a surge of resentment at seeing firsthand what Bob had found so appealing, she didn't have to feign liking them, which totally surprised her. She'd anticipated it would take months before any true feelings of friendship towards them developed.

"Denise," said Houston, "let me introduce you to Monday and Tuesday Quinn. Girls, meet Denise Jones."

There was a time when she'd have found it odd the three of them were all wearing striped sweaters and jeans, but not now. She relieved the detective of his burden, taking his trench coat and hat as well. "Make yourselves comfortable while I put these away. What can I get you to drink?"

"I'd love a cup of hot tea," Monday answered. "And if it's all the same to you, I'd prefer taking it at your dining table."

Expecting an aloof snob, Denise appreciated her down to earth directness. She dropped the coats on the recliner, and placed Houston's hat atop the pile. "Hot tea it is."

Tuesday grinned at her sister. "Can you believe she's wearing stripes?"

"Pretty ironic, isn't it," said Denise with a smile.

Monday cast one back at her. "It certainly is."

Houston nervously cleared his throat. "Must have a lot in common."

The Quinn's cut their eyes to him. She did likewise and said, "Well we do have one very important thing in common."

"Yeah, Bob." Monday put her hands on her hips while saying it. "Denise, I can easily see why he was so smitten with you. I need to ask your forgiveness because I've hated you ever since he told Tues and me he was in love with you."

A warm rush of affection welled up inside. "I need to ask your forgiveness for feeling much the same about you and Tuesday. Would you believe I now feel spiritually bonded with the two of you, like we're kin to each other?"

Monday nodded. "I feel it too."

"So do I," said Tuesday.

She gave each Quinn a hug and motioned for everyone to follow her into the kitchen.

"Have a seat . . ." she went to the sink, filled a teapot with water, set it on the stove to boil, and joined them at the table. "So what did you girls think of Poppy? Wasn't he a treasure?"

"Yes, but why are you referring to him in the past tense?"

Houston coughed and quickly said, "Um, Monday, the reason she did was because he moved over—"

"Can it, Detective, this is my show—you just sit there and listen. Us women folk will do the talking, thank you very much. You might just learn something."

Monday and Tuesday giggled, which made her like them all the more.

* * * *

Denise was right about it being her show, but he hoped she had more sense than to tell the Quinn's she thought Poppy was an angel.

She meshed her fingers, rested her hands on the table, and said, "Poppy's no longer with us."

The sisters gasped.

"When did he die?" asked Tuesday.

"No, Poppy's not dead, and he can't die, because he never lived."

Fuck me to tears, she's gonna do it!

"As a man, that is. Poppy's an angel, and has returned to heaven from whence he came. That's most likely the easiest thing for you to believe of all that I'm about to tell you. Now let this sink in before you say anything. He took on the form of the man we all knew as Poppy Quinn, and somehow made himself forget that transformation. Not only did he do that, he also became another person whom he, Bob, and I referred to as The Biker—a mysterious man, whose face we never saw because of a masked motorcycle helmet he wore. The Poppy we knew thought he was just a man until the very last, when he faded away."

Expecting the Quinn's to demand he rescue them from this madwoman by taking them home immediately, Houston couldn't believe what happened. Instead of outrage, the sisters gawked at each other—eyes glistening with excitement, lips spread with knowing smiles.

"That explains it then," said Monday.

He frowned at her. "Explains what?"

She leaned towards him. "I thought you were told to shut up and listen, mister."

Denise and Tuesday laughed at her remark, while he could only sit there, dumbfounded.

"Tuesday and I had the same dream on the same night, and it was about Poppy Quinn. I knew then, as has just been confirmed, that the dreams had to be prophetic. He spoke to us, but we couldn't hear him with our ears, only in our minds. He was wearing a motorcycle helmet just like you described,

Denise, so we couldn't see his face—but we knew it was Poppy. Whatever he said was extremely important, yet neither of us could remember it when we woke up. Anyway, because of that dream, I believe you."

"And so do I," said Tuesday.

Denise was beaming. "Thank you, Lord! This is going to be so much easier than I thought."

"Go on, tell us the rest," Monday urged, blushing with anticipation.

A strange feeling came over him that he was somehow connected to their dreams, but he couldn't figure out why. It dissipated when Denise started speaking again.

"Poppy, Bob, and I saw each other for the first time in the Mojave Desert, after fleeing for our lives when we saw . . . ."

He listened as Denise told the tale, never deviating one iota from what she'd laid out to him. Monday and Tuesday seemed to be taking everything she said at face value, totally blowing his mind. Suddenly, the Quinn's dreams gnawed at him again.

The whistle on the kettle blew. Denise kept talking while serving their tea, with Monday helping in spite of her protests that she was company and should let her work alone.

By the time she neared the conclusion of her brainwashed saga, he finally figured out what was bothering him. He'd dreamed about Poppy too, but had forgotten all about it—and like the sister's, couldn't recall a single word the professor had said.

". . . Then I came back from Brooklyn, and just knew one of you would be pregnant as well. Since you're not, that leaves only one possibility as I see it."

The Quinn's looked at her with intense expectation, but instead of answering she sipped tea, which prompted Monday to say, "Well don't leave us hanging!"

Denise sat her cup on the table and folded her arms. "Bob said you read the Bible a lot, so you understand how it is with marriage. The woman is bound to her husband as long as he's alive, but she's free from the marital bond if he dies, and can marry again. I think I know what Poppy was telling the two of you. I've got a feeling you'll remember his words, just like our memories returned when Bob and I first saw each other here in Chicago. Do Olive Trees ring a bell?"

Not only did the Quinn sisters suddenly recall what Poppy had said in their dreams—a fact easily discerned by their shocked expressions when Denise said the two words—but so did he. Poppy had told him he was the progenitor of one of the Olive Trees, while the other was to come through Bob Talasota's line.

"And you, Detective, are bound to be wondering where you fit into all this, am I right?"

He started to tell Denise his dream, but she continued before he could utter a word.

"The Olive Trees are two prophets who will call down plagues during the first half of The Great Tribulation, then they'll be killed and raised up to heaven, three and a half years before Christ returns to set things straight. The baby in my womb will be one, or the father, grandfather, or ancestor of one.

"Only God knows the time of the end, but if my son is one of the two prophets spoken of in Revelation, then the time is at hand for the rise of The Beast and False Prophet. The Olive Trees will call down plagues as a testimony against the antichrist, to show the world that the peace and prosperity being experienced by those who worship him are false and temporal, and that they should repent and worship the true God, who created all things. Their ministry will be like that of Moses and Elijah, and many people believe they'll actually be those two great prophets reincarnated, an opinion I don't particularly agree with.

"Anyway, since Bob is no longer with us, and I'm only

carrying one baby—and neither of his other two wives are pregnant—he obviously can't sire the other Olive Tree. Poppy said you were called to this, Houston, so it's up to you to fill Bob's shoes."

"Denise," Monday blurted excitedly, "before Houston gave me your letter, Tues and I were trying to seduce him. We believe we belong to him now. Does that mean you belong to him too?"

The elder Quinn spoke like he wasn't even in the room, but finally acknowledged his presence with a concerned frown. "You do like us, don't you, Houston . . .?"

THIRTY THREE

They strolled along the grassy banks of a river that flowed towards a shimmering horizon of multicolored brightness. Though they'd been walking for quite some time, neither he nor his companion felt any fatigue. Physical limitations were behind them now. He carried a motorcycle helmet in his left hand, and had his right arm draped across the broad shoulders of his charge.

* * * *

They'd driven straight to the Cook County Clerk's Office after a shocking discovery at Northwestern University.

"This can't be." Houston gawked at the recorded deed which showed Winona Gleason had taken possession seven years ago. He searched all the way back to the nineteen-thirties, but no one named Paul Quinn had ever owned that property.

The day after introducing Monday and Tuesday to Denise, he finally told John what he'd secretly been up to. The Quinn sisters had so unnerved him with their strange belief that he was destined to be their husband, he hadn't dared mention his dream about Poppy, knowing it would be like pouring gasoline on their delusional fire. Instead, he'd finally presented his one solid piece of evidence to Denise. But even after telling her Talasota had bought Peter Quinn's Jeep and had given it to Poppy before she met them, she still refused to believe they were victims of mind control. When the Quinn sisters had sided with her, despite the impossibility of any of those weird events in the Mojave really happening, it'd dawned on him he could no longer handle this solo.

His partner had theorized much as he'd anticipated: a covert arm of the industrial military complex must have been surreptitiously conducting experiments in mind control. When he'd mentioned Dean Hayden telling him Quinn had resigned from Weinberg College, John had looked at him funny and said, "The dean you talked to was a man?"

"Yeah, Sorrel Hayden."

"I don't recall the name," John had said, "but I remember reading that a woman runs that section of Northwestern. You must have gone to one of the other schools under its umbrella. Not that it matters, I suppose."

An argument had ensued when Houston insisted he'd been told the news by the dean of Weinberg. To settle matters he'd called the university and learned John was right. Insisting his partner accompany him, Houston had gone back to Weinberg College and directly to the dean's office, only to find another name on the door. The dean hadn't been there, but her associate had never heard of the man he'd talked to.

Mystified at how the imposter had managed to pull off such a feat—and stupefied as to why—he'd checked out every professor the bogus dean had told him about. Though their names had corresponded to those recorded in his notebook, they weren't the eggheads he'd questioned, and none of them knew anyone named Sorrel Hayden. Flabbergasted and unable to comprehend how such an intricate hoax could have been planned in advance—since nobody had known he was coming to the university the day he met Hayden—he'd received an even greater shock by their statements about Poppy. When they'd heard a colleague with whom they weren't acquainted had been murdered, each had assumed Paul Quinn worked at one of the other ten schools comprising Northwestern, since he didn't teach at Weinberg. That had driven John and him to the business office, where they'd learned Paul Quinn had never been employed by the university at all. The person who'd told him over the phone that Quinn worked at Weinberg had to have been part of the scam too.

Houston finally quit staring at the real estate data and rose from the chair. "What's going on here? I swear to you, an old man that looked enough like Paul Quinn to have been his father answered that woman's door the first time I went there."

Evidently still not grasping the full gravity of the situation, since the look on his face seemed to stem from irritation over a clerical error rather than the baffling perplexity he should have felt at the moment, John smugly said, "I don't know how Missing Persons got the wrong employer and home address when they wrote up Quinn's file, but since Winona Gleason lives alone, you must have gone to the wrong house that day."

His stomach tightened with anxious frustration. "No, I went to the right place all right. I'm positive because I've been there twice since. And you saw Paul Quinn's driver's license just like I did. It had the same fucking address on it, John!"

Fearful confusion blanketed John's face, turning it a whiter shade of pale.

"Finally starting to sink in, is it."

"What the fuck is going on here, Houston?!"

* * * *

"Yeah, that's true, Pops, I've always believed in Him, but I don't remember accepting Jesus like you say I did."

He grinned at Bob affectionately. "A little friend of yours talked you into asking Him into your heart when you were a young child."

"That's all it takes, huh? I wonder how many people are

like I was—saved without knowing it. Wish I'd known. Maybe then I would have lived my life for Him, instead of for myself."

"So do I, but there's nothing we can do about that now. Please be merciful to me."

Bob shot him a confused frown. "What do you mean, be merciful to you?"

"It's written: 'Know ye not that we shall judge angels?' I'm your angel, and after you pass through the judgment, you and all your spiritual brethren will judge me and mine. The blood of Christ was shed for your sins, and His righteousness has been imputed to you. Your sins won't be remembered—they're covered by the blood of the Lamb of God—but I, on the other hand, will be judged solely on what I did, since unlike you, I have no sin nature."

"I don't get it, Pops. If my sins aren't going to be judged, what is?"

"Your sins have already been dealt with—Jesus bore that penalty for you at Calvary. But your life will be examined at the Judgment Seat of Christ, so that you may receive, or be denied, various rewards as the case may be."

Eyes glazing over with angst beneath arched brows, Bob stretched his lips into a sneer. "What, you got me all calmed down after learning I died, just to start scaring me again, Pops?"

"There's no reason to be afraid, Bob. It's strictly for your sake. To quote the Apostle Paul: 'Other foundation can no man lay than that which is laid, which is Jesus Christ. Now if any man build on this foundation gold, silver, precious stones, wood, hay, stubble—every man's work shall be made manifest, for the day shall declare it, because it shall be revealed by fire, and the fire shall test every man's work of what sort it is. If any man's work abide which he hath built upon it, he shall receive a reward. If any man's work shall be burned, he shall suffer loss; yet he himself shall be saved, yet as by fire.'"

"Come on, Pops, spit it out in plain English. I haven't got a clue what you just said."

"The foundation is Christ who saved you. Your earthly deeds are the works evaluated upon that foundation. Now these particular deeds have nothing to do with sin. Paul used the allegory of gold, silver, and precious stones as the good works. Wood, hay, or stubble represents worthless deeds. He then uses the symbol of fire to test them. Obviously, wood, hay, or stubble would burn up, so such a work wouldn't stand, and no reward given. The others could withstand the fire and would remain, meaning those works would be rewarded. But even if all is lost, Paul said, 'he himself shall be saved, yet as by fire,' likening the experience to a man fleeing naked from his burning house. He may have lost everything he owned, but his life was spared."

Bob grimaced with a sickly expression. "Oh jeez, then I'm gonna be butt naked in eternity for sure. I never did any good works."

"Did you ever do something nice for someone?"

"Uh, sure . . . lots of times."

"Then maybe you'll at least get a diaper to wear."

He coughed out a nervous laugh. "Well, if I wind up being a nudist so be it. Beats the hell out of going to that other place, if you'll pardon the expression."

"Good attitude. I recall several good things you did, stop worrying about the Bema."

"The Bema?"

"The Judgment Seat of Christ."

They walked on . . . .

"Pops, will I always be like this, the same as I was when I was alive? I always figured all the people in heaven would wear robes, and the men would be like eight feet tall with white hair and beards."

"You'll be glorified and given a new name. You're a son of the Living God, a coheir with Jesus Christ."

"What do you mean by glorified?"

"You'll be given a new immortal body."

Bob donned a gleeful smile. "Wow, so I am gonna get a new chassis, huh. Is that the way you really look?"

"No."

"Can I see what you really look like?"

"You'll see me transformed when we get there. For now, this is more comforting to you, as is this contrived landscape we're walking through."

"So why do you look the way you do now?"

"When I incarnated I looked exactly like you, since I'm your guardian, but that would have scared and confused you. I bought the Jeep from a man named Poppy Quinn. After I left him I took on his persona and willed myself to forget I was an angel. I retained only his memories, yet without his personality. In order to navigate the three of us through the desert experience—which was designed to force you and Denise to accept the reality of the spirit realm, and therefore prepare you for what lay ahead—a part of me became the biker."

"But you didn't know it, right, Pops? While we were in the desert."

"No. I was just as frightened and confused as you and Denise. My thoughts and reactions were the same as the real Poppy would have experienced."

He heaved a sigh. "Jeez, that's wild. So what happens to Denise now? When does she buy the farm?"

"That's not for you to know. Earthly things are no longer your concern."

Raising his chin, Bob perused the color-streaked sky and sighed again. "Well I just hope she winds up having a happy life. I really loved her, you know?"

"I know."

"So what's the deal with the Olive Trees? I thought we were supposed to be them."

"In your dream I told you—that is the biker told you—to tell me as Poppy Quinn that I was the Olive Tree. That's because the real Poppy will become instrumental in what is about to happen. And as for you, Denise is carrying your son."

"Whoa . . .!" the proud grin on Bob's face was so wide it made the bottom of his earlobes curl. "So I'm gonna be a daddy after all. Will he be an Olive Tree or will that come further down the line?"

"That's not for you to know."

"Aw come on, Pops, tell me."

He gave Bob's shoulder a pat, and lowered the arm he'd held there since acquiring him an instant before his Buick hit the eighteen wheeler. "I cannot tell you what I do not know."

"Ah, so you don't know either. What about the creature we saw? Is he the demon you thought he was?"

"No. He was merely an illusion created by me, as was the town. Of course I didn't know it at the time. The RV, people at the store, the store itself, even the garden were likewise. Besides forcing the two of you to accept the reality of the spirit realm, it was also designed to bind you and Denise together. Ordinary circumstances wouldn't have sufficed. Her temperament would have put you off had you approached her in the real world, and you're not the sort of man she'd readily accept. The biker hid your t-shirt so the sight of your bare chest would ignite the spark in her that eventually turned to flaming desire."

"So *that's* why it was under the seat. Then none of it was real?"

"The riverbed and sandy Mountain were quite real, but the rest of it was a contrivance. My commission was to create the scenario after you and Denise were both on Interstate Fifteen at the same time. After I bought the Jeep in Texas I transported to the outskirts of Barstow, California—"

"What do you mean transported?"

"Let's just say it didn't take me long to get there."

Bob shook his head with amazement. "So you made the Jeep fly, huh. What a trip."

"In a manner of speaking. Actually it went from Texas to California instantly, and when I got there I willed myself to retain only the conscious memories of the real Poppy Quinn. So when I pulled into the convenience store before entering the town, it was all as real to me as it was to you and Denise."

"I don't get it, Pops. Why'd you do that?"

"Out of necessity. As your angel, I'm bound to guard over you, so the only way I could let you go through the process without interfering was to make myself forget what I really was, and think I was a man. I was allowed only so much leeway in protecting you in the normal world, because mishaps and mistakes resulting from human freewill, must be permitted. As it's written: 'what ye reap, so shall ye sow.' But that spiritual principle didn't apply to the Mojave experience because it was paranormal. The fear and confusion you felt would have enflamed my protective instincts, and I couldn't risk my empathy for you in any way affecting the construct I'd created. Denise's angel had to back off totally throughout the ordeal, and not witness any of it for the same reason.

"Everything had to happen precisely as it did. You both had to believe it was all real so that when your memories returned, causing Denise to also get arrested for my murder, you'd be totally unable to successfully defend yourselves. The two of you had to be convicted, or the seed wouldn't have been planted."

"What seed?"

"The beginning of a warning that the end times are approaching. Houston Shoat won't give up trying to find out what really happened, and he'll eventually see the light. Once he realizes that God orchestrated the whole Paul Quinn scenario, he'll be converted. Eventually he'll come to understand time is rapidly running out, and tell others. Those with eyes and ears will believe him."

Bob frowned. "What do you mean by eyes and ears?"

"Merely a euphemism for those who are spiritually alive that can receive the truth that's incomprehensible to spiritually dead minds."

"So Denise and I had to go through all that just to arouse the curiosity of Houston Shoat?"

"Partly, but it goes much, much deeper."

"So lay it on me."

"You wouldn't understand, even if I was permitted to tell you."

"So you can't tell me?"

"No, not about that."

* * * *

"What do you mean neither of you wrote this file? You were the initial investigators on this case." Houston had to hold his frustration in check to keep from screaming it out.

Detective Bryant wrinkled his bulldog face into a defensive scowl. "Look, we were handed this file when Paul Quinn was officially listed as missing. I could have sworn the officer who took down the information signed it, but I guess he didn't since his name's not there now."

John shot him a challenging look. "Who gave it to you?"

"Hell, I can't remember."

"What about you, Lowe? Can you remember?"

Detective Lowe shrugged his narrow shoulders. "I've slept since then, sorry."

"Aw hell!" Houston let out a groan. "You guys better *start* remembering. We've got a fucking mess on our hands that you two are going to share the blame for starting otherwise."

"All I know is it was someone from Missing Persons. I've never seen him before or since. I wouldn't know him if he walked up and bit me on the ass."

* * * *

"Okay, Pops, I get that you had to turn up missing and all that, but couldn't you have done it easier, and still not have fouled up anything, by just making yourself forget you were my angel and not one altogether?"

"No, because Denise had to be exposed to Poppy Quinn. Although I didn't have his personality, I had his mind and character, so for all intents and purposes she became very well acquainted with the real man through me."

"So why didn't you take on his personality as well?"

He felt a sly grin form on his borrowed face. "The real Poppy is a little too, what you'd term hoakie or corny for Denise. At least when he first meets people."

"You're saying the dude's a hayseed?"

"Yes, that's pretty much how he's viewed until people get to know him, and learn of his tremendous intellect and spiritual prowess. He's a very humble man, so he purposefully tries to refrain from using anything but simple, down to earth terms, until confident he won't appear condescending to whomever he's conversing with. That, coupled with his country mannerisms which he never sheds, would hardly have impressed Denise. I chose to take off the rough edges, if you will, so that she could see what the man essentially is, and not shy away from him when she finally meets the real man.

"You see, she thinks she's supposed to marry Houston now—that he's taken your place. But the plan all along was to get you and Denise together to produce your offspring and have Poppy Quinn raise him in the knowledge of the Lord. Very soon she and the real Poppy will meet through Houston Shoat, who's already made his acquaintance, and she'll eventually fall for him the same way she fell for me. Only this time she won't be disappointed. Poppy Quinn will fall in love with her as well."

Bob ran a hand over his head and blew out a wistful sigh. "The real Poppy Quinn is one lucky, lucky guy. Say, that bout you had at Denise's when it looked like you were gonna croak, what was up with that?"

"We were nearing the end, the time of your departure, of course I didn't know that at the time, and the two parts of me—the biker and Poppy Quinn—had begun to reintegrate. I went through a similar experience in the garden, but the biker was only detaining me until you got convicted. Anyway, once we merged together, the biker became dormant until later that night, and then my incarnation disintegrated. Denise witnessed the whole thing."

"Wow, that must have really freaked her out."

"Yes, I'm afraid it did."

They walked on . . . .

* * * *

Houston eyed the young officer suspiciously. "How can it have just disappeared?"

"I don't know, Detective Shoat. None of us here can explain it. I wrote her down as the family member who reported him missing, I'm sure of it. Ask Hunt over there, he saw me do it."

Officer Hunt nodded. "That's right, I witnessed the whole thing. She said she was Paul Quinn's aunt and feared for his safety because he must have gotten stranded in the Mojave Desert, since he hadn't called her in three days. He was supposed to check in with her every evening because his Jeep was on its last legs. He didn't have a cell phone and had last called her from Barstow, California, so she knew he had to be somewhere between there and whatever town he was heading for, which I can't recall now. You can check with Lieutenant Nye, he's the one that called Los Angeles to get a search started."

"I was there too," said a female uniform. "I watched him fill out all the information on Paul Quinn because he was teaching me how to do the missing person reports. He wrote her name down and signed it, I'm sure of it."

"Yet neither it, nor his signature is on the file now," said John indignantly, "and none of you can remember what her name is. How do you explain that?"

"Like I said before, we can't . . . ."

* * * *

"Does John Crate fit into any of this, Pops?"

"No, other than being instrumental among those in the Chicago Police Department who'll testify the events surrounding the case of Paul Quinn can only be explained as supernatural. Houston Shoat, however, has a much more important role. One Olive Tree comes through your line, the other through his. Monday thought you were the one, but she and Tuesday were meant to be with him. Even though they both believe they are now his, it will be quite some time before they realize they made a mistake in choosing you. In the dream I had where the biker told me to look up Leviticus eighteen-eighteen, he also told me that you and the Quinn sisters were married. That was me deceiving myself for the purpose of setting the stage for Houston to wind up going there."

"Gee thanks, Pops, makes me feel like a million knowing I was just a mistake they made."

He beamed at him. "Joy unspeakable awaits you, Bob. You were nobody's mistake. As it's written: 'Eye hath not seen, nor ear heard, nor hath entered into the heart of man the things he has prepared for those who love him.' They saw your picture in the paper and made plans to meet you, little knowing that divine providence was leading the way for them to hook up with Houston Shoat. You see, he'd met Monday some years before, and the reason he was there when you woke up on your last morning on earth was because he thought you might be in danger.

"Monday couldn't help feeling a pull towards him she didn't understand, and when Tuesday met him she felt the same way. Incidentally, she met him just a few hours after your death. They took a vacation after your demise, and during that time rationalized the feelings they had for him as a precognitive sign from the Holy Spirit that he was there to take your place, not realizing you were there to lead them to him all along. Of course your interaction with them was also designed to provoke Denise to such intense jealousy she forced herself on you, thus producing your offspring. These are the reasons known to me. The Almighty has endless reasons for all events, known only to Him."

"You say Monday met him years before? Why didn't they hook up then?"

"It wasn't the proper time, but it set the stage for Houston to come to her house that night you were there, as I said."

They walked on . . . .

"So when did it all come back to you? You being an angel, I mean."

"Your last night on earth."

"Wonder if Denise will ever figure out what you are. She must know you weren't exactly human, since she saw you disintegrate and all."

"She knows. I was permitted to put some thoughts into her

mind at the last."

"So what gives with the real Poppy Quinn? How come he gets to have Denise and raise my son?"

"Because he's closer to the truth than any man alive on earth at the present, though he doesn't know it. He's a brilliant theologian, and an excellent teacher."

For a moment Bob looked jealous. Then an inquisitive gleam appeared in his eyes, denoting mere curiosity. "Does he know how to speak Italian, or were you using your powers when you spoke to me?"

"Oh yes, and many other languages. During my incarnation I was never able to do anything the real Poppy couldn't do. As far as I knew I was really him—his memories were my memories, his fears were my fears, his likes, dislikes, even his taste in clothes were all mine as well. I also had his spiritual gifts. The man has a very strong anointing."

"Sheesh . . . what a trip."

"And he is related to Monday and Tuesday, by the way."

"So they had seen you before like they thought?"

"No. I knew I'd seen them too, but couldn't recall where. Now of course I remember everything. The Quinn sisters saw Poppy—and he saw them—in a dream the three of them had simultaneously. Tuesday was only eight at the time, and neither she nor Monday remembered dreaming it. When they saw me the memory stirred, as did mine as Poppy Quinn, but none of us realized it had taken place in a dream. That shared vision was for Poppy's sake. It will help him realize the Lord has called him to bring the two sisters, and their soon-to-be husband, to the full truth. Monday's scriptural understanding has hit a ceiling she won't be able to get past until the real Poppy guides her beyond it."

"How are they related?"

"Their father and Poppy had the same paternal grandparents. They were cousins, but neither knew the other existed."

"So are the Quinn sisters Irish or Cherokee?"

"Neither. They're Jewish."

"No, I mean from their father's side. Sheesh, I'll never forget how I freaked when they said their mother was Jewish."

"There father was as well. So was Poppy Quinn's, though he doesn't know it. Three generations before the real Peter Quinn was born, a young man named Jerome Lipkowitz changed his last name to Quinn because he was ashamed of his heritage. He later married and had children. When one of his grandsons tried to trace the family tree and couldn't get further on the surname than his grandfather, he wanted to know why. Jerome, forced to admit he'd taken on the name Quinn, made up a story about his deceased father being a Cherokee without a last name, so he'd chosen one. Your ancestor did much the same thing."

"Huh?"

He looked upon the unwitting vessel the Lord had selected before the foundation of the world—choosing a spiritual weakling to confound the wise. "You're Jewish, Bob."

"Ah, you're teasing me now," he said with a grin. "That can't be right. My mom did my family tree. It goes way, way back on both sides, and it's Italian all the way."

"No. Your mother's family stems from the tribe of Judah, and your father's from Levi, though neither knows it. Your ancestors moved to Italy a thousand years ago, and your paternal forebear took on the name Talasota, while your great-great-great-great-grandfather on your mother's side changed his surname to Pacino."

Bob slapped his forehead with both hands. "Blow me away! My mom had me circumcised even though she was Catholic. I wonder if she knows subconsciously that we're Jewish."

"No, she thinks it's merely a Pacino tradition."

"I'm really not related to Al Pacino, you know."

He smiled at him. "I know."

"So why Paul Quinn, and why make him a professor from Evanston? Just a name and occupation you picked out of the air, or what?"

"The surname Quinn was chosen to entice Houston Shoat to come to his brainwashing conclusion and eventually contact Peter Quinn. I picked Paul arbitrarily because of the apostolic ties of Christ's renowned disciples, Paul and Peter, but it was inconsequential. The name Houston had to hear in conjunction with Quinn was Poppy, the real Peter Quinn's nickname.

"After the biker sank into the hill, he immediately began setting the stage for the Chicago authorities to think Paul Quinn both existed and was missing. Houston was prevented from discovering the truth by the biker making him think he was talking to the dean and several professors at Northwestern University, when it was actually only him in disguise. When Houston went to what he thought was Paul Quinn's house I—that is the biker—entered the body of the woman who lived there, and made Houston think he was seeing an old man who resided with Quinn.

"Many people in authority are going to have to admit that something supernatural transpired when they discover you and Denise were arrested, tried, and convicted for the murder of a man that never existed. It's all public record and can't be covered up. Houston will soon discover there is no Paul Quinn and that—along with some key revelations Poppy Quinn will receive in the near future and pass on to the detective—will sound an alarm that will reverberate from Chicago, through the nation, and eventually the whole world. Those with eyes and ears will awaken, while those without will remain what I call sleepwalkers."

"Sleepwalkers?"

"Yes. People who think their earthly existence is all there is, even though most of them profess to believe in an afterlife. After spending their years pursuing their own ambitions instead of seeking God's will, they are rudely awakened at the end when confronted with the truth, as if they'd been asleep their whole lives."

Bob made a sour face. "Guess I was one of those sleepwalkers, huh, Pops."

"Yes, to a great extent you were, but your eyes were forced open in the Mojave. Unfortunately, much of the Body of Christ is half dozing. It's time for a sleeping church to wake up. That's why God ordained for both Quinn sisters to marry Houston Shoat, even though only one is required to bring forth the special son—to offend the status quo."

* * * *

"Look here, Shoat, I'm as concerned as you are, but I know none of my people are responsible. What could possibly have prompted any of them to do it?"

Houston had to admit Lieutenant Nye had a valid point about there being no apparent motive, but someone managed to erase the name as if it had never been there, it hadn't just vanished on its on.

"If you want to talk to her so badly, why don't you get a copy of the trial transcript? She testified, didn't she? Her name has to be on it . . . ."

The court reporter swore she'd recorded the testimony of Paul Quinn's aunt, even though it was nowhere to be found. "Someone had to have tampered with the transcript, Detective Shoat. I would never make such a mistake to begin with, but even if I had, one of the attorneys would have spotted it and brought it to my attention during the trial." Like himself and everyone else involved with the case, she couldn't remember the woman's name . . . .

The assistant district attorney's witness list was minus one very crucial entry that had been there before. Nobody could explain why . . . .

No one at the Sun-Times or the Chicago Tribune could account for the mysterious lady disappearing from their archives . . . .

* * * *

An official investigation was launched, and every Paul Quinn in the state of Illinois was contacted—but none of them had abandoned a Jeep in the Mojave Desert, or been reported missing by a worried aunt.

* * * *

Winona Gleason called the police because two unoccupied vehicles were sitting in her driveway: a blue Honda and a white Jeep. The Jeep had Texas tags.

* * * *

"You know, Pops, I can't remember anything except seeing that truck, then hearing you tell me it was time to go home. You'd think the moment of your death would stick with you for life."

"A humorous way to put it."

"Guess that did sound dumb."

"It's written: 'He that believeth on me, though he were dead yet shall he live,' and again, 'He that believeth on me shall never see death.'"

"So what's your real name anyway?"

"Shamarbacharel."

"That's easy for you to say," he chuckled out. "Sheesh, what a mouthful."

A short laugh emerged. He gazed fondly at the royal seal on the coheir's forehead. Visible only to angels and demons, the mark separated believers from heathens, Abel's from Cain's, the wheat from the chaff. "It means *Protector of God's chosen.*"

"That's beautiful, Pops. Say, why are we walking? Can't you just zap us there—you know, transport us."

"Is that what you wish, Bob?"

Looking this way and that, he took a deep breath and sighed. "Nah, let's just walk . . . for now."

About the Author

Arley Owens, Jr. is a musician, composer, author, and rancher who resides in his native Texas with his lovely wife Cristi. He's a member of the musical group TORN PAGE.
http://www.tornpageband.com

Other Books by Arley Owens, Jr.

The Cyrus Syndrome
A Texas Ghost Story
Incident in Baltimore
Death Ranch

Read Arley Owens, Jr. on your Kindle
http://www.amazon.com/author/arleyowens

SHORTY MAE PRODUCTIONS
P.O. BOX 81102
MIDLAND, TEXAS 79708

www.ingramcontent.com/pod-product-compliance
Lightning Source LLC
LaVergne TN
LVHW020703110826
845149LV00012B/2099

* 9 7 8 0 9 8 4 8 1 9 5 2 2 *